D1094327

Ursel Anderson

By ROBERT ANDERSON

NOVELS

Getting Up and Going Home
After

PLAYS

Tea and Sympathy
All Summer Long
Silent Night, Lonely Night
The Days Between
You Know I Can't Hear You When the Water's Running
I Never Sang for My Father
Solitaire/Double Solitaire

Getting Up
and Going Home

Robert Anderson

SIMON AND SCHUSTER
NEW YORK

Copyright © 1978 by Robert Anderson
All rights reserved
including the right of reproduction
in whole or in part in any form
First trade edition
Published by Simon and Schuster
A Division of Gulf & Western Corporation
Simon & Schuster Building
Rockefeller Center
1230 Avenue of the Americas
New York, New York 10020
Manufactured in the United States of America

2   3   4   5   6   7   8   9   10

A limited edition of this book has been privately printed.

Library of Congress Cataloging in Publication Data

Anderson, Robert Woodruff, date.
    Getting up and going home.

    I. Title.
PZ4.A54945Ge   [PS3501.N34]   813'.5'4   77-16359
ISBN 0-671-22853-6

For My Editor, Nan Talese

1

The candle on the bedside table had guttered out soon after they had stopped making love. The only light now was from the small aquarium across the room and from the streetlamps below, where the garbage trucks were banging and grinding.

Jack looked across Kimberlee's back at the photograph of her husband and seven-year-old son. Scott would return from his six weeks' trip tomorrow, and Colin was sound asleep upstairs.

Jack had not slept. It had been more than a month now that he and Kim had been making love, first downstairs in the starkly modern living room of this Upper West Side brownstone which Scott had remodeled, then soon after, at her daring suggestion, upstairs in this big bed. And he had never been able to sleep after. Perhaps it was because he always knew that at four o'clock he would have to get up and go home, making way for Colin, who sometimes padded down the stairs near dawn to snuggle with his mother. Jack had felt sure that one morning he would meet Colin in the hall. Or he would meet Frank, the college student who looked after Colin and lived in the room next to him. He sometimes rose early to jog in Central Park a few blocks away.

He lay there, happy, sad, bewildered, at the moment drunk with Kim's body, intoxicated with every curve and fold, enchanted by what he had come to think of as the calm excitement she aroused in him, permitting long, almost aimless times of sensuous enjoyment, sometimes ending in orgasm for one or both, almost as an afterthought.

He resisted the temptation to touch her, to gather her gratefully to him. What a gay, bright and lovely soul! Her father had called her Sunshine. And how beautiful! She sometimes objected to being called beautiful because she felt in some way it was disparaging to her fine mind. When she had asked him, "Why do you love me?" he had said, "First, for your beautiful mind, and first, for your beautiful body, and first, for your beautiful eyes." The startling cornflower-blue eyes could be laughing or pleading, challenging or frightened, or suddenly filled with despised tears ("sloppy and self-indulgent").

And the tall, slender but wondrously fleshed body. He had laughed with delight when he had first seen her lean forward to cup her elegant breasts in her bra. Her hair, which she seemed to wash constantly and which she said was never the same color two days running, now seemed a shiny chestnut brown streaked with gold. She said it went ash blond in the summer when she and Scott spent time sailing.

Would he see it in summer? Would he ever make love to her again?

For the whole month of April now he had had her to himself. An unreal month. Tonight, when they had finally stopped making love, she had looked at him, eyes barely open and murmured, "You want to send me back to him a ghost, don't you?"

He did not want to send her back at all. But tomorrow night she would be in this bed with Scott, whom she loved,

8

and he would be some sixty miles away in Ridgefield, in bed with Catherine, whom he loved and had loved for nearly thirty years.

It had been an exhilarating and bewildering month. All his life he had tried to avoid living the clichés, and here he was in the middle of the oldest. He had found the "new morality," if that was what it was, confusing. He had found it difficult to live in an atmosphere of suspended judgments or no judgments at all, particularly of himself.

As long as he could remember, he had led a rather carefully examined life, had always felt that with a minimum of resentment he had been a good son, a good man, a good husband and father. Until he had met Kim, he was a man who knew that if he slept with another woman, he could not go back to his wife.

And yet, at forty-nine, he had fallen in love with Kimberlee Cooper so easily, so guiltlessly. He had become hopelessly infatuated.

It had really happened that first night, six weeks ago, when her husband had taken him home for a late potluck supper after one of their squash games at the club. He already knew something about Kim, had formed some picture of their life, from occasional remarks Scott had made over drinks. "We're driving into the country tomorrow if Kim managed to get the garage man to fix the car." . . . "I'm in no rush. Kim gets home from the office around five-thirty and fixes supper for Colin and Frank, a college boy we have living with us to look after Colin. She and I eat later." . . . "Kim is off to hear Colin play in a school concert. Something they call an open string orchestra, for kids. They don't have to do any fingering. They just saw away on the open strings. I begged off."

As they had entered the ground floor of the brownstone, Kim had called out, "Hello. We're back here." There was a lilt, a crisp cheerfulness in the voice. Scott had not told him she was, *had been*, English.

They moved back down the hall, past a small front room, which was Kim's study, to a large family room kitchen, opening onto a walled garden. Kim was perched on a stool at a counter next to her young son, Colin. Her dark lustrous hair was pulled back and tied in a bright ribbon, and she wore snug black velvet pants, a faded rose-colored turtleneck sweater and ballet slippers.

As he approached, he saw the eyes, the incredible light-blue eyes set off by long dark lashes. And the smile!

But it was the whole scene. The radiant woman-wife-mother, the kitchen, the manly little blond boy, reminding him of his own son and earlier days with Catherine. *Home at evening.*

"This is Jack Montgomery. He was alone in town, and I suggested he come by for supper."

"What a nice idea! It's good to meet you at last." She held out a fine-boned, well-cared-for hand and looked at him as though she had been waiting to meet him all her life. "And this is our son, Colin."

"How do you do, Colin?"

Colin dutifully slipped off the stool and shook hands politely.

Scott peered at the television. "What are you watching?"

"An absolutely brilliant show that I, like an idiot, decided not to produce."

While Scott got a beer for himself and made vodka martinis for Kim and Jack, Colin disappeared upstairs, and Jack explained that he and Cat really lived in the vicinity of Ridgefield, Connecticut in a big Victorian house, but they kept a pied-à-terre in town. Cat was often busy working late, taping interviews for a literary talk show she conducted on a local radio station, and since as a lawyer he had many committee meetings which seemed to drag on into the evenings, he often stayed in town for the week. When she could, Cat joined him midweek for theater or a party.

Kim said she had heard Catherine give a reading of her poetry when she was in college.

Scott then whisked him off to show him the house. "This was once a very elegant neighborhood. Then it turned into rooming houses, and then for a time I think this was a whorehouse." Scott's smile was embarrassed. At the club Jack had always noticed that Scott, a tall, blond, obviously sexually attractive man, was very reluctant to be involved in any discussion of sex. Friends and associates of his had implied that when he went away on one of his long trips in the States or abroad, looking at sites for new projects he was designing, he "managed very well" but very discreetly.

"We sheared off the front steps, as you saw, and I've opened it up, exposed the brick walls, painted others white." The first floor above the ground floor was one huge room from front to back. "When we bought this for a song, it was a honeycomb of small rooms, each with a washbasin."

On the next floor was their bedroom. Totally different. "Kim did this room. I think she finds the rest of the house a little cold. The fireplace works, and it's nice on winter nights."

Jack smiled at the room. It was warm and colorful and cozy. Apple-green carpet, comfortable chairs with white muslin slipcovers, books, a large basket of geranium plants by the window and, dominating the room, a large bed with a raspberry-colored quilt and plump oversize pillows. There were also examples of Colin's latest drawings taped to the bookshelves and small family pictures on tables and

11

dresser. A closet door was open, and he saw Kim's brightly colored clothes. On one of the chairs was a pillow on which had been stitched.

BLAME NOBODY
EXPECT NOTHING
DO SOMETHING

There was a pleasant scent in the room, the same Jack had noticed when he had taken Kim's hand in the kitchen. The door to the bathroom was open, and he could see the huge old-fashioned tub, the glass shelves with bottles, the full-length, ornately framed mirror. He was noticing Kim's short nightshirt hanging on the bathroom door when Scott casually closed it in passing as they moved back into the hall.

After Scott showed him Colin's domain on the next floor, complete with bumper pool table, and then his own studio on the top floor, he took him back to the kitchen and excused himself to make some calls to California.

Kim was putting dinner together, still watching the television show. Jack offered to make the salad, said he was pretty good in the kitchen, had done a lot of cooking throughout their lives because Cat had often been away teaching or giving poetry readings or conducting interviews in distant places. "Cat taught me how to make a cream sauce, and I was off and running."

"Scott hardly knows the stove from the refrigerator, and I like it that way." She smiled. "I'm the original male chauvinist pig."

Jack sat on a high stool and watched her. He was fascinated by the way her graceful fingers held the tomatoes as she sliced them. He wanted her to go on slicing tomatoes forever. "Scott told me that you were once an actress."

"Oh, I had a *succès fou* as a child of ten at the Arena

Stage in Washington. My father was with the British Embassy at the time, and they needed a precocious English brat. The experience rather turned my head. They took the play on to New York the next year, and they wanted me to go with it, but my father wouldn't let me go."

"But you went on to Yale Drama School."

"Yes. But unfortunately by then I was very definitely an English ingenue type. I was terribly good in Restoration comedy, but when I finally came to New York to make the rounds, they didn't seem to be doing much in the way of Restoration comedy." She smiled. "But it was quite sweet. These very nice older producers would have me come into their offices, and they would sit there regarding me as though I were some precious piece of porcelain from a bygone age. They'd say, 'You would have been lovely in . . .' And then they'd name a series of drawing-room comedies of the thirties."

"How did you get into television producing?" She was through with the tomatoes, but her hands were just as graceful tearing apart the lettuce.

"Since I was so limited as an actress, I decided to be a director. After all," she said cockily, "I'd taken a course in directing at Yale." She smiled at herself. "I hounded agents to let me read anything and everything for a possible off-off-Broadway production. I finally found something, but I thought it would be better on TV, and I took it to a TV producer. They did it. Of course, I wasn't allowed to direct it, but they took me on in the company, and as the saying goes, I worked my way up. It's a much more sensible life for a wife and a mother."

"Scott says you're something of a paragon. Able to carry off everything in your complicated life with great éclat."

She looked at him, as though to see if he were teasing her. "That's not so. Far from it. Scott keeps me up to snuff.

13

I think without his prodding and poking, I'd be rather a sloth." She frowned and shook her head. "What's your area of law?"

"Literary. Copyrights. Contracts. I mostly handle writers, novelists, playwrights, songwriters."

"That must be interesting."

"I wanted to be a writer."

"Did you? Well, you see, we're all failures." She smiled. "Scott wanted to be a painter. Why didn't you go on with your writing?"

"My father sent some of my stuff to a friend who was an editor. He said I had a nice gift for the personal essay, but the world was not in need of any more pieces on Poor Relations or Eating Roast Pig." She laughed. Encouraged, he went on. "I also wanted to be a singer."

"A Jack-of-all-arts."

"But when I was eighteen, my father had a group of his musician friends in one Sunday afternoon, and with my mother accompanying me, I sang 'Who Is Sylvia?' and 'Where E'er You Walk.' The unanimous decision was it was a nice voice, but the world was not in need of another nice voice."

"Well, at least you function among writers and musicians."

"Yes, with a certain amount of envy, I'm afraid. I also wanted to be a tap dancer."

"Oh, no!"

"But I didn't tell my father that."

"Do you still tap-dance?"

"Only in the shower."

She laughed. He noticed the snug curve of her bottom in the black velvet pants. She was not wearing a bra, and the large, firm nipples, which he would later come to relish, appeared and disappeared as she moved.

14

He remembered when his daughter, Jorie, first insisted on not wearing a bra. She had had a conflict. She wanted to be "with it," but she had been embarrassed at how her nipples showed under her blouses and sweaters. Catherine had helped her resolve the conflict by suggesting that she wear Band-Aids over her nipples.

Does one tell the young wife of an acquaintance that she is beautiful and slices tomatoes exquisitely? "That's a great sweater. I love that color."

She blushed. "Thank you."

"Perhaps my favorite color."

"It's ancient. Very faded. I have no patience shopping for clothes, so I wear them forever and ever."

"I saw some of them hanging in your closet. Very bright and pretty." She looked at him and blushed again. "Your closet door was open. I liked your room."

"It's a kind of hodgepodge."

"I noticed the pillow. 'BLAME NOBODY,' et cetera. Did you make that?"

"Yes."

"I go along with 'BLAME NOBODY' and 'DO SOME-THING.' I'm not so sure about 'EXPECT NOTHING.'" She looked at him. "If there were no expectations in a relationship . . ."

"It doesn't say 'NO HOPES,' just 'NO EXPECTATIONS.' I believe in hope."

He sat there drinking his drink, looking at her, smiling, wanting to touch her.

She made him think of Cat years ago in the kitchen of her charming small apartment on Beacon Hill. As a sophomore he had trooped over to her place with a group of "literary" Harvard students interested in gathering together to read their poetry aloud with this beautiful "older woman," who, though only twenty-three, had already published a volume of verse and who knew both Frost and Auden personally.

He had come back to Cat's place the night after the poetry reading to bring her a book she had admired. She had invited him to stay for supper and had offered him a highball, his first. And he had helped her in the small kitchen. The highball had been strong, and he had spent ten minutes trying to figure out how he would manage to touch her. Maybe kiss her. Then she had reached up and across him to get something from a shelf, and he had kissed her shoulder through the sweater. She had stopped and looked at him, surprised, touched, amused. He vaguely knew that she was supposed to be in love with some "older man," a writer who taught at Yale. But he had had to touch her because he knew he was going to marry her.

And now he was wondering when he might touch Kim because he knew that it was inevitable that sooner or later he would. He wanted to move into this house, to become part of her home. To sit here and watch her slice tomatoes, to lie close with her in that bed upstairs, eat supper with Colin and go to his school and listen to open string concerts, and drive off into the country in a car she had managed to get fixed.

Why? Dear, lovely Christ, why? He had not been looking for this, had always avoided it. There had been other opportunities, and he had moved away from them quickly, going back to Cat. He was a house-husband, loving his marriage and his home.

Two days later Scott left on a six weeks' trip to the Middle East with a team of architects, and Jack sent Kim a short novel by one of his clients as an idea for television. He did not have much hope that she would take it, but it was an excuse to be in touch with her again. He *had* to see her again.

They met over lunch to talk about the book, and since it was a story about love and marriage, they soon found themselves talking intimately about their own feelings. She said, "You know, I've always rather disliked stories where the husband and wife get back together at the end."

"Really? Why?"

"I don't know. It's funny. I have a very strong marriage. A sometimes reluctant husband, but a strong marriage. And yet I have this feeling about those stories. Odd?" She cocked her head and smiled. "No doubt it should tell me something about myself." She sipped her drink.

"What do you mean 'a sometimes reluctant husband'?"

"Oh, I think there are times he'd like to be off and away. Don't most men have that feeling?" She looked at him.

"I don't know. My marriage and home seem to have been pretty much the center of my life. Perhaps if I'd managed to make it as a writer or a singer, something all-consuming. . . ."

"Or a tap dancer." She smiled.

"Yes."

"I think men need a long leash."

"Do you? A couple of times I've found myself attracted to someone. Once at a conference in Aspen. I left a day early and rushed home and took Cat off to Bermuda for the weekend."

She looked at him. The incredible blue eyes studied his face. "That's nice. You've been faithful, then, all these years?"

He felt uncomfortable. "It sounds rather smug to say so. Very unfashionable." He smiled. "Maybe it's just a lack of energy." She laughed. He went on. "It's been rough some-

17

times. We've been separated a lot since the beginning. Our work."

"We're separated a lot." She stopped and looked off, then went on coolly. "I know there are girls on his trips. I feel sure there are. But I don't feel threatened. He doesn't love them. He wants me to go with him on these trips, but I have my son and my work. It's a choice I have to make."

"What makes you think there are girls, women?"

"Oh." She shrugged. "Why not? Sometimes he's away a long time, like now. Six weeks."

"Why don't you give him the benefit of the doubt?" She looked at him and smiled. "I always felt that if I were ever with another woman, I couldn't go back to Cat." He looked at her, aware of his hypocrisy. He was talking about how much his marriage meant to him, how faithful he had been, and he was falling hopelessly in love.

"He once said to me, early on, 'If you don't come with me, I'll . . .' So I just assume. But, as I said, I don't feel threatened, because they're just girls." She smoothed the tablecloth. Somehow it was too cool. She went on. "Of course, it would be different with me. Different from Scott, I mean. I couldn't be with a man unless I loved him." She looked up. "But then, that's the difference between men and women, isn't it?"

He studied her for a moment. "Not necessarily."

She smiled. "I'm sorry. Generalizations. I don't like being lumped with 'women' either." They were quiet, and then she said brightly, "I'd better be getting back to the store."

Cat went to California, and a few days later, on a Friday night, Jack stopped by Kim's office to discuss with her associates the possibility of the purchase of the novel, and he took her home in a taxi and stopped in for a drink. She suggested that he stay for supper. Colin was off with a school friend for the weekend. He looked at her, sitting at the other end of the couch in a soft light-blue wool dress, and he knew what would happen if he stayed. He said "No" almost rudely and hurried out of the house.

If Cat had been home, he would have gone home, and that would have been that. But she was not home, and he found himself in a phone booth on the corner, calling Kim to say that he would like to have dinner with her, explaining that he always had difficulty saying yes the first time to an invitation.

She laughed and said she usually asked only once. "But I'm delighted you changed your mind."

He went back, bearing a bottle of vodka and a big bunch of daisies, and midway through dinner they looked at each other and felt the sinking sickness of love and desire and left the meal unfinished and made hurried and urgent and somewhat awkward love on the couch.

After, when they were lying there in a confusion of clothes, looking at each other and smiling and shaking their heads in delight and wonder, she said, "You're a surprise."

"Am I?"

"Yes. I never would have guessed . . ."

"I know. I look detached, aloof, stern. There's not much I can do about it. I try to smile as much as possible."

She laughed. They looked at each other with foolish and happy smiles. "When did you first know?"

"When I saw you slicing the tomatoes. When did you know?"

"When you said you tap-danced."

In the days and nights that followed, they were like adolescents in love, only better. If it is true that youth is wasted on the young, the feeling of youth, of being newly in love again, was not wasted on Kim and Jack. With delight and gratitude they rediscovered a playfulness in themselves that they thought they had lost forever. Lying in bed one night, she said, "You make me feel and seem something I'm not except when I'm with you."

Flattered, he held her and kissed her and after a few moments said, "Tell me what you'd really like me to do."

"What do you mean?"

"When we make love."

"What you do do."

"No, really. Tell me."

She hesitated and blushed, then finally said, "I like to be kissed and held. Real kinky, eh?" And embarrassed, she turned her head into the pillow.

And he kissed her and held her, and they made love, and he whispered into her ear, "Don't try so hard," and she laughed and a few minutes later for the first time with him she "slid downhill."

She snuggled close to him. "Mmmm. That was nice. I rarely manage it. I take forever, and—" She stopped.

Later, stroking her hair, he said, "You know, I've never been pursued before."

She looked up, surprised and smiling. "Do I pursue you?"

"Yes, and I love it. I've never met anyone so unselfish."

"I'm very selfish. I pursue you because I want to be with you."

"You make all the arrangements, make it all possible."

"Well, that's the way it works. The man declares his intentions in one subtle way or another, and the woman makes the arrangements." She laughed.

"You should have a younger lover."

"Anyone can have a younger lover."

20

He was conscious of his age, that he was forty-nine, his tall body and craggy face looking every day of it, while she was thirty-three, looking a mature twenty-five on particularly bad days. But he knew that it gave her some kind of perverse pleasure to have an older lover.

He brought her silly gifts and kept her bright and cheerful bedroom awash with daisies and even brought her two black angelfish for her aquarium. "To look after you when I'm not here."

She broke engagements to be with him, and when she couldn't, she might call him from the restaurant. "I'm in the ladies' room at Caravelle, and I'm just calling to say I love you, Jack Montgomery." And she'd hang up.

Being newly in love, he discovered an intensity missing in his life. He had not realized it was missing, had been missing for some time.

He took delight in her various facets, her various tones and manners. As a bright, young television producer she was direct and forceful. As an occasional luncheon partner in out-of-the-way places she was often glib and amusing, as though she were the actress she had wanted to be, playing drawing-room comedy. As a lover in bed she was complicated, sometimes silent and generous, the beautiful blue eyes behind the dark lashes urging him to enjoy her body. And then there might suddenly be tears for a sorrow she would not discuss, which made her infinitely dear to him and which he assumed had something to do with her marriage.

The other compartment of her life was her letters. From their first days together, they had written letters to each other to be read "later" when each was alone. In her letters, written in a rounded, almost schoolgirl hand, she was truly naked, revealing in deceptively measured prose her deepest feelings.

My dearest, dearest Jack:

I have never felt so safe in my life. I never would have dreamed that love could be so complete and undemanding. I have always thought that demands were something I could never accept, but that they were good for strengthening oneself.

But now I realize that I have never experienced loving and being loved without demands, and I still marvel at the peace and security of it.

They had spent a good deal of time in bed, not just making love, but talking, laughing, reading poetry to each other. "Scott hates poetry." But she also insisted that they sometimes enjoy each other "standing up." They took long walks in parts of the city where nobody knew them and drove out to Long Island to buy plants for her garden or small antiques for her bedroom. "Can you be on the corner of Ninety-second and Park in twenty minutes? I'm going for the car now."

She was happy with what she called their "marriage within a marriage," but as the weeks went on and the time for Scott's return approached, he began to fret, to be jealous. It was a new and difficult concept for him that she could love him and her husband too. One day he would decide that she didn't love Scott. The next day she didn't love *him*. And then sometimes he would wonder if she even knew what love was. He knew this was the conventional Jack wondering. A person who could love two people must be shallow. But her love was not shallow.

One day, walking in a small village on the Island, he taunted her by asking, "If you have such a strong marriage, why do you need me?"

She replied, "It's not enough. One hundred percent has never seemed enough." Then she stopped. "I'm sorry. That sounds terrible. If you don't know why I need you . . ."

She looked at him despairingly. "I know your views on the excitement of commitment, the satisfactions of wholeness. . . . But I think it's asking too much to find everything in one person."

They walked on, and he turned to her, smiling. "You know what I think you would really like?"

"What?"

"You'd like to have me in the attic and Scott in the guest room."

She beamed. "What a lovely idea!" They laughed, and she took his hand.

"I'm not sure how I feel about being your second best lover."

"If you were, you wouldn't be here." They both laughed at the glibness of this, but he was deeply touched and suddenly stopped and embraced her. "I shouldn't have said that. It's unfair to Scott . . . and it's also belittling to you." She drew back and looked at him a long time. "You've saved my life, John Montgomery. Do you know that?"

He didn't know it. He couldn't understand how he had saved her life. But he didn't ask, knew he mustn't ask. He just held her again, his eyes closed, feeling joy and pain.

Now he turned and reached for his watch on the bedside table, where it lay with the Kleenex box and the large Baccarat goblet that had been filled with vodka and ice and slices of lemon peel. They had passed the vodka from glass to mouth to mouth, laughing, sometimes almost gagging each other, cooling and freshening their mouths, heavy with the musky taste of sex.

Nearly four. The alarm would go off soon.

Dazed with making love and lack of sleep, he stared into the shadows of this room he had come to love, this cozy and warm room within a cool house, this home within

23

a home for their marriage within a marriage. Within two marriages.

He turned and moved against Kim's body. She stirred in her sleep, pressing herself against him. He gathered her to him, wondering at his growing, almost desperate need for closeness. Had Plato been right when he had said that man and woman had originally been one being and had been split apart and had since then been trying to re-form that union and achieve wholeness?

He reached over and turned off the alarm and kissed her. She awoke and smiled at him, hovering over her. "Did you sleep at all?"

"A little."

She touched his face. "Don't be sad."

"I'll try."

"Just remember, it's different."

"All right." But he knew how he would feel as he looked at the clock that night.

They didn't say anything while he dressed. He had to hunt for one black sock, which he found under the bed. He tied his tie, looking at her, put on his worn and rumpled Burberry raincoat and sat on the bed next to her.

She smiled. "At least you won't have to get up and go home anymore."

"I don't like that 'anymore.'"

"No. I don't either. We'll see." They had not discussed the future. She took his hand. "We were incredibly lucky."

He leaned over and kissed her. He felt heartsick. "Thank you."

"We don't thank."

"I know." He looked at her. "I love you, Kimberlee Cooper."

"I love you, Jack Montgomery."

He got up and moved away. He tapped the aquarium

24

and said goodbye to the two fish he had brought her, then quietly opened the door to the bedroom, waved and went out, closing the door behind him and starting down the stairs.

He turned out the lights on the first floor, then proceeded down to the ground floor. On the hall table was a pair of wooden bookends Colin had made in school for Scott. There was a sign scrawled on a shirt cardboard. "For Daddy."

He closed the door and found the key on his chain. The bolt was stiff and made a loud noise as it clicked to. He turned up his raincoat collar and, hunching over, stepped away from the entry as quickly as possible.

Each morning, when he had left, he had thought the street with its trees and bright lamps looked like a movie set. Each time he had headed somewhat warily for the avenue, hoping he would not have to wait too long for a taxi. Twice there had been someone coming in the opposite direction. Once he had crossed the street, and once he had not. This time there was a taxi stopped for a red light.

As the driver drew up before the East Side brownstone where he and Cat had their floor-through apartment, he noticed a streetlight was out. His entryway was in deep shadows.

"Would you wait until I'm inside, please?"

"I always do."

"Thanks. Good night."

He walked up the three flights of stairs to his apartment, past the Maxwells. The Maxwells were the reason Kim could not come to his apartment. She knew them.

He opened the door, threw his raincoat over a chair and went into the kitchen. Debbie, his ancient Irish setter, cocked an eye and barely managed to wag her tail. He had taken her for a walk at nine before he had gone to Kim's, but she had still wet the floor. Cat had said she should be put away, for her own good, but they had had her fifteen years, originally for the children, and he couldn't . . . yet. He spread some newspapers where it was wet, scratched her behind the ear, fixed a bowl of cereal and sat staring at the wall, eating. He thought nothing. It was too late, too early, to think. He was hungry. He was eating, and in a few minutes he would go to sleep.

The phone rang. He looked at it, and his stomach tightened. It might be an emergency. He should answer it. What could he say to Cat? She might have been calling all evening. He had never had to lie to her. It had never rung before at this hour, and she had never asked him what he did with his nights in town. He picked up the phone, base and all, and turning it over, switched off the bell.

He felt ashamed, angry and annoyed. He put the bowl and spoon in the sink, turned out the light and went to the bedroom. Christ, he didn't want to hurt Cat. So far he felt he hadn't hurt Cat. That had been the surprising thing about it.

He washed his face. Kim was still there, in his mouth, on his lips. He brushed his teeth, took a Valium and crawled naked into bed.

2

The next morning when he entered his office on the thirty-first floor of a glass and concrete building on Park Avenue, he was glad to see a number of messages already on his desk. It would be a busy day.

It had been a mistake to see Kim last night. With Scott coming home tonight, they had said they would not see each other. He smiled at this "nicety." But they had seen each other, and though he had showered and scrubbed, she was still very much with him, and the thought of her with Scott tonight would be pure bloody hell.

Miss Lorenz, his secretary, had cut out the *Times* and the *News* reviews of one of his clients' plays. He had seen the play in previews and the last minute had begged off going to the opening when he and Kim had decided they had to see each other. The playwright had been upset. With these mixed reviews, he should be grateful that Jack had convinced him to make a preproduction deal for the movie rights. His agent had urged him to wait and hope for a big smash.

"One o'clock. Partners' Lunch."

At the partners' weekly sandwich lunch, he was to give a short analysis of the new Copyright Bill, about which he had conferred a number of times in Washington.

"Kimberlee Cooper called."

She knew he didn't want to talk to her today! He didn't want to be conscious of her today. And why hadn't she called the apartment? He remembered he'd shut off the phone and had forgotten to turn it back on. He should call home just in case there was something wrong up there.

He looked up to see Oliver Bolton standing in the doorway. Oliver, now seventy-five, was one of the founders of the firm and, in many ways, Jack's surrogate father. "Morning, Oliver." Jack stood up.

"Have you got a moment?" Now that he was retired, he was very apologetic about breaking in on the time of what he considered the "working lawyers."

"Of course." Jack motioned toward a chair and started to sit down.

"No. No. I won't stay long." Jack straightened up and remained standing. "I sat next to Millicent Rogers at a dinner party last night."

Jack smiled. "Dear God."

"She was after me to get you to change your mind about taking over at Buckminster."

"Oliver, I have no qualifications to be a college president, even an acting president."

"She said it would only be for five or six months to help pull them out of this fiscal mess. She said you had agreed to talk about it."

"Yes, I did, in a weak moment. As president of the Board of Trustees I felt a certain responsibility. But—"

"It might be just the change you need." Jack looked at him. "I don't want to intrude on your personal life, but over the years we've talked rather frankly. You've been very helpful to me." He cleared his throat. "I think a sabbatical might be a good idea. You know, some firms require the partners to take sabbaticals. I think it's a damned good idea. I took one when I was about your age."

"Well, there's so much to do. . . ."

"None of us is indispensable." He smiled.

"Oh, I realize that. It's just the timing. They've asked me to come down to Washington to help negotiate some of the provisions of the new Copyright Bill, and—"

"You've given a great deal of time to them down there already. If you didn't want to go to Buckminster, you could just go away and work on your copyright book, if the idea of doing nothing for a year disturbs you, as it well might, being Richard Montgomery's son." He looked at Jack for a moment. "I sense you're in a period of churning, Jack. Up to this time the momentum of career and family and home keeps a man moving along almost automatically. But around fifty. . . ." He smiled. "It's like second-year Law School. Remember. Nothing seems to be happening. Or your third year as an associate." Jack nodded. "Well, I won't keep you. I'll see you at the Partners' Lunch. But think about it." He raised his bushy eyebrows and looked wisely at Jack.

"Thanks, Oliver. You know I always appreciate your advice."

Oliver left, and Jack sat down. He was embarrassed about this whole situation, that he had ever told Millicent Rogers that he would even consider the acting presidency. He had reluctantly allowed himself to be trapped into being president of the Board of Trustees because his daughter Jorie had gone to college there, and he had felt some obligation. But it was ridiculous to consider this. As a matter of fact, he was weary of his various presidencies and chairmanships and had jokingly told Cat that when he became fifty, he was going to say, "Now everybody off!"

But Millicent had caught him at a bad time, perhaps a time of "churning." In quick succession his partners had refused to take into the firm a young lawyer who had been with them a few years as an associate and whom he liked enormously. Then they had voted against his taking on as a client a young author who had brought him a case he felt could break new legal ground. It was rare in the work he usually did, authors' book contracts, playwrights' production contracts, movie sales, that you could set any legal precedents. It was mostly haggling with publishers and producers, trying to restore to contracts clauses that had been agreed upon but then deleted by company lawyers out to make points.

Also, he had been fed up with his firm's becoming so specialized that he felt he was more of an administrator than a lawyer, passing his clients on to others in the firm who were specialists in tax planning, real estate, trusts and wills, and divorce. Once at a Partners' Lunch he had said that the day would probably come when he would be allowed to write contracts only for comedies while some other partner would handle the tragedies.

He had discussed the possibility of the acting presidency with Cat, and she had said that it might be a good idea for him. He was fed up with the office. It would give him a breathing space. They would manage to see each other some weekends.

For more than twenty-five years, since the very beginning, they had accommodated themselves to each other's work. He knew that this accommodation had been an unspoken condition of their marriage. Cat had not really wanted to be married, had seen her fragile, beautiful mother, now living alone in a mansion in Worcester, totally dependent on her father for everything, and she had vowed it would never happen to her.

She resisted dependency of any sort. Even did not like him to make love to her with her doing nothing in return. "It makes me feel self-conscious." She would never allow a friend to be one-up on her in the matter of gifts or invitations to dinner. She had been upset when, a few years after their marriage, he had started earning more than she did. And when she stopped work briefly to have Rich and Jorie, it had been difficult for her to have him deposit money in her account.

Jack had been proud of her various careers and interests over the years (poet, editor, teacher, political activist, translator, expert interviewer). And he felt he had always supported her in her work.

But that was not absolutely true. Sometimes in the early days he had protested when she had repeatedly not come home for dinners he had prepared, or later, when the marriage bed had become too heavy too often and too late with books and clipboards.

"Do you want me to quit?"

"No, I don't want you to quit. I just think that your priorities should shift occasionally."

"Then I'll quit."

"Why is always that? Quit? All or nothing. There is something in between."

He must call Millicent and say a firm no.

Miss Lorenz buzzed him. "Kimberlee Cooper on three."

He sat and looked at the phone for a moment; then he punched the button. "Hello."

Kim waited for Miss Lorenz to cut off. "I'm sorry. I know you don't want to talk to me today." He said nothing. "I just thought I ought to tell you I was the one who called last night. I didn't realize till I'd made the call that you might think it was Catherine. I'm sorry. It was very poor judgment."

"It's okay. I sweated a little."

"I just wanted to call to say I love you. I mean last night. Today too. You seemed so blue." Pause. "I'm sorry, I shouldn't have called. Now, I mean." Another pause. "Do you not ever want to see me again? Shall I hang up?"

"No. I don't know. You shouldn't have called. Today, I mean."

"All right. I'll hang up."

He closed his eyes. Jesus! Couldn't she understand! He stood up abruptly and looked out over the city. A man who never pounded walls, he wanted to pound walls, smash glass, in anger and frustration.

Hanging up like that, as though she were scolding him. She hadn't been upset when halfway through their month Cat had returned and he had gone to her and things had gone well. Kim had said, "Why should I make myself miserable by being jealous?"

He was jealous. That was supposed to be a terrible admission in this day and age, to be sexually jealous. But he couldn't help it. He remembered years ago, before their marriage, when Cat had told him of her affair with Ned, the man at Yale. He had wanted to throw up. He wanted to throw up now. He had not changed. Perhaps if Scott were some faceless husband. But he wasn't. He saw Scott's lean swimmer's hips . . .

His eyes closed, and he shook his head, trying to ward off the image. Then he stared at the wall across the room. It had to be over! That was the only way he was going to survive tonight and all the other nights. "It's different. Just remember it's different."

How could it be different? She loved Scott. She was not

32

just servicing some unloved husband. He knew how it had been with Cat when they had come together after their many times of being apart, rushing up the stairs to the bedroom . . .

For a moment he loathed Kim, saw her as a woman who cheated, lied, connived to be with a lover. But then he had been that lover, and it had not seemed like that at all. She was a woman who loved two men, apparently very deeply, very needfully. It would all be a great scandal on page three of the tabloids, but as they had lived it, it had seemed beautiful and innocent.

He had told himself that it was over before. Two nights before Cat had come back from her trip, he had walked down Kim's street, away from her, and he had meant to stay away from her. He could not go back to Cat, make love to her, on any other terms. It was too cynical.

And the excitement of recommitting to the marriage, of feeling whole again, the joy of having Cat back and of being back with her, had carried him through the night.

But he had gone back to Kim. And had tried not to think about it, what he was doing.

He knew that many of his friends had made their "arrangements," usually as they got into their early forties, sad, reluctant compromises with their consciences and deepest desires.

One had told Jack he could not handle an affair emotionally and had a pleasant call girl he saw more or less regularly. It had not been all gain. There had been some loss. Before, when he had wanted to make love to his wife and she had demurred, he had urged, pleaded, even cried (he said), and if her reluctance was based on anything more than fatigue or "just not wanting to tonight," it had come out in the open, and they had perhaps worked out something important in their marriage. But now, if she turned away from him, he just went to sleep, knowing that he could see his call girl the next day. "No sweat."

He reached for a yellow legal pad.

Dear Kim,
This is impossible. I adore you as I have never adored anyone . . .

That wasn't true. He had adored Cat.

. . . but I can't take it. You have always been honest. I knew this time was coming . . .

He could hear Kim say, "But what do you want me to do?"

He didn't want her to leave Scott. He knew that was impossible. They were in many ways the perfect modern couple, young ambitious, successful, cool, making it in every department.

And he didn't want to leave Cat.

"I want you."

"But you have me."

Maybe other people could do it. He couldn't. He hadn't been programmed for it.

He took a deep breath. He could call Cat. Maybe they could drive up to Williamstown for the weekend, just be by themselves. Or they could go on one of their "what-the-hell" trips, just getting in the car and driving in whatever direction pleased them. Just be together.

He wouldn't finish the letter. He knew that if he did, he would end up more in love with Kim, pleading with her, whining unattractively about who was more in love.

"Would you get me Mrs. Montgomery at home, please? And if she isn't there, try the radio station."

After the weekend with Cat he would have lunch with Kim, talk to her. It was not a question of what he wanted. It was a primitive, irrational gut feeling. The whole situation was impossible. She didn't really love him, and . . . Back to that. Dear God!

"Mrs. Montgomery is not at home or at the station. Shall I leave a message?"

"Leave a message at her service that I'll pick her up at the studio, and see if she can manage to get a lift so that we'll have only one car."

"Peter Thayer is here for his appointment."

"Ask him to wait a minute, please." He tore up the letter and sat for a moment, collecting his thoughts. Let's see, Peter. Peter wanted to talk to him about a divorce. A preliminary talk, of course. If it became definite, he would have to pass him on to an expert. But after handling Peter for ten years as a writer, he thought that he understood Peter and his moods better than one of his partners would understand him.

Peter, who stood at the bar at the club, where he now lived, drinking and talking till the last member had departed for home. He had become a separation/divorce bore, touching at first as he had talked about his marriage and how it had "just died." But finally, a bore.

"Ask Mr. Thayer to come in. And remind me to call Millicent Rogers before I go to lunch."

3

Jack opened the door to the beat-up Volvo station wagon and helped Debbie into her seat. It *was* her seat. She sulked if she was made to ride in the back. Now for a while she would sit up, alert, checking the stops and turns, glancing over at him as though to say, "That's right." Later, after the Triboro Bridge, she would curl up and go to sleep, waking only to make sure he had paid the tolls. He would have to take her to the vet's tomorrow.

As he tossed his small suitcase and raincoat in the back and got in, he thought how Debbie had affected their lives. Bought for the children fifteen years ago, when the family had moved to the country, she had been left behind as they went off to schools and colleges. ("How's Debbie? Give her a hug for me, and tell her I'll see her at Christmas.") And now she was like some old family retainer, living out her life being cared for by those who had once been her charges.

They had found that she was morose when left in kennels, so instead of staying in hotels when they had come to New York, they had had to find a pied-à-terre. She wasn't allowed to ride on trains, so they had to take the car. Now Cat, with a cleaning woman only twice a week in the country and being away from the house so much with her work, couldn't handle Debbie. Debbie had been hit by a car two years ago, and though Jack had not blamed Cat, she had said, "I can't handle it. I can't keep checking if she's in or out or on the road." When she was in heat, naturally she wandered. Looking over at her, Jack was touched by the fact that here she was, almost dead, and she was just coming out of heat. She was a little testy because she had had her usual false pregnancy, had scratched her nest behind the big chair in the living room, teats hard as rocks.

The traffic on the FDR Drive was, as usual, impossible. After years of trying to figure out when to leave and when to return to outwit the thousands of other drivers, he had eventually given up and left whenever it was convenient, slowly moving into line and hitching his car to the back of the one in front. It would ease up after the Triboro.

It was good to be heading for the country. Travel, even a short trip to Connecticut, always gave him a feeling of cutting ties, leaving behind the confusion and mess of the week. Of course, coming back into town gave him the feeling of leaving the confusion and mess of the weekend.

It was perfect spring weather. He would sit in the control room and watch Cat do the last part of her interview. He loved to watch her work, with precision and authority, the almost angry-looking frown of concentration. Then the sudden big smile.

He had made a reservation at La Crémaillère. It was a place they saved for "events." He hadn't been able to reach her, so she would be upset that she wasn't dressed properly. But Cat was always dressed properly. She had style.

And then tomorrow, if they couldn't take off for Williamstown, they would play tennis in the afternoon, be with friends for dinner. Sunday and the *Times*, more tennis, maybe an auction or antiquing, if she wasn't working on an article or a book review.

Suddenly at the Ninety-Sixth Street entrance he started to jam on the brakes. He almost bumped the car in front of him. Debbie looked at him reprovingly. He thought he had seen Kim's dark-brown Alfa Romeo heading into town, returning from the airport.

It had not been Kim's car, but it would be soon. Or it had been a few minutes ago. He saw her driving, coolly, aggressively, sometimes impatiently taking risks, the delicate, long fingers on the stick shift.

As he left the Bruckner Expressway, the air began to freshen and the traffic broke up. He loosened his tie and took a deep breath. It was good to be going home. It had been a fantastic experience. But now . . . He cherished wholeness. Chaos, fragmentation had disturbed him all his life. He couldn't handle them.

It would be good with Cat. He would make it good. For a while now she had seemed more reticent sexually, had seemed to be withholding more and more of her body from him. In their early days in Boston she had been so sophisticated and knowledgeable, almost leading him and indoctrinating him in her role as "older woman." She had been rather smugly proud of having an illustrated copy of *The Perfumed Garden*, which they had read in bed and then had tried all the described positions until they had knocked themselves out laughing.

Was it that she no longer found her body attractive? "I don't feel very nice there," though he tried to reassure her that she was, showing the pleasure he took in it. Or was it something more subtle, something about not feeling loved, shrinking from such intimate exposure unless she felt the security of the most accepting love?

Sometimes he had wished that sex had been more routine for them, something they just rolled together and did. There had always, almost always, after marriage especially, been some tension and tentativeness. "Do you really want to?" Both needed to know they were wanted. Both were retreaters in the face of the slightest sign of anything that could be interpreted as disinterestedness.

They had started together at a time when men were being lectured in books and magazines for their insensitivity to a woman's needs. In story after story, the sign of the uncouth man was his boorish insistence on sex when he wanted it, regardless. Enlightened young men of the period, like Jack, were very much on their guard against such primitive "forcings." (It was also the period when everyone strove for simultaneous orgasms. And the period of the mood-ruining diaphragm. How had anyone survived?)

"Do you really want to?" For years his almost instant erection at even the thought of making love had made the question irrelevant as far as his "wanting" was concerned. But when his responses had started to slow down and she had interpreted it, he thought, as lack of interest, he had panicked, and at a time when he wanted reassurance, wanted in a way to be glutted with sex, he had found himself sometimes holding off, unsure.

One night, a while ago, as he had touched her breast, she had said, "Have you forgotten romance?" He had not moved, had not taken his hand away, had lowered his head into the pillow in the dark, hurt and angry. Moments later he had turned over and stared across the room. He felt that he had *not* forgotten romance, that he wanted romance more than ever, that he had always, or almost always, been loving in their sex. Of course, it was not the way it had been when they had first met, almost thirty years ago. She was not so naïve as to expect that. Or was she? And was he? And sometimes it was.

He knew he shouldn't lie there saying nothing. He should turn over and try to convince her that he had not forgotten romance. But what would it mean in response to such a plea? He would have to wait until it was spontaneous.

What did she want? He knew, of course, that he wouldn't respond this way if he did not feel some guilt. Sometimes his "romance" was perhaps perfunctory. His mouth was sometimes everywhere on her body that she would permit now, except her lips. Once she had taken his head in her hands and brought it up away from her body and brought his lips down to hers.

But no matter how it started out, it was never perfunctory later. For him there was always a mystique about sex. He had always been slightly in awe of what happened. Some very profound communication beyond words.

He thought of the last "honeymoon" they had gone on, to an almost deserted beach in the Caribbean. He had wanted to walk naked. Had wanted to be with her in the long grass above the dunes. On the deck of their cottage overlooking the water. "No." In bed, "Yes," and he had loved her with all the intensity of the early days, but she had stroked his hair, at times looking off into space.

Though a warm and affectionate person, she had never had his "body hunger," the sometimes intense need for physical contact, touching, holding. Some nights when they did not make love, he had playfully instructed her that the two proper ways for them to sleep were with him curled around her, spoon fashion, his hand holding her breast or lodged between her legs. Or she could curl around him, clutching his cock and balls. She had tried the latter once, but it had excited her, which excited him.

And now, thinking about it . . . he was sure everything would be all right tonight.

Debbie sat up and checked that he paid the toll, glanced around, sniffed, then laboriously lay down again, this time with her head in his lap. She heaved a big sigh and went to sleep. Tomorrow she would make a feeble effort at chasing a few groundhogs. Dogs and people liked to think they could always do what they had once done.

4

At the radio station Jack sat on a high stool in the darkened control room and looked through the glass wall at Cat, sitting at a green felt-covered table with a microphone in front of her, listening to a man across the table from her, presumably Dr. David Raskin, who had written a book on alternatives to marriage. The sound was off in the control room.

She had had her hair cut. She had said that she was going to. The beautiful white hair, now in a crisp, stylish bob, or whatever it was called this year. For a time now she had parted her hair in the middle and looped it over her ears and caught it in back with a light blue ribbon. He had liked that, but this was nice, too.

The white hair and still young face and figure were so striking. Once a man had come up to her in the baggage area of an airport and had said, "Excuse me, but you look terrific." That was all. He had then moved on. Cat had told Jack this but immediately had said, "He must have been crazy. I was all rumpled and a mess." Cat was never rumpled.

The dark-framed glasses were stuck up in her hair now. In a moment, when she would read a question from her list, written in her beautiful slanted hand, she'd flip them down, then back up. They were her plaything, her prop, along with cigarettes and a cup of coffee, when available.

Light-blue blouse with Peter Pan collar and a stylish dark-blue short cardigan sweater matching the wool skirt. Blue. "I hope someday to find a dress that isn't blue." But she rarely did. And why should she? The white-white hair and the blue eyes. She had always had a tendency to wear a "uniform." It had been gray sweater sets and gray A-line skirts before her blond hair started turning at thirty-four. Then the components became blue. In New York, blue suits or sometimes black, though she liked to stick to blue because it made the shoe situation simpler.

And shoes were a fetish with Cat. She had exquisite legs and ankles. "But don't look above there." For no reason at all she was self-conscious about her upper legs and thighs. She said she had once been fat. He could never believe that this tall, small-breasted New England woman had once been "porky," as she put it.

She stood beautifully erect, had spent a year in England at a school where for half an hour a day the girls had had to sit in wooden chairs with no back legs. If they did not sit erect, they toppled over backwards.

Jack smiled as he saw Cat looking sidewise at herself in the glass wall. It was an old trick. He used to kid her when they were courting in Boston. She rarely passed a window or a mirror without a glance. He liked this vanity.

He remembered how Cat's hair had affected their sex life. The first years, when he was in law school and she had taught, and later, when she had gone to an office for a while as an editor, she had come to bed with her hair up in pins and tied with a scarf. They had made love around the "hair problem," either right after dinner or if at bedtime, she would get up after to put it up. Except on Thursday nights, because she had her hair done on Friday morning before going to work. (But even then she liked to read, had to read before going to sleep, and he would often wake up after making love and find her curled up on the couch in the next room "getting sleepy.")

Cat glanced down again at her list of questions. She was a compulsive list maker, not just for her interviews, but for the myriad things she did during the day. He sometimes pictured her as running across an open field pursued by swooping and darting pieces of paper on which were written her lists of things to be done today, tomorrow, sometime. All her projects, interests, responsibilities.

They were opposites in temperament. Cat never foresaw the possible disasters waiting at the end of an overcrowded schedule. She undertook everything with gusto. Jack always foresaw the disasters and so tended to say no to projects. Neither of them was right. Disasters did occur sometimes, and Cat would have to be bailed out. And his life was sometimes empty because he had not gone ahead on a proposed project. Friends would say, "What a great combination! You can strike a happy medium." But they never did, or rarely. For Cat, life was only interesting when overcrowded. For Jack, not having some space and air around him panicked him.

He had sometimes urged that they both strip their lives of all extraneous elements, sit quietly together for a while and work from the core of their lives outward, expanding, growing from the center and not losing sight of the center in confusion and frazzling activity. By the core, of course, he had come to realize he meant them, their marriage, though he had not said so. She had said, "I'd like to. I'd really like to. But there's so much that has to be done before we can do that." Was she afraid of the core or maybe that there was no core at all?

44

Cat was signaling to the engineer to turn up the sound in the booth. She wanted to talk to Jack.

"Hi, Jack. Listen, uh, this is going so well, I want to make it a two-part interview and go on now. Is that okay with you?"

He felt the skin on his face tighten, but he nodded his head and smiled and waved. The engineer said, "Okay," over the mike.

It was not okay, but . . .

"Jack, if you want to go out for a drink, go ahead. We're all going to have dinner together after."

"I'll just stay here."

"He'll just stay here."

This often happened. It was one of the reasons they had decided that he might as well stay in the city a few nights a week. Cat didn't take on these dinner engagements just for business reasons. She did it on impulse. "He had no place to go." "They seemed lost." "They seemed to want to go on talking." She had a tendency to take in strays.

Of course, he understood, had understood for years. And she would have had no way of knowing how important it was that they be together alone tonight. He expected people to sense too much, to read his mind even miles away. How often when things had gone poorly with them, he had decided on his own to make some big effort at reconciliation, flying home a day early, leaving the office at three and dashing over to her office, only to find her not there or annoyed at her plans being upset or irked by his intrusion during work hours.

Without really knowing it, he was watching the sweep-second hand go around. He felt depressed. Of course, it was absurd and even ludicrous that he needed and expected Cat's support tonight. Outrageous to want a wife to overwhelm him with love and affection to help wipe out the image of a woman in bed with her husband.

Maybe he should take the Ritalin he kept wrapped in a small piece of Kleenex in his wallet. He had taken only three of the thirty the doctor had prescribed four years ago, when he had been so depressed "about nothing. I've got a good job, a fine wife, great children."

"Well, middle age, certain realizations of limitations."

He had started carrying the Ritalin in case he felt depressed. It was like the thought of suicide. Nietzsche had said that the thought of suicide had seen many people through terrible nights. It was there if you wanted it.

That time Cat had been away taping interviews. She had stayed away a long time, much longer than he had expected. And when she came home, she had confessed that she had almost not come back, that she had felt that she was causing his depression, ruining his life. He had been shocked that she would think of leaving him just like that, had hoped that instead of leaving, she would have sensed his need to have her come closer. Possibly she had sensed that need and feeling unwilling or unable to come closer, had thought the best thing was to leave entirely.

He had put his arms around her and lovingly assured her she had nothing to do with his depression. He didn't know what it was. "Male menopause." He smiled and hugged her tight. She hadn't been convinced, and for the first time there had appeared a kind of closed-lip smile, sweet but tentative.

He had wanted to say, "Just go easy for a while. Let's do things together. Just be close and undemanding. I need reassurance, in all departments. I sense that nothing exciting is going to happen from here on in, certainly not in my work. Make me feel that what I have is enough. Help!"

46

He had not said this, had not asked. In his book things asked for were not worth anything. A person should sense a need. But instead of sensing it, in some perverse way she had seemed to heap things on him, as though testing his strength, as though she were feeling some panic of her own at his sense of weakness.

But things had worked out.

The engineer had left the sound up, but Jack had been too absorbed in his own thoughts to notice. Now he heard Raskin say, "There must be some reason why married couples are living apart and single people are living together."

Eight o'clock.

"Well, as always in these sessions, we have to close with a lot of questions left unanswered. I should say before we leave that Dr. Raskin is married and the father of three children." She looked away from the dust jacket of the book to see Raskin frowning. "Read the book *Alternatives*, by Dr. David Raskin. Until tomorrow on *Books and Things*, this is Catherine Ives saying, 'Good afternoon.'"

5

When they came out of the restaurant after dinner, they found that Debbie had peed in the front seat. Jack kept a roll of paper toweling for such occasions, but Cat said she would sit in the back and perhaps sleep. She was tired. He had hoped that she would sit in front and doze with her head in his lap.

She lit a cigarette. "I'm sorry about that, bringing him along for dinner, but . . ."

"It's okay. He was interesting."

"Will it bother you if I open the window back here? It smells."

"No." Please let's not have an argument tonight about the dog or anything. Let's have a good evening, a nice night. I need it to be good tonight.

"I should listen to BAI. There's an interview with Kaplan. They want me to do him too. But his book is dull."

Jack reached for the radio knob. "Do you want me to turn it on?"

"No, thanks. I've listened to enough today. I did two interviews this afternoon to get ahead for my trip."

Jack tried to concentrate on his driving. The dinner with Raskin had been interesting but disturbing. It had

48

turned out that Raskin was married but on the point of separation. "It's all a question of whether or not one deserves a great love." He had smiled. "You do not expect an analyst to have such adolescent ideas. My own analyst is, I'm afraid, slightly critical of me. But of course, he won't express an opinion." He had laughed.

Cat had asked if he had found his "great love," and he had said, "Yes. And I'm ashamed to say the whole thing is completely banal. I mean, she's a woman half my age. I am fifty-two." Perhaps he was ashamed. but Jack also sensed that he was rather pleased about it.

"I have a feeling it's my last clear chance." He had turned to Jack. "You know the term in law, of course. The person who has the last clear chance to avoid an accident is responsible. As I said, I'm fifty-two, and my options are dwindling."

Cat had asked, "Are you moving on to a divorce?"

"Unfortunately, my wife does not want this separation."

Cat had frowned. "I could never understand that. It seems to me that if you knew someone no longer loved you . . ."

"Ah, well, what is love? asked Jesting Pilate. I don't think love has a great deal to do with the marriages of most of the middleweds I know. As a psychiatrist I know how adolescent and unaccepting it is for me to feel this way. A great love! But I do feel this way, and I know it is serious, and I would ignore it at my own peril. It is not like a bad cold."

Jack had said very little. He had almost spoken up when Raskin had said that he almost wished that his wife were having an affair of her own. He had almost said, "I don't think if you really loved a woman, you could say that." And he had noticed the time on Cat's wristwatch.

Now he looked back to make sure Cat had not fallen

49

asleep with the cigarette in her hand. He wished they were on their way up Route 7 to Williamstown for a weekend alone. They had spent their brief honeymoon in Williamstown, at the old Williams Inn, which was no longer an inn. The morning after their wedding night Cat had been driven over to Bennington for an interview for a teaching job. It would have been difficult with Jack at Law School in Cambridge, but they could have managed it. He had been eager to establish right off that their marriage would not interfere with her career. She had been turned down for the job and, instead, had gone to Vermont to teach poetry for a few weeks at a writers' workshop.

Jack knew this road well. They had looked at houses in this area but had wanted someplace more rural so they might grow vegetables, maybe have a horse for Jorie. Rich had never cared for riding. It seemed to be mostly young girls who liked horses. He remembered the pleasure in Jorie's eyes when he said they would get her a horse, and how she cared for it and won prizes.

He thought of what Raskin had said about fathers and daughters and how loving daughters sometimes helped fathers over bad periods. Jorie had certainly helped. She had flirted with him, tried out her early sexual wiles on him, encouraged roughhousing and wrestling until one night, when he had put his arms around her as he had done a thousand times before, she had changed, had withdrawn into herself, was suddenly her own girl or woman.

How beautifully she had sat her horse! All the cups and ribbons in the attic, and Jorie in Holland married to a Ph.D. in chemistry who couldn't get work in the States. Jorie teaching gourmet cooking classes to the wives in the small Dutch town where they lived. Hoping for a child. She would be lovely with children. Whenever they

50

had worked together over her college applications and they came on the question "What other interests do you have?" she would answer, "People."

Thinking of Jorie, he suddenly couldn't remember the turns and angles in the road before him. He put his foot on the brake. He felt a momentary sense of panic. He had been careful not to drink too much. Would take a drink to bed when they made love. Then he recognized a house and relaxed and picked up speed again.

They *would* make love. Usually they didn't on Friday nights. Both too tired and frazzled. They usually waited till Saturday morning or Saturday night, when they had had a chance to grow together a little. After the usual party. If it had been her party and it had gone off well, Cat was unusually ready.

But they would make love tonight.

Debbie woke and started sniffing a mile from the house. Cat stirred only when he slowed to turn into the long driveway. Jack loved the picture the Victorian house made at night. Lights on, glimpses of warm interiors, the old stained glass windows on the landing. Sometimes lately, when he was most depressed, alone in the house, he would turn on all the lights and then walk some distance away and stand and look back at it. It looked so like a home. As a home should look. And he would turn and see their field and remember the baseball games, or Jorie in her smart riding outfit, or Debbie dashing after blackbirds or groundhogs.

Over the years, in gusts of domesticity that didn't last very long, Cat had torn the kitchen apart or started to remodel the attic. The attic was still unfinished. Soon after she had started, she had gone to Smith College for a term as writer-in-residence and on her return had lost interest in the attic. Now she was redoing a part of the barn as a studio for her various projects. "It will be deductible." She also wanted to restore an old bowling alley that was on the property.

Cat went into the house while Jack stood in the drive and watched Debbie shuffle around for a few moments, her nose to the familiar turf. By the garage light Jack looked at the notices that had been stuck in the garage door. The oil had been delivered today, and the apple trees had been given their second spray. It was a clear and beautiful night, stars and a full moon. Cat knew all about the stars. Many times the family had lain on their backs in various fields while she had pointed out the constellations to them.

He saw Cat turn on the light in the bathroom and pull the shade. Debbie squatted, looking at him with the same modest embarrassment she always assumed on these occasions. He looked away. Then she trotted past him toward the back door and into the house. Sleep was important to a dog her age.

Jack left the garage door open for the birds that were nesting in the rafters. He crossed the gravel drive to the house, locked the back door, turned out the garage lights. He looked through the week's mail on the kitchen table. Bills, requests for money, a letter from Jorie in Holland, saying how much she was looking forward to Cat's visit, asking when Barbara's baby was due "exactly!" and how was Debbie? And please, Mom, bring pictures of everyone and the house when you come. He smiled at the way she used a piece of paper. Filled it, then started writing around the margins till there was no more room.

He heard Cat running her bath upstairs. He looked at the clock on the oven door. Eleven-fifteen. He closed his eyes against the image of the clock on Kim's bedside table and looked at the week's batch of magazines, *The New*

Yorker, Time, Newsweek (she liked one; he liked the other), a new House and Garden with a marker inserted. He opened it. A section on remodeling barns. He leafed through the New York Times Book Review, which Cat got early. No reviews of hers but, in a full-page ad for a book she had reviewed, a blown-up quote from her. He smiled, remembering when she had started reviewing books for the Atlantic, years ago, and her reviews had been repeatedly quoted in the advertisements and the editor had called her in to say they weren't in the business of composing blurbs. She had said that nothing could make her say nice things about a book she disliked, but if she liked it, why not say so interestingly?

He took a glass from the cupboard, filled it with ice cubes. He had resisted getting the ice-dispenser attachment. One more thing to go wrong. He was glad he had lost the argument. How many arguments they had had about the house, about every place they had lived, from Boston to New York and now Connecticut.

He turned out the kitchen light and went to the liquor table in the living room. It was an elegant, yet colorful room. High ceilings, French windows, warm lamps and furniture they had brought from the city with a few antiques they had bought at country auctions. Everything was neat and orderly except for piles of books on every table. It seemed to him that Cat received every book that was published.

He filled the goblet with vodka. Upstairs the water stopped running. He didn't really want to make love tonight; that is, there was little physical urgency. By and large, with some notable exceptions, it had been this way with them for a while. They had not known when they went to bed what was going to happen. There was often that small tension, the "I don't really feel like it tonight, but what will she think?" No doubt she had the same thoughts, but since he was almost always the originator, it was up to him. He resented this, but had come to accept it as unfortunate cultural conditioning rather than as lack of affection for him. He was always glad that he had made the move, always felt closer to her and to himself after. But as he approached fifty, he had wished that his body would help his mind more. It had never really failed him, but of late it had rarely originated the idea. Of course, once they were in bed and close and touching . . .

He took a drink and then poured more vodka into the glass and started turning out the lights in the living room. As he moved into the entrance hall and up the stairs, he could hear Cat sloshing around in the water. He went into their bedroom and found a place to put his glass on his bureau, cluttered with notes to himself, mementos and general debris. Once a month Cat asked him to tidy it up. He more or less hid the glass there, wanting first to approach Cat and not to have her emerge from the bathroom and immediately see the glass on his bedside table. When they would "neck" on the couch or just caress in passing with an exchanged "mm" or a smile, they would know, and his bringing the glass to bed was a continuation of something mutually understood. But when only he knew . . .

A woman client seeking a divorce had once told him that she had been driven crazy by her husband's habit of bringing an apple to the bedroom whenever they were going to have sex. He liked to eat an apple after, and whenever she had seen him arrive with the apple, she had frozen.

Jack took a drink. He wanted to be numb but also more alive than ever. He wanted to wipe out the image of Kim and Scott in bed and at the same time to love Cat, show Cat and himself that they were still lovers, as eager and as fierce as Scott and Kim . . . if they could only be open to each other again. If she would only not look at him with the slightly questioning smile which seemed to say, "Do you really love me?" Be open tonight. Please. He closed his eyes against the image of Kim's eyes looking at him, heavy-lidded, almost pleading with him to use and even abuse her body.

Cat had turned down the bed. In addition to the bed-side lamps, she had turned on her spot reading lamp, which he had devised years ago so that she could read after he went to sleep without going in the other room. He had been proud of his ingenuity and had laughingly said it would save their marriage. She had admired it but added, smiling, "It may also ruin my eyes."

On her bedside table were the clipboard, the glasses, the ashtray, the jar with pens and pencils. What was she writing now? Poetry? Articles? She never discussed work in progress.

When it was done, she read aloud completed poems and showed him articles or reviews. She was not a confessional poet, though he felt she might want to be. He had once overheard her say, "How nice to be a composer. You can't hurt a person's feelings with a B flat minor chord." She was more a nature poet with nature used as the metaphor. The small bird fallen from the nest that they had tried to nurture with an eyedropper and warm milk and had failed; the raccoon half-dead by the side of the road that the vet had instructed them to gas by putting it in the trunk of the car with a vacuum-cleaner hose attached to the exhaust. Though she had a great sense of humor and sharp wit, her poems were mostly sad, the touching moments in daily existence. Only once had she let her emotions go, in a poem about Vietnam, which had been widely published in newspapers and which had brought her hundreds of letters and a sudden burst of fame.

He smelled the smoke from her cigarette. A neat trick of hers, smoking while taking a bath. He undressed and went into Jorie's old room and took a shower in the bathroom he now used. He shaved first. As he got older, his stubble was harder and sharper, and once Cat had said, "Would you do me a favor and get up and shave?" He had laughed and bounded out of bed. Her fair skin was delicate.

Toweling himself, he rubbed the steam from the full-length mirror and looked at his long and spare body. Last night he and Kim had stood naked in front of her bathroom mirror, fondling, exciting each other, and he had said, "What if by some magic our images were caught in this mirror and tomorrow night . . ." "Perish the thought!" And she had run from the bathroom and thrown herself on the bed.

He saw that the thought of last night had excited him. He slipped on his blue terry-cloth robe Cat had given him and padded into her steaming bathroom. She was still in the tub, her hair wrapped in a towel. He stood beside her, his robe open. She looked up at him then at his beginning erection and then back at his face. This automatic engorgement used to amuse her, and she'd smile and call him Johnny-Jump-Up. He knew it also excited her. And when by a tightening of the muscles he would make it bob up and down, she would burst out laughing.

Now he saw that almost plaintive smile again, her eyes studying his face. He thought, Oh, please, please don't question like that. Believe! He reached down and took her hand and brought it to his cock and held it there. Then he knelt by the side of the tub and leaned over and kissed her nipple. She withdrew under the water, and his mouth followed. He came up spouting water and laughing. "Do you want to drown me?"

"Let me get on with this."

His hand reached under the water between her legs where the hair was still ash blond. "Don't let me bother you."

"Come on. I'm about to get out." She pushed his hand away.

"Okay." He kissed her and stood up and grabbed a washcloth and smiled at her. "How about my staying to help you dry?"

"No. Go on."

He wanted to stay. Now that contact was established he wanted to keep it, to fondle and stroke and caress, to become an unthinking animal. The vodka was numbing his thought processes. He just wanted to be a body with a body. In the early days she had wanted to be very private in her bathing and preparations, but she had finally come to accept and even enjoy his intrusions, his offers of help, even giving in when he had suggested that he learn how to place the diaphragm (the doctor had suggested he might do this). He wanted to be part of it all. Did not want to be left on a bed while she disappeared. To him it was all sensuous and beautiful, every part of it.

He left the bathroom. He was already losing his erection. Under usual circumstances this was all right. It would return. But tonight was different. There was the edge of doubt, of panic that it wouldn't work. He wanted her help, her understanding. Of what? What was she supposed to understand? She was simply a wife taking a bath. Or was there more than that in her look?

He took the drink to the beside table, turned out the light on his side and lay on top of the bed in his bathrobe. He had always felt more sensuous with something on, had never been eager for Cat to strip her nightdress off the minute he touched her.

The tub was emptying. He'd forgotten to call the plumber about having the drain fixed. She would be in her nightdress now, standing tall and graceful in front of the mirror, appraising herself coolly, possibly sizing up the new haircut. Now she was brushing her teeth. Impatient and needing contact, he wanted to leap off the bed and go in and stand behind her and reach around and, pressing himself against her lean flanks, stroke her body through the sheer nightdress.

The light went out in the bathroom. Cat opened the door and came into the bedroom. "Where's Debbie sleeping?"

"In the kitchen."

"She'll mess. She should be in the cellar."

"I'll clean it up."

"It's going to be hard for all of us, but I think you should consider putting her away."

"We're seeing the vet tomorrow." Please, dear God, let's not argue. He held the glass out to her. She shook her head. She stood at her side of the bed and wound the alarm clock, looking at him; then she slipped into bed and pulled the covers up.

He moved over and lay close to her, idly stroking her belly. "What's the plan for tomorrow?"

"The Cowleys' at night. There's a church antique auction in the morning."

"And you made a tennis date?" He had to be careful. She was ticklish near her navel.

"Yes. I told you."

He snuggled closer. "A nice day. Is my racquet back?"
"Yes."

"Mmmmm." He nestled above her shoulder. "You smell good. What's that?"

"Same as always. Soap."

"And you." His hand continued to move idly over her body. "You know, I love sitting in the booth there, watching you function. Your frown of concentration, the lively questions you ask. I know you don't like me to be around while you're working. . . ."

"No. It's just that it breaks the concentration, which is so hard to get in the first place in these interviews."

He had gone to her early poetry readings after her first volume appeared, and he had been charmed by a little gesture she had used while reading, a slight movement of the hand and arm as though she were conducting the music of the poem. And he had told her how delightful it was, but she had said it made her self-conscious to have him point out her mannerisms, even if he liked them. And later she had said she would feel more comfortable if he didn't come to hear her. In introducing the occasions for each poem, she wanted to feel free to say whatever she wanted to say, however personal, and she felt constricted with him there.

His hand moved over her body. Touch me, please! Do something. "I like your hair." He moved his hand to ruffle it. "A great success."

"It's not quite right, but it will be better next time."

"Anybody stop you today and tell you how terrific you look?" She smiled, remembering the incident in the airport. He kissed her neck, her ear. She turned out the bedside light. He reached up and turned out the reading spotlight. The bedside clock glowed in the dark. Eleven-thirty. He closed his eyes and moved down and rested his face against her belly, his hand moving along her thigh.

The moonlight filtered into the room. "What a beautiful night!"

"Yes." At last her hand began idly to stroke his hair.

He pressed his face into her belly and groaned. "Mmmmm." He looked up at her. Her face was turned away from the windows. He moved up and tongued her breasts though the thin material. She sat up suddenly and stripped the nightdress over her head and tossed it on the floor, then lay down again. He shrugged off his robe and moved on, caressing, fondling, mouthing, uttering little groans of pleasure and appreciation. He did appreciate the sleek coolness of her body, the long gracefulness of it lying in the moonlight. Cool Cat. The fresh, cool sheets, the plump, oversize pillows. Growling playfully, he straddled her rib cage and rubbed her nipples with the head of his cock. Sometimes she used to raise her head and take it in her mouth for a moment. He lowered himself so that he still straddled her, his cock pressed against her ribs and belly, and he kissed her neck and hair. She turned her head to look at him, studying him. He kissed her lips. "Mmmm." He skimmed his nails lightly over her body. She had taught him how to do that to her. Her nipples rose. She was quick to arouse. No credit to him. But he felt again as he had felt recently that her body in its headlong rush to orgasm was responding in spite of herself.

Her hips moved. He got off her and tried to turn her on her belly.

"No," she murmured.

"Yes." He urged, and reluctantly she allowed him to turn her. He leaned over and kissed her bottom. "You have a fantastic bottom." She was proud of it, went to exercise classes twice a week to keep it in shape, but lately she didn't seem to like his fondling it. He massaged her

60

shoulders, then ran his hand down over her back and reached between her legs. She tightened. He had always liked stroking her this way. She had never liked his coming in her from that angle. It hurt, she said, but he had wondered if it didn't somehow convey debasement to her.

After a minute or two she twisted around and lay on her back. Jack, fully aroused now, quickly moved his head between her legs.

"No."

"Please!" He pushed her legs apart.

She twisted, but he moved on, his tongue moving up her inner thighs, and in a moment his face was nestled in her warmth. She stopped resisting, a small sound, a moan of protest and pleasure. Barely raising his head, he murmured, "You used to like this. Ask me to do it." She used to say, "Eat me!" and then laugh at the idea of her giving such orders. It obviously excited her. With one hand he reached up to stroke her breast, the other tried to slide under her bottom, but her hand reached down to stop him. She had never liked to come this way, and he had never particularly liked to come from sucking. It was too sharp, lacked the warmth and connectedness of fucking. And now tonight he did not want her to come this way. He wanted to "mount" her, "plow" her. It must be some violent physical taking. He wanted to hear her cry out as she sometimes used to, "Oh, yes, fuck me! Fuck me!"

"Come in me. Come in me."

He moved up and, kneeling, entered her, shoved into her with unaccustomed force. He reached down with both hands grabbed her bottom and pulled her up and toward him, their bodies lunging against each other. No lingering, long sensuousness, holding off as long as possible. No playfulness.

61

With the fingers of his right hand he started to probe her.

"No," she cried softly.

"Yes!" But he didn't, just ground their bodies together, finally letting go and lying full on top of her, his toes digging into the bed as she came with a series of small, almost protesting cries.

He paused, pressing deep into her, allowing her to move against him as she would. "Come now! Come!" she called out almost petulantly. Other nights he might wait, if he could, and bring her around again and possibly even a third time before coming himself. But she was right. This was not one of those nights. It was a night of rutting. He thrust quickly. Cat could take deep thrusts.

After, he let himself down full on top of Cat, sweating, his breathing short and shallow. She felt lifeless under him, her head turned away on the pillow. It had all been rushed, driving, in some way frenzied. He was both exhilarated and ashamed. Confused. He saw the glass with the vodka, the ice now melted.

He turned and kissed Cat's neck, her ear, tasting the salt. He lay his head in the crook of her shoulder. He suddenly felt infinitely sad, not just the "little death." It was something more. He sensed that in the middle of the taking, the anger, the lust, the wanting to love, something had been lost.

After a while he slipped out of her, reached down and pulled up the covers, drawing them carefully over Cat's shoulder. She turned away, and he curled up behind her, pressing against her back, kissing her shoulder, looking past her to the wall.

6

When Jack woke up, he sensed that he was alone. He turned; Cat was not there. The clock read three-thirty. The bathroom door was open. She was not there. She had thoughtfully pulled the covers up on her side.

Why had he forced her? Why had she almost made him force her?

What had been going on? It had all seemed so desperate on his part. Her part was . . . what? Passive, protesting. Her body finally acquiescing, hurrying as though to get it over quickly. So many times before it had reaffirmed something between them. Sometimes when he had felt least like making love but most like loving. No physical urgency but an urgent need to connect, to reaffirm, and the next day they had seemed to be closer, touching in passing, smiling knowingly. He opened his eyes again and looked toward the open bedroom door. No sign of light. Was she sleeping in Jorie's room or Rich's or some other room in this huge old house?

Something had happened tonight, not what he had expected. Not the exorcising and punishing of Kim and the proving of his love for Cat. There had been anger and desperation. Over the last five years of what he sensed as her withdrawal, he had never before said things like, "You used to like it." He had accepted it, sometimes gently, wordlessly persuading her.

He wished that she were there in bed so that by moving to her and holding her close, he could somehow communicate his sadness for what had happened. He couldn't say anything. It was all too complex. How much more meaningful it would be, just holding her like that, so much more loving than all the urgency and violence of three hours ago!

He smelled cigarette smoke. She was awake somewhere. Should he go to her? Talk. What was there to talk about that could be said? So much emphasis on communication these days, but if all you communicated was sadness and unhappiness . . . It would be better just to show how he felt, tomorrow, by kindness, consideration. At the auction, after she had dropped out of the bidding on something she really wanted, he would put in one final winning bid. Later, on the tennis court he would enjoy the beautiful arc of her body as she reached up to serve, might even risk touching her, though she loathed what she called "PDA," public display of affection. They would gentle each other, relax, not try to prove anything. They had so much.

He looked out the bedroom door. She had left his bed to be alone, away from him. Yet somehow he couldn't stand the idea of her being sad and alone somewhere in this big dark house. One instinct told him to wait until tomorrow, then be close. But his responsible, protecting self told him that Cat was somewhere needing comfort. Or maybe he was exaggerating, imagining, and she was simply somewhere reading or writing.

He got up, put on his terry-cloth robe and, without looking for his slippers, went out into the upper hall. He could see now there was a light somewhere downstairs. He could smell coffee along with the cigarette smoke. He hesitated. Usually when she got up to read or smoke or have a cup of coffee, he did not follow her. In the early days he had, but he soon learned that she was a night person, did not need much sleep and didn't like his padding after her, asking "Are you all right?" He started down the stairs.

He walked through the dark living room and approached the door to the kitchen. Cat was sitting under the lamp at the kitchen table, her pink flannel robe wrapped around her, smoking, drinking coffee and looking at the real estate section of the paper. She looked up and smiled. "Hi. Did I disturb you? Sorry."

"No." He came to her and, touching her shoulder, bent down and kissed her hair. He saw they had caught a mouse in the trap. He moved to pick it up. It was his job to dispose of caught mice. "I hope with the nice weather they'll be moving out of the house." They had argued often over using poison, but she insisted the mice died in the walls and smelled up the house.

Debbie opened her eyes without lifting her head, thumped her tail once and went back to sleep.

"Do you want me to warm up the milk for you?"

"No, thanks. I'll just have it like this."

"You should have your slippers on."

"I'm only going to be here a minute." He ran his hand across her shoulders as he moved to the table and sat down opposite her. He flipped open the magazine. "I didn't get a chance to study the pages you marked about the barn. But they looked interesting."

"It was just an idea." She looked across at him. She seemed unusually relaxed, strangely calm. He sensed that something was about to happen. She reached out her hand and took his and, smiling sadly, said, "I think that we should think about a separation or divorce."

He frowned and opened his mouth to protest but found himself saying nothing. She went on, calmly, coolly.

"A few years ago when I brought it up, you were against it. But . . . I don't feel we've had a life together for quite a while."

She squeezed his hand and smiled, as though to soften what she was saying. "We're good in bed. And we've made love a great deal lately. But it's seemed to me a rather desperate effort to keep something going between us, to try to persuade ourselves that what we knew was happening wasn't happening." Now mingled with his other confused feelings was hurt.

"I'm sorry. Does that sound ungrateful? I don't mean it to be. It's a lot. We're lucky that way. But I have sometimes come to dread it. I'm sorry. Because somehow our lives seem to depend on each time we're together . . . you're trying to prove to yourself and me that you still love me."

He drew his hand away from hers. "That's not true."

"I'm sorry. What can you say? You've always found it difficult to admit that what is is. You've always felt that with a little effort you could change things."

He sat there while she went on. He was shocked at her coolness and, in spite of himself, angry at her characterization of their last years together. He had tried.

Then he wondered if this was just another way of saying, "I want you to love me more. I want you to overwhelm me and reassure me." If it was, he couldn't do it. Couldn't once again overcome the questioning look in her eyes. Not without help. Two years ago he had. They had ended up hugging and kissing and making passionate love. But not now. Why? Along with the protest, he felt something welling up inside him, stemming from his resentment at her rejection of his love. "Let it go. Let it all go."

He was stunned and angry and wanted to defend himself. But why be angry? She only wanted him to love her the way he wanted to love her. What was he angry at then? The impossibility? Did he want to vindicate himself or save the marriage? Any attack would only confirm her point of view that he didn't love her. Of course, he had thought about separation and divorce. What married man or woman hadn't? But only as a fantasy. She had never wanted the marriage. Thank her father and mother for that! But he had done everything he could to make their marriage different. He felt a kind of rage in him, and yet perhaps he should shut up and let it go and take the blame.

He looked back at her. She was hurting him, breaking up their marriage and blaming him. He wanted to defend himself with countercharges. Had *she* tried? But at the same time his instinct was to comfort her for what was happening to them.

She looked at him, trying to persuade him. "We haven't had a marriage in a long time. Just a kind of loving accommodation to each other." It had been a long time since she had talked to him like this, subtly inferring her greater wisdom, her maturity and understanding. "You've been thinking about it, too, haven't you? Be honest."

She seemed to want him to say, "I don't love you anymore. Your suspicions are true and accurate." But they were not true. And he felt hurt that his efforts had been judged inadequate and somehow guilty that they had been inadequate. And yet somewhere also he was crying out, "I have done my best."

He said, "I don't seem to be relating to anything much in my life at the moment. I don't know why. Age." He shrugged. This seemed to be asking for her understanding, denying and affirming nothing. But it was true, except for his feelings for Kim.

He knew that he would get no understanding, and perhaps shouldn't, for this semi-evasion. Cat had never responded sympathetically to his periods of self-doubt, dissatisfaction, moodiness. Cat was not sympathetic to brooding indecisiveness. She felt there was always something that could be done. (She was like Kim in that respect. Both of them mistrusted anyone who was sick in bed for longer than a day. They had no patience or time for illness.)

She sat across the table, seeming strong and determined. He saw in her the woman who many years ago, before he knew her, had declared her father dead as far as she was concerned because of a dispute over what she wanted to do with her life.

She lighted another cigarette. "All this week I've been thinking, making lists in my head. If Onlys . . . if only you would do this or that. If only I could do this. It all seemed so petty, but then I realized, that it all seemed to add up: If only you would not be you and I would not be I."

She seemed to be carefully avoiding arguable issues. It was just "something." He remembered his client's comment about his marriage. "It just died." He looked at Cat. It was as though they were taking part in a ritual, the specifics avoided, all cloaked in symbolic generalities. There was so much to be said. Each bursting with things to be said, but each aware of the futility of saying more. They both seemed to have some instinct not to tear each

68

other apart, to leave each other whole, as a last act of love. Still, he said, "We have so much."

"I know, but . . ."

"I think our marriage is as good as most of the marriages we know. Better than most. Better than my parents'. Better than your parents'."

"But not good enough. Is it? Perhaps if one of us were willing to settle. It would be easier if I hated you or you hated me. Of course, on occasion we have hated each other." She tried for a joke. "We could buy another house and remodel it. Some couples do that. It's too late for us to have another baby. Maybe we'll be better friends. You'll come to see me only when you want to see me."

He sat there staring into the shadows of the kitchen. It couldn't all be just slipping away like this. But it was. She had not wanted to discuss it. She had wanted to declare it, still with the charge that "It's you." "You'll come to see me only when you want to see me." Something kept his tongue from moving, from blurting out his usual protestations of love. He had loved her, and it was not enough. He looked at her. His silence seemed to acquiesce in her feeling that he didn't love her. He did love her. But he couldn't go on his knees and hug her and promise it would all be different. They had what they had, which was a lot.

"I should have brought this up a long time ago, only I was afraid."

"Afraid of what?"

"I don't know. How I'd live, how I'd manage."

He looked at her. He was filled with a mixture of pity and anger. Had she been staying with him," "letting" him make love to her because she was afraid she couldn't "manage" by herself? The idea was both repulsive and somehow sad. He leaned toward her. "I wouldn't want to change your life at all. The house, the apartment, if you want it. I'd take care of the bills same as now." He knew what he was doing. His usual. Rejected, he rushed away. I won't trouble you anymore. But in a kind of reverse vindictiveness he could not explain, he assured her that he would still be as kind and protective as always.

"No. I don't want to live here without you."

"I don't want to live here without you."

"Well, then we should sell it."

He couldn't believe it. They were rushing on to the logistics of their separation. They had discussed nothing and were already talking about where each would live. "No. I don't think we should sell it." She looked at him. "Until we know. Until we really know."

Suddenly she started to cry. She turned, trying to hide her face. He moved to her quickly and, crouching beside her, hugged her to him and buried his face against her shoulder. She stammered out, "I hate what's happening to us."

He drew her closer to him, trying to cradle her, all resentments and angers and hesitations dissolved by her tears. "Let's try. Let's try again." Still crying, she shook her head. He went on. "Let's go over things and see." She sniffled and again shook her head.

She was infinitely dear to him at that moment. Nothing in the world was worth causing these tears, the blank look of despair in her eyes. Why had she never cried before? She had always seemed strong and assured. Would tears have shown her needful? She didn't want to clutch anyone for comfort. Even now it was he who was clutching her, holding her. Her hands were at her face, trying to hide, or reaching for Kleenex in her robe. He shifted from a crouching position to kneeling. She looked toward him. "You're uncomfortable there. . . ."

"I can't stand seeing you like this."

"It's very self-indulgent. I didn't do it to have you fling your arms around me."

"I know." He rubbed his face against her shoulder. "Can't we try?"

She looked at him, trying to smile, and shook her head. He felt utter desolation. Almost ever since he could remember she had been the condition of his life, the reference point. He did not want to be free, had never dreamed of being free. Had only wanted things better with them.

She blew her nose. "Debbie wants to go out."

Jack looked around and saw her standing at the door, staring at it dumbly. Cat rose from his embrace and took the cup and saucer and glass to the sink. He opened the door for Debbie and turned on the outside light.

"Mother, of course, will say, 'I told you so.' Always said I made a lousy wife."

He came up behind her and took her by the shoulders. "That's not true." She looked at him, smiling disbelief. "Let's not tell her . . . until we know."

"I can't lie to her."

"I don't think we should tell anyone yet."

She studied his face. "I still want to see Jorie in Holland as I've planned."

"Of course. But don't tell her or Rich . . . yet." Debbie barked once. He let her in, locked the door and turned out the outside light.

Cat turned from the sink. "We've got to call Bill. The drain's stopped up again." They put their arms around each other and left the kitchen.

"And the brake on my car."

71

"I'll talk to Chuck about it tomorrow."

"Hunter says the apple trees should be pruned if we want any kind of apples." They were going through the living room toward the hall.

"That's okay."

They walked upstairs and into the bedroom. He headed for the bathroom. "I'm going to take half a Valium. Do you want one?"

She looked at the clock. "I may not be a very good doubles partner."

"I think we need it." He brought the pills and the glass of water from the bathroom. They swallowed the pills and got into bed. She turned her back to him, and very gently, but all-enveloping, he wrapped his arms around her and pressed against her.

"Your feet are cold. You should have worn your slippers."

"They'll warm up." He moved them away from her.

They lay like that for some minutes. He thought, I haven't felt so close to her in months. She started to cry again, softly, and he held her closer, but neither of them said anything, and they finally went to sleep.

7

The next day when Jack awoke around eight, Cat was already out in the garden, cleaning up the beds to ready them for spring planting. Last night they had agreed to separate, yet they would spend the morning tending the gardens and shrubs as though nothing had happened. Perhaps nothing had happened, and it would all be forgotten.

After breakfast he joined her in the garden. Debbie waddled over to be petted, and he put his arm around Cat's shoulder and kissed her sweaty cheek. "Good morning."

"Good morning. Did I disturb you when I got up?"

"No. Did you manage to sleep at all?"

"Yes, some." He hugged her. She pointed to the flower bed. "Are those weeds? I can never tell."

"Weeds." And he leaned over and, loosening the earth around them, pulled them out.

For an hour they raked and cultivated, and he carted the debris off to a compost heap at the back of their property. Then, at nine-thirty, he helped Debbie into the station wagon and took her to the vet's. Cat and he exchanged glances over the dog, but she didn't say anything. She just looked at Jack and then at Debbie and scratched her behind the ear and patted her as though it might be the last time.

But the vet decided that she was still enjoying life, and as long as Jack was willing to put up with the trouble of giving her extra attention, he saw no reason for putting her away. When they returned to the house and Debbie eased herself out of the car with Jack's help, Cat looked at him and smiled and shook her head once, but that was all.

At the church auction Cat bid for an antique cradle. "I know that Rich and Barbara would never use it, but it would be fun to take to them tomorrow." Then the bidding got too high, and she said, "Oh, let them have it." And then, as he knew he would, Jack put in the final bid and won. "You shouldn't have done that. It was too much." But she was obviously pleased, and as they sat on the church lawn under the huge maple tree and ate their sandwiches, she looked at the cradle, now piled high with old quilts, an antique doll, an ancient apple corer, and said, "If they don't use it for the baby, they can use it to hold geraniums."

He smiled at her. "I think you're more tickled about becoming a grandmother than you were about becoming a mother."

"I know. It's indecent. Of course, I'm not really a grandmother, am I, since they're not married. I wonder what I am."

Later in the afternoon they played doubles on the neighbors' rather beaten-up old court, and he didn't once tell her to rush the net when he rushed the net, nor did he correct her calls when she repeatedly gave their opponents the benefit of the doubt. He found himself praising her shots, and she reciprocated by urging their "team" on with

74

"We've got them on the run now. Your serves are really terrific today." As a matter of fact, they were.

Before they went to the Cowleys for dinner, Jack retired to his study to write a birthday jingle for Mark Cowley's birthday party. Everyone had been asked to write something. Jingles and occasional verse had always been a specialty with Jack since his days at boarding school. Custom decreed that they be a little stilted, formal with an outrageous rhyme here and there.

The guests at the party were mostly old friends; some they had known since college, where Cat had been their lodestone, her apartment a gathering place for drinking and talking about the arts and LIFE.

The men had wanted to be poets or playwrights or novelists. They had become doctors, businessmen, lawyers and professors, but when they were with Cat, they could once again "gather 'round" and remember the days at her place when they were artists. She was the only one who had "made it" with three books of poems, a collection of short stories and her various jobs in the arts, editing, teaching, interviewing.

Jack always wondered how Phil Merriam felt after Cat would look at him late in the evening at one of these parties and say, "This one could have made it. This one had it, really had it." Did he sleep well that night? And sometimes she would look at Jack and say, "He could have made it, too." And he would be aware again how in a way he had failed her in that department. In her diary, which she had kept during her love affair with Ned, the trips back and forth to New Haven before she met Jack, she had written of Ned, "It would be so exciting, the two of us plugging along together, writing, talking writing." Jack was supposed to have outstripped Ned as a writer, but he'd chickened out. Ned's last book had been dedicated to Cat, though she wouldn't read it.

The party broke up around midnight. Cat had had an exciting time, the center of attention, yet always modest, turning away compliments with a girlish phrase she had used as long as he could remember, "Oh, pooh!"

Jack walked around the grounds with Debbie, making sure that she didn't amble onto the road, and then put out the lights and went upstairs. Cat was in the bathroom with the door closed. He heard the water running in the basin. He undressed and went into his bathroom and came back and got into bed and lay there waiting.

It had been one of those great country Saturdays. And they had gentled each other, treated each other with such consideration. It was impossible to think that they could be separating. Would they? Had this closeness been brought about by the clearing of the strain, by the knowledge that they were going to part, or what? There had been no carping, no complaining, no running arguments over the usual list of "differences." They had just enjoyed each other's company. It was the way they were on trips. She had always said, "We're good in hotels." Was last night just another "scene," different, quieter? What did he want? Here he was lying in bed again, waiting. He picked up his glasses and a magazine and flipped the pages.

The water stopped, and in a moment Cat opened the door. The light was out in the bathroom, but behind Cat, Jack could see there was a light on in the room beyond. She was wearing a nightdress and flannel robe. "Good night."

Jack just looked at her.

She came to her side of the bed and took her glasses and the clipboard. "It was a lovely day."

Jack watched her. "Yes. Great."

76

"Thanks for indulging me about the cradle. I know it's silly, but . . . thanks." She was back at the bathroom door. "Let's not forget to take it to them tomorrow. We can pick up some geraniums along the way."

"Yes."

She stood in the doorway for a moment. Then: "Good night."

"Good night." She closed the bathroom door.

He felt sick and hurt and angry. For a long time he just lay there staring at the closed door. What did she want? Did she want him to come to her, kneel by the bed, plead, bring the matter to a tearful crisis and finally to a commitment? His instinct had always been to heal, to patch up, to achieve a wholeness with himself, with a relationship.

But now something in him kept saying, "Let it be." He continued to stare numbly at the bathroom door. Then he turned out the light and pulled the covers over his shoulder. Why had she brought up the whole subject? He would never have brought it up. They could have managed, were managing. It was a long time before he went to sleep.

8

Sunday he found himself touching her, kissing her cheek, putting his arm around her shoulders, wanting to be close.

They visited Rich and Barbara in their rented dilapidated cottage in Branford, gave them the cradle filled with pots of pink geraniums. Jack and Rich walked along the beach. He did not mention the separation. If it did not go through, there was no sense in upsetting "the children." Rich talked about his feelings for Barbara and the expected baby and how he wanted them to marry. "But Barbara doesn't want to. She's afraid."

They admired Rich's very modern sculpture in the barn and listened to Barbara talk with excitement about her work repairing and restoring paintings for the art gallery. And they each felt the baby kick in Barbara's belly. A neighbor took a family picture of them all pressed together, arms around each other, smiling. This would go with Cat to Jorie in Holland.

Jack always drove away from the children's cottage with a jealous pang, for what they were doing, for what they were and for where they were in their lives.

On the way home they talked about the children, about Cat's trip. "Can you pick up some things I'll need in the city?" And from time to time he held her hand.

Arriving home, he couldn't stand the tension he felt within himself, and unwilling to face another night like the previous one, he ate a quick sandwich with Cat, gathered together his clean laundry and Debbie and headed for the city, feeling relieved but miserable.

The next morning was the first of many mornings he was to awaken at four-thirty, depressed. For half an hour he lay there bewildered, unable to come to grips with anything. Finally, he went into the second bedroom and opened his attaché case, which he hadn't opened all weekend, and tried to do some work.

At the office he propped Cat's list against the picture of her and the children.

> Take blue shoes for lifts
> Tapes (10)
> Elizabeth Arden (I will call order)
> Prescription 583689
> Blue wool dress. Clean and bring to country.

He found it difficult to concentrate, wanted to go out and run Cat's errands.

But he had to concentrate. The ten-thirty meeting with Spivak and the tax adviser was not the happiest. Spivak, a novelist turned screenwriter, had apparently been listening to some Hollywood types who had excited him about the possible deals and arrangements that could be made. When Jack's partner had said they were not the kind that he could recommend, involving, as they might, fraud, Spivak had been angry. They might lose Spivak.

Looking at his old messages from Friday and seeing Kim's name, he realized that he hadn't really thought about her since three-thirty Saturday morning in the kitchen. Up until then, Kim and Scott had been very much on his mind. Too much. He closed his eyes. If Scott hadn't come home that night . . . If he hadn't been so upset about it. If . . .

But really, Cat and Kim had nothing to do with each other, did they? It's not as if he would be running to Kim to say, "I'm free!" Did he want to be free?

At lunchtime he took Cat's list and bought the tapes and went to Arden's, but she hadn't called in her needs yet. Then he walked around the corner and sat in the mini-park where the Stork Club has been and ate a sandwich and stared at the waterfall. All he could see was the image of Cat sitting at the kitchen table in the middle of the night, sobbing. Nothing, nothing was worth that. He should go to a phone and call her.

His sense of failure in the marriage, the loneliness which was beginning to invade him, his sense of guilt, every instinct told him to call. But he didn't.

Normally, being a man who dealt in rational analysis day in and day out, he might have mentally made Column A and Column B, as he and Cat had done when they were debating things like the move to the country. But his mind was a blank, resenting and resisting a choice.

Back in the office he found it difficult to sit still. He called Arden's to ask if Cat had phoned in her order. She hadn't. He wanted to talk to someone, but what could he say? What could anyone say to him? He had listened to men who needed to talk about their marriages, and all he had been able to contribute was: "Yes." . . . "Well." . . . "It's difficult." Nobody could ever know what went on in another person's marriage. Usually the men had talked themselves into their own answers, revealing to themselves how much they really loved or hated their wives and their marriages.

Late in the afternoon he got up abruptly and went to the club to knock the ball around the squash court by himself. He didn't want to play a match. He just needed to bang the ball around. Work off some tension.

He had been hitting the ball for a few minutes when he let the ball roll dead and found himself just standing in the middle of the court, staring at the floor.

The door to the court swung open, and Scott stepped in. "Jack?"

Jack looked up. "Scott! How are you? Welcome back." He shifted his racquet and extended his hand.

"They said you had nobody to play with. Can we play?"

"Sure." He realized that, taken by surprise, he was being overhearty. "How was the trip? You look great. Terrific tan." It was a strange feeling. Scott was no longer a casual acquaintance, a twice-a-week squash opponent. Since he had seen him last, he had learned a great deal about him, and he had occupied his mind with intimidating images. They began hitting the ball.

"Fabulous country over there. I had no idea. Rich as hell with all that oil money. An architect's dream." They rallied for a few moments.

"When did you get back?" Jack asked casually.

"Friday."

Jack wanted to ask, "What time?" but he didn't.

"It was great to get home. Colin had made me a set of bookends. Sitting in the hall, waiting for me."

He knew he should ask, "How's Kim?" but he couldn't carry it off.

In the showers Jack was acutely aware of Scott's well-tanned athletic body fifteen years younger than his, and for the first time he was embarrassed in his naked presence. It was strange. He had been sleeping with this man's wife, yet he felt intimidated by him.

Over a drink in the bar he said yes the first time Scott invited him to come home for dinner.

81

In the taxi he changed his mind. He didn't want to see Kim with Scott. "I think this is an imposition, just to barge in on her like this."

"No. She prides herself on being able to rise to the occasion. You remember the last time."

When they both appeared in the family room kitchen, Kim frowned and then quickly beamed a big "Hello."

Halfway through dinner there was a call for Scott from Seattle. He apologized, explaining how difficult it was to connect with people on the West Coast, who were just getting to the office when he was on his way to lunch and so on.

Kim looked at Jack. "Why did you come?"

"I'm not quite sure." He smiled. "You like risks."

"How are you?" There was a tone of sympathetic concern.

"All right. How are you?"

"All right. Friday night I looked at the clock hoping you were asleep."

He smiled. "I looked at the clock knowing you weren't."

"Did you go home?"

"Yes."

"Good."

"And at three-thirty in the morning, Cat and I were sitting in the kitchen"—he was going to say, "having made love," but didn't—"and she said she thought we should separate or divorce."

"Oh, no!" Kim frowned and reached out to touch his hand, then drew back.

"She's brought this up before. The last time we went to the mat and yelled at each other and ended up, of course, in bed. This time there was no passion to it. Just sadness, a strange closeness as though we wanted to leave each other as whole as possible."

Kim shook her head and looked at him, still frowning, waiting for him to go on.

"Saturday we had a beautiful day together. Then she went into a guest room to sleep. And I just turned out the light and didn't do anything. I seem to want it to happen, and I don't want it to happen. And somewhere in between I'm paralyzed."

She looked at him. "Is it my fault?"

"No. Perhaps if I hadn't met you, I would have insisted on another trip to Bermuda, another try. You *have* reawakened feelings, possibilities I had forgotten."

"Maybe all she wants is reassurance."

"I don't seem to be able to give it to her. Or to want to give it to her. She says we haven't had a life together for years. I thought we had." He shrugged. "All I could give her is what I have given her. And that doesn't seem to be enough. And maybe it isn't enough. We haven't mentioned it since. This weekend she leaves for Holland to see our daughter and to tape some interviews in Europe for her program."

"Maybe she'll just forget about it."

Jack played with his spoon. "I'm not sure I want her to forget about it. It's odd. I go around picking up things for her for her trip, lovingly adding small gifts I know will please her. But I don't know if I want her to forget about it." He looked at Kim and smiled and shook his head. "Also, I seem to resent being put in a position of making a choice." Under the table his leg accidentally touched hers. "I feel strange talking to you like this about Cat and me."

"I've talked to you. Besides, I'm selfishly concerned. When you left the other night, I had a feeling you never wanted to see me again."

"I didn't think I wanted to. I felt it was the only way."

Scott came into the room with more apologies, and after dinner he and Jack watched some baseball on the family set, while Kim retreated to her room to watch a show she had to "check on."

Around ten o'clock he left and headed down the street again toward a taxi and home, feeling confused and more lonely than ever. They had said goodbye to him at the door, arms loosely around each other. "Good night. See you at the club."

"Yes. Good night."

9

Friday night Jack arrived in the country with Cat's dress, shoes, prescriptions, cosmetics, odds and ends she had asked for (she had added to the list over the telephone) and various small presents he had bought for her.

She was late getting home from the radio station, where she had been taping interviews all day, and he cooked dinner. Almost immediately after dinner, around ten, exhausted, Cat went upstairs to take her bath and go to bed. Jack stayed downstairs watching baseball, and when he went up around eleven, he found Cat asleep in their bed.

His feelings, slightly numbed by a couple of strong scotches he had taken to prepare him for his lonely bed, were confused. He felt a surge of love and relief, a grateful return to simplicity and wholeness. And yet there was an awareness that Cat was calling the turns, leaving the bed when she wanted, returning when she wanted. Where were they?

He undressed in Jorie's room. When he slipped into bed, Cat turned toward him and half asleep embraced him.

They made love wordlessly, not with the rush and abandon of reunited lovers, but tenderly, gently. After, she murmured, "Maybe we could go on being lovers, even though we're separated."

He smiled and kissed her cheek, almost a reflex action to such a suggestion.

But he became aware of some resistance to this idea. Part of him wanted to stay married, to enjoy days and evenings and nights like this, his home, his wife, the complexities of married life. But if they broke the marriage . . . What then? He wanted to be free. He wanted the texture of his marriage, of his home and family, or he wanted to be free. They made love in the context of their marriage, their sharing, their memories, their hopes and fears. As lovers, it would be completely different. Now he loved her and slept with her out of the wholeness of their life together. There was nothing condescending about this idea. True, it was different. There was a richness of association no love affair could have. Even the rueful awareness that they were no longer young, no longer new to each other, evoked a tenderness and compassion which gave a complex and darker tone to their lovemaking. Sometimes they made love like triumphant survivors surprised at the new tones and colors they discovered together.

They shifted into their sleeping positions; he snuggled against her back. But he didn't go to sleep. She had as much as said they were still separating, and he had said nothing.

Saturday they were late arriving at Kennedy, and Cat barely had time to hurry to the ladies' room before going through the security checkpoint. Jack bought her the *Times*, jammed it in her tote bag and went with her to the checkpoint. "I feel like a refugee with all this junk."

He looked at her, her white hair freshly washed, her trim, figure sensibly but beautifully dressed for the trip. "Lady, you look smashing." She laughed.

As they approached the gate, they found that today they were allowing only passengers through the checkpoint. They stopped. "Thanks for helping me get off. I never could have done it alone. For a woman who is famous for organization, I certainly went to pieces." They kissed. "Where will you be?"

"In the apartment probably. Maybe in the country, weekends. I've got to clean out the pool."

"I'll write to the apartment."

"In ten days or two weeks I go to Cambridge for some meetings."

"You have my schedule?"

"Yes. My love to the kids."

"Do I have that picture for them?" She hunted in her purse and found it. "Yes." They kissed again. "You know you need a haircut."

"I know."

"I might spend a few days in Rome if I can get an interview with Moravia."

"Let me know so I can meet you."

"I can manage." She picked up her purse and camera, and he picked up her tote bag, and they moved to the security checkpoint.

"Have a great time."

"I will. You know how I've been looking forward to it. Take care of yourself. See people. Call people. Don't stay alone."

"I will." They kissed again.

He watched her go through the security check, smiling, chatting with the guards. On the other side of the screening arch, she picked up her things and moved down the corridor. She didn't look back. He watched her until she merged in with the other passengers and passed out of sight.

He stood at the window, staring at her plane, watching it finally move out toward the runway, disappearing behind a building. There was something symbolic about it

87

all, the leave-taking, the leaving. He remembered three years ago when they had come to see off her ailing brother. Cat had insisted on going up to the observation deck and watching until the plane had disappeared in the sky. Then she had turned and said, "I have a terrible feeling I'm never going to see him again."

And she hadn't.

Sunday evening Jack ate supper at a hamburger joint and went to a movie. On his return to his apartment he saw a letter half pushed under the downstairs front door. It was Kim's familiar blue stationery and her handwriting. "Mr. John Montgomery."

He knew the Maxwells were not at home. She didn't. She had taken a big risk. It was the first letter since Scott's return.

As he climbed the three flights of stairs, he wondered what it would say, what he wanted it to say. Cat was away again now. But Scott was home; for how long, no one knew. There might be times when they could be together.

He was in a sense "free," but in a strange way what he did now was more related to Cat than what he had done before that Friday night in the kitchen. Somehow before, his life with Cat seemed more or less distinct from Kim. Now, if he were going to try to hold his marriage together, he felt he could do it only by recommitting himself entirely. He could not be so cynical as to see Kim.

But as of now he had made no move to hold his marriage together, nor had Cat. He opened the letter.

My dearest, dearest Jack:

He shook his head. Always just reading these words, in some way so formal, in another so loving, made the hopelessness of their situation vanish.

This has been a wretched week, not being able to see you. Only those few short impersonal calls at the office. I miss you so painfully, and I know now that you are indeed essential to my life. And I keep trying to devise a way to have all my lives together.

I keep hoping (fantasying) that you and Catherine will not part and that we can go on with our marriage within a marriage.

You see, I said I was selfish, and you never believed me. But I say this for your sake too. You love Cat and your home. I know that this annoys you to have me acknowledge your love for Cat. You think it seems to diminish your love for me.

Of course, you may not want to see me again, ever. I wonder.

I know your wish for wholeness in your life, to find everything in one person, and I respect it . . . if you find it. But you seemed so happy with us even after Cat returned. Or was it difficult and you didn't let me know?

I would like "us" to work, if you want it to. In a sense, you made "us" work after Cat came home. I feel it is up to me now that S. is home. That is, as I said, if you ever want to see me again.

I can no longer lead a single life. Simultaneous time with you is essential. But I cannot leave my other life. And I realize it is unfair to S. and to you, because the domesticity you love so cannot be shared, and yet for S. he loses the one part of me he probably wants most. But this is yours.

May we try?

My love,
K.

Monday morning Kim called before Jack was out of bed. "Did you get my letter?"
"Yes."

"Do you want to see me?"

"Yes."

"I loathe the idea of sneaking in and out of hotels."

"So do I, but . . . What time?"

"One o'clock?"

"Any idea on hotels?"

"No."

"The Plaza?"

"No. We'd be sure to meet somebody in the lobby."

"The Waldorf?" It occurred to him that he had never stayed in a hotel in New York.

"You don't have to impress me."

"Let me think and call you at the office."

"I'm not going to the office this morning. I've got to go to school with Colin for a conference with his teachers and then to a meeting out of the office."

"Down in the village. The Fifth Avenue Hotel?"

"Too far. I'll only have an hour and a half or so."

He remembered that at the Biltmore the elevators were not directly opposite the registration desk. "The Biltmore."

"All right."

He tried to figure out the logistics. Kim was obviously on edge, anxious to get off the phone. "Let's see, I'll check in around twelve-thirty. You call after that, and I'll tell you what room."

"Good. It'll be lovely to see you."

"What if I can't get in the Biltmore?" But she had hung up.

While he shaved and bathed, he thought about calling the Biltmore, going over what he would say. He stumbled each time he said, "Uh . . . we'd like a double bed."

He made the call, sounding very casual, as though he

did this sort of thing all the time. No problems. "We'll be checking in around one o'clock."

What do you do next? He rummaged around in the closet and found a small overnight case, Cat's. He tossed in a pair of shoes, some underwear, a shirt, his toilet-articles kit. He shook his head at his compulsion to be "legitimate." Why not just a phone book?

While he was walking Debbie, he tried to figure out what he was going to do. He didn't want to walk into his office with the overnight case. He'd check it at the club and then leave the office early and pick it up and go to the Biltmore. He'd have to pick up a bottle of wine. And a bottle of cashew nuts for Kim. What about lunch? They wouldn't want room service busting in. He'd stop at Charles on Madison Avenue and get some tuna sandwiches, which she liked.

At the office there was a lot of petty detail which was irritating. Jeremy Simmons stopped by to complain about the size of his bill. Jack told Miss Lorenz to dig up the billings and send them to Jeremy. Jack never questioned the price of anything. It embarrassed him to have someone question his charges. His first impulse was to tear up the bill and say, "You don't owe me anything." But he couldn't do that.

Then Mary Kinsella called to say that it had just dawned on her that she had never used the company that Jack had persuaded her to form for tax reasons, and why had they gone to the expense of forming it in the first place?

He was late getting away from the office, and by the time he hurried into his club to pick up his suitcase, his irritation had spread to Kim. Instead of excitement, he felt annoyance and embarrassment that he was scurrying around midtown, picking up his bag, buying wine *and* a corkscrew, then waiting in line at Charles with all the secretaries who were ordering their lunches, then finally going up the steps to the Biltmore feeling that everyone knew exactly what he was there for.

The bellman rushed for his small suitcase, and he handed it over. Normally he would have said, "I can manage."

"I had a reservation for Mr. and Mrs. John Montgomery." He had given his real name. He could not bring himself to be "Mr. Jones." He filled in the registration blank. His hand was sweating.

The clerk checked through his cards and returned. "You asked for a double bed." Jack was sure he blushed. "There's no room with a double bed made up yet. I can give you twins. You see, our checkout time is one o'clock."

It was ordinarily Jack's nature to take whatever was offered. But he heard himself saying, "My wife and I are changing for a reception, so we'll need the room now. And we like a double bed." The sweat ran down his back.

The clerk looked at him for a moment. Of course, he knew what the hell was going on. "All I can do is ask the bellboy to find the floor maid and see if she'll make up your room for you now."

"Thank you." He started away, then stopped. "And will you see that the operator knows what room I'm in? I'm expecting a call."

Going up in the elevator, he made embarrassed small talk with the aging bellman. As they were about to enter his room, the maid emerged from the room opposite. The bellman called across to her. "Would you make up room 802 as soon as possible for this gentleman?"

"I got a lot of rooms to do."

Jack had been getting his money out, ready to tip the

bellman, and slipped a five-dollar bill into the maid's hand. "I'd appreciate it if you would." He couldn't go into the business of changing for a reception again.

"All right. As soon as I get through this one."

"Thank you."

The bellman opened the door, and they stepped into the room. It was a shambles. The bed looked as though there had been an orgy, dirty towels, washcloths. On the bedside tables and bureau, empty bottles and beer cans, cigarette butts, dirty dishes. The place reeked of dead cigars.

"Some people are pigs." The bellman opened the window and left the key on the bureau. "She'll have it cleaned up in a few minutes." Jack tipped him, and he left.

His impulse was to walk out and never return. But he had to stay to get Kim's call to tell her which room he was in. He had always felt a certain sexual excitement on entering a hotel room. He and Cat had been good in hotels. But this mess . . .

The maid came in and started to clean up as though she saw sights like this every day of the week. Jack stood there watching her. He wanted to shave again. But there were no clean towels, and the bathroom was as big a mess as the bedroom.

"If you want to go down to the lobby, I'll be through in a few minutes."

"I'm expecting a phone call."

A few minutes later, as the maid was cleaning the bathroom, the call came.

"Hi. I just got here. Room 802. It's godawful, but I'm here. The maid's cleaning it up now."

"Listen. I can't come. It's terrible, but I can't."

"What happened?"

"I tried to catch you at the office, but you were taking no calls, and I couldn't very well leave a message. Scott's insisted I have lunch with him. He's in a foul mood."

"That's okay. It's bound to happen."

"I tried to reach you before you'd taken the room. I hate the idea of your spending the money for nothing."

Jack was embarrassed. "Oh, come on. How about lunch tomorrow, at a restaurant?"

"I don't know why, but I'm uneasy about that just now. Are you going to be in tonight?"

"I can be."

"Scott has a meeting, I think. I'll call. There's a chance he might go to Texas for a few days." Jack said nothing. "It all sounds terrible, doesn't it? Sneaking around corners. We were spoiled. But I want to see you. Do you want to see me?"

"Yes."

"I'll call you tonight, or try. I hate to think of you sitting and waiting for a call. I wanted everything to go so well."

"I'll be home."

"It won't be before nine." Then quickly and softly: "I love you, Jack Montgomery."

"I love you, Kimberlee Cooper."

He hung up the phone, amused, annoyed and relieved. It was a farce, scampering around like a guilty adolescent, only to be "stood up." Why the hell at his age was he waiting in hotel rooms and staying home for phone calls? He knew why. He had once kiddingly asked Kim, "Why do I put up with all this?" And she had laughed and said, "Because you love me." She was right.

He opened his suitcase and took out the bag with the sandwiches. The maid was passing through with towels. "Would you like a tuna fish sandwich?"

"I don't care for tuna fish, thank you."

Feeling somehow virtuous, he went to the Century for lunch and sat at the long table with twenty distinguished men and listened to two lawyers discourse learnedly on Baroque music. He felt stupid not being able to join in and on his way back to the office stopped in at the Record Hunter to buy an album of Telemann and Handel.

Kim did not manage to call that night. She called the next morning while Scott was out jogging. "I'm sorry. It was just impossible. And it looks hopeless until Thursday noon. Do you want to try again Thursday? Please!"

He was waiting in the hotel room. He had the wine and the cashew nuts and the tuna fish sandwiches. He had tried the lights various ways, had left the door ajar so that she would not have to stand in the hall.

He lay on the bed in his shirt sleeves, his shoes off, tension mounting. She was late; he had become used to that, but now he sensed a hostility growing in him, centered seemingly on her lateness. But he knew it wasn't that. It was anger that she had gone back to Scott. It was a kind of revulsion for what she was doing now, coming to him, perhaps from Scott this morning.

He got up and poured himself a glass of wine.

Then she walked in, carrying a bunch of daisies. "To cheer up our home." Her bright, perky smile. He stood there looking at her. Her smile vanished. "You really don't want to see me, do you?"

He looked at her for another moment, and then suddenly it was all very quick, and he took her, and she offered herself to be taken, to be repossessed. And as he thrust into her again and again, all he was thinking was, I am fucking his wife. I am fucking the sonofabitch's wife.

After, he told her everything he had had to block out

95

to be with her. How it had had to be the way it had been. She understood. She had wanted it that way.

They held each other, looked at each other, studying each other's faces in detail. "Did you and Cat say anything more before she left?"

"No." He did not want to tell her that Cat had suggested they be lovers. That was private.

"Maybe you'll stay together."

He smiled, knowing what she was thinking.

"You wouldn't want to see me if you did stay together." He looked at her. It seemed impossible that he could ever not want to see her. "Then my best hope is that you not stay together. But I don't want to hope that because that may be wrong for you."

He traced the outlines of her face with his fingers. "If Cat and I do separate, how often could we see each other?"

"I'd come to you whenever I could."

He smiled. "Would you go to the movies with me? That's when I'll know you love me. When you go to the movies with me."

She slapped him playfully. "You can find someone else to go to the movies with you." She became serious. "I realize there would be other women. You're not going to sit alone night after night. But I wouldn't feel any more threatened by them than I do by the women I'm sure Scott has when he's away. When a person wants a lot, she has to put up with things."

He smiled and drew her to him and kissed her. "You've either got a great deal to teach us all, or you're crazy, or you're fooling yourself."

"About what?"

"About loving Scott or me." She said nothing but nestled close. "I'm sorry."

"No, it's all right. You think if I loved him or you, I'd be

96

jealous. I think I love you both, and that's enough. But I can't prove it to you."

"Maybe it's different with a man. I don't know, but when I think that you'll be going to him tonight—"

"Shhh. Don't!"

"Or that you came from him this morning—"

"I didn't. I didn't." She kissed him. "You mustn't."

For a while they didn't say anything. "I wouldn't have other women. I'd wait for Tuesdays or Wednesdays. If I love a person, I'd rather wait for that person. Cat and I have been separated many times for long periods."

"And you waited?"

"Yes. Does that sound self-righteous?"

"No. It's nice. I waited, until you." He kissed her. "But now if we were ever together, living together, you would never trust me, would you?"

He stroked her back. "I suppose I flatter myself that you wouldn't want to go to anyone else."

10

They didn't see each other again for a week. Kim rushed off to Florida to do some troubleshooting on a film her company was producing. Scott went with her, a chance for them to see something of each other for a change.

Jack went to Cambridge to chair one of the several committees he served on at Harvard. He enjoyed the five or six trips he made to Cambridge each year, attending classes, meeting with students and faculty, giving reports to the president or the Board of Overseers. He wasn't sure it all did any real good, but it was pleasant to return to Harvard and to talk with the interesting committee members who had gathered from all over the country.

He had left Debbie with the vet and had driven up from Ridgefield in the early evening, keeping to the back roads till he reached Hartford.

It was a soft and hazy evening in Cambridge, and after an hour or so of walking around, stumbling over the uneven brick sidewalks, nostalgically touching bases, he felt a great loneliness and longing. And back at the Faculty Club, after a vodka and tonic, he scrawled in large letters with a felt-tipped pen a silly/joke letter to Kim:

WHERE ARE YOU?????
YOU SAID YOU WOULD MEET ME HERE AT SEVEN!!!!
AND YOU ARE NOT HERE.
AND I MISS YOU!!!!

He drew pictures of a clock, of himself waiting, a moon-face with the mouth turned down. Then he went to the bar and had another drink and went to bed.

The next morning, while he was having breakfast in the Faculty Club dining room, he found himself staring at an advertisement in the *Harvard Crimson:*

> Summer sublet furnished. Studio. Sep. kitchen. Air-cond. Near Square. July, August. $250 month. 263-5678

All day the idea of this studio apartment stuck with him. He had spent seven years in Cambridge, and though he had been miserably lonely until he met Cat, he remembered mostly the good times that he and Cat had had. Maybe their best times.

When he had come up for his meetings and had attended classes, he had always had a longing to buy a big fat notebook and sit for a year listening to people telling him things, things they knew and things he could believe.

Sitting in again on Castner's class on property had reminded him of the excitement of his first year at Law School. Before the churning had set in.

Several times he had suggested to Cat that they come to summer school, lead the simple but fulfilling life of students, which had brought them together.

Maybe if he and Cat separated, he could come up here, take a sabbatical from the firm, "loaf and invite his soul" or work on his book on copyright or maybe even take a writing course. He had always hoped that one day he would "get back" to his writing.

At lunch he asked Jill, the department secretary, to find out if he could see the apartment before he returned to New York.

The place appealed to him. It was a large one-room studio in an apartment house which seemed to cater largely to transients. There was a bank of floor-to-ceiling windows across the rear wall, looking out onto the tops of trees and the backs of large old houses. There was a good bathroom and a small, tidy kitchen. It was sparsely but attractively furnished: a mattress with an orange spread on the brown cork floor, a couple of white wicker armchairs with bright cushions, an old sea chest for a coffee table and a large worktable with architect's extension lamps. The woman who rented it and was not there was obviously a graphic artist or designer of some sort. He liked the atmosphere. It was an artist's pad, a place where he could feel all right alone, almost as though he were back in school. He told the super he liked it, but he would have to let the woman know. He left Jill's name and number as the contact.

On Sunday evening Kim called. "I am about to offer you your heart's desire."

"What?"

"Guess."

"I can't."

"You may take me to the movies."

He laughed. "How come?"

"Scott went on to Atlanta for a few days."

He met her outside the Regency Theater on the West Side and hurried her into the ten o'clock show as though she were a movie star trying to remain incognito. During the movie he held her hand under the raincoat. She was uneasy, checking out every newcomer and rising just before the end of the picture to pull him out of the theater before the houselights came up.

It felt strange to be back at her house now, alone with her. He was uncomfortable. It was no longer their home. They went through their usual routine of getting the ice out, peeling the lemon, pouring the vodka into the goblets. She seemed moody.

"What's the matter?"

"Nothing. I don't know. I'm sorry." She flashed her smile.

"You didn't want to see me tonight."

They moved to the couch. "Yes, I did."

"I don't like being something you feel you have to do, an item you have to tick off on your daily list of things to be done." He smiled.

"I don't feel that way."

"You know you're pretty overextended. Most modern women are satisfied to be able to handle a husband and a career, children and a home. You want a lover, too."

"I didn't want one. But I've got one. A rather unhappy one."

"No."

"Yes. I don't do you much good."

"What's the matter? Tell me."

"I don't know. Right now I'd like to run away to a desert island. Be absolutely alone. Regroup my forces." She took his hand. "Just when you need me, just when I wanted to show you that everything could work."

"What happened in Florida?"

"Oh, God, I don't know. Everything. Scott kept saying how nice it was, being away together, all leading up to his wanting me to cut down, be more available to him."

"I can understand that."

"The point is, you can't cut down in this business. The competition is fierce, especially from women in the field who have no families, who can give their whole time to rooting out material, riding herd on production people, developing ideas. Scott's decent about it. He's proud of my work. He chortled down there at the way I managed to cajole the director into getting back on schedule. He knows he'd be bored stiff with a wife who didn't work. He accepts it intellectualiy but not emotionally. He doesn't understand you can't cut back."

"What was it the Red Queen said in *Alice*? You have to run as fast as you can to stay in the same place."

"Exactly! There are some very talented unattached women working as production assistants in our place, just waiting for me to drop the ball. They're there Saturdays, Sundays, morning, noon and night."

"But they don't have your brains, and . . . style."

"Oh, don't be too sure. They're sharp, and their careers are the only things in their lives."

"Pretty boring."

"Yes, well, I wouldn't like it. But . . ." She frowned and became more intense as though defending herself against some accusing voice. "I've made a damned good wife for Scott. It's not a good feminist attitude, but I've felt it was a privilege to be able to work as I do. We don't need the money. And when I come home, I feel I have to earn that privilege. And I think I do . . . in every department. God, I know some wives who stagger home from the office with the idea everyone should make it up to them for having worked at something they love all day. I can't stand that. And I don't do that!"

Suddenly there were tears, and she tried to turn away.

He moved along the couch and took her glass and put it on the table and held her and kissed the side of her head.

"I'm sorry. Very sloppy." She tried to smile like a good little girl taught to be ashamed of tears.

"Why? Why be sorry?"

"You didn't come here tonight to have all this dumped on you."

"I came to be with you."

After a few moments her tears subsided. She reached for her glass and just sat there, shaking her head and trying to smile at him. Finally, she said, "Shall we go upstairs?"

He smiled. "No."

"You don't want to. I don't blame you. God, what a mess!"

"*You* don't want to."

"Yes, I do." Her eyes were pleading. "We won't do anything if you don't want. Just hold me. Please!"

She wore her nightshirt to bed, and though they intended just to hold each other, they made love. He felt a great tenderness for her and wanted to comfort her. But in the end he was not sure that he had not been serviced.

He kissed her lightly. "I don't like you making love when you don't feel like it."

"I did feel like it. It's just that there's not much of me right now." After a few moments she asked, "When's Cat coming home?"

"Sometime this week, I think. Depending on whether or not she went to Italy."

"What's going to happen?"

"I don't know."

A few minutes later she turned over and went to sleep.

He knew he wouldn't sleep, but he stayed beside her there for a while and then got up and dressed quietly without disturbing her and left.

11

When he entered his apartment, all the lights were on, and there was a note on the floor of the living room.

Hello!   1 A.M.
    Sorry. Meant to go directly to country, but plane late and I am exhausted. Waited up, but couldn't make it.
                                                    Love,
                                                        C.

For a moment Jack stood with the note in his hand and looked at Cat's suitcases, lying open around the room. Why had she written "Sorry"?

He hung his raincoat in the closet and moved quietly toward the bedroom. The door to the study/guest room was closed. He stared at it. Then he moved down the hall to their bedroom. The lights were on, and his side of the bed turned down. Propped against the pillow were some pictures. He picked them up and looked at them. Jorie and her husband, their new house in Holland, their dog, and a few of Cat and Jorie. Dazed, he put them on the night table and just sat for a moment. He was hungry, wanted a bowl of cereal, but decided to go to bed as quickly as possible. He couldn't see Cat tonight. He could not be her lover tonight.

The door to the kitchen was closed, and Debbie safely in there. He had walked her before leaving to meet Kim. He turned out the lights in the living room, went to the bedroom and undressed. He went to the bathroom as quietly as possible and washed himself. He brushed his teeth and washed his face, went into the bedroom and closed the door and went to bed. He looked at the pictures again for a moment, then turned out the light.

What had Cat thought as one o'clock came around and he was not home? Would he say anything in the morning about where he'd been? He would not have humiliated her for the world. Couldn't stand the thought of her arriving home from Europe, full of news of the "kids" and sitting there, wondering, knowing perhaps, where he was. The note said "1 A.M." Had she gone to the bathroom at 2 A.M. and he still not home? He suddenly felt cheap.

The next morning the sound of a bureau drawer opening wakened him. Cat, fully dressed in a blue wool suit, was rummaging for something.

"Hi."

She looked around. "Sorry. But I had to get this sweater."

He held out his hand. "How are you?"

She came to the bed. "I'm fine. Sorry to wake you."

She took his hand; he pulled her to him and kissed her.

"Why didn't you let me know so I could meet you?"

"I thought I was going to stay a couple of more days; then I changed my mind. Then the plane was hours late. Rain. No cabs. Last limousine for Connecticut had left."

"Did you have a good time?" He should draw her into the bed beside him.

"Wonderful."

"The pictures are terrific."

"I have more. That's just a taste." He brought her to

106

him again for a hug and a kiss. She moved away. "Do you want some coffee?"

"Okay."

She started for the door and stopped. "When I came in last night, the phone was ringing. I wrote the message down in the kitchen. Did you see it?"

"No. I didn't go in the kitchen."

"Some girl in Cambridge who was looking for apartments for you, says she had to know if you want the one you were interested in." Jack frowned. Cat went on. "I think I'm going to take a small house in Redding. I looked at it before I left, and she cabled me that she might be willing to come down to my price."

They looked at each other for a moment. Then: "Orange juice?" He nodded, and she left the room.

He closed his eyes. What had he expected her to do? She was making her plans. He was making his plans. They both would go on making their plans until someone or something stopped them.

12

Saturday morning they planted some rosebushes and shrubs they had ordered from a catalogue in the winter. Though they were walking out on their marriage, they continued to tend the house and the grounds as though they were going on forever.

In the afternoon Cat took him to see the house that she was planning to rent. It was really a barn and stables, which the owner had converted into a spacious cottage. While she showed him the various features of the place, Jack felt acutely uncomfortable and sad. He was also amused that Cat was seeing herself in this very simple place. It was an image she had of herself. But then, he had his own image of himself in the studio apartment in Cambridge.

"See this wall oven. I've always wanted one like that." She stopped. The kitchen had always been a bone of contention, but they were past that stage now.

She marveled at the closets, which Jack knew were too small and would hold only a tenth of her clothes. He called her attention to various drawbacks. "Oh, that won't bother me. It would bother you, but not me."

He felt numb. Somehow it was all too civilized. He went

out and stood on the small deck and looked out over the pastures and fields.

Suddenly there was blaring hard rock music coming from the main house maybe fifty feet away. Cat looked at the lady of the house who was with them. "That's my daughter and her friends. It's only weekends, and I've learned to put up with it. I'm just glad they're at home and not someplace else. A small price."

Cat looked around at her dream house as it slowly vanished from the future. Jack felt sorry for her. She was having such fine fantasies. He knew she could never take that music, was very sensitive to sound, on trips had sometimes made him change their hotel rooms several times because of people playing the television or radio too loud next door.

"I'll let you know tonight for sure. All right?"

"No later, please. I want to make plans before I leave next week myself."

When they got in the car, he said, "I'm sorry."

"God damn it." And she sighed.

Now knowing she wouldn't take it, he said, "It's a cute little place."

"Why does she let them do that?"

It was strange to comfort her for her loss of her dream cottage. She pouted and was annoyed and during their movie dinner at a local bistro, she went on and on about too-permissive parents. She even toyed with the idea that if *she*, an outsider, talked to them, they might . . . But finally, just before they went to the "flicks," with tears in her eyes she called and said she'd changed her mind. She didn't mention the rock music.

During the movie he held her hand or put his arm around the back of her seat. It seemed impossible to believe that they were separating . . . and without some further attempt at talking things out. It seemed weird that here they were about to do something which would change their lives, and they were avoiding the subject while going on and making plans. Was it that neither of them felt up to "going into it all"? Neither of them could find the end to the tangled ball of string? A place to start unraveling the complexity?

And yet he knew that the complexity was both the weakness and the strength of the marriage. Every argument had come to involve everything each of them was. His overdeliberateness, her compulsion to jump in. His sense of insecurity (bred from watching his father during the Depression?) her not giving a damn about the future. "I'll take care of it when it comes."

Yet troublesome as these "Here we go again" aspects of their marriage had been, he was smart enough to know that in these conflicts there had been life and the process of living. He thought again of his friend who no longer discussed with his wife her willingness or lack of willingness to make love. He simply went to his call girl the next day. But he had admitted his marriage had lost something.

If he opened it all up again, they would lose this good feeling, drag out all the dirty linen, go over it piece by piece, possibly end up hating each other, separating in anger. Was that better? A wound would heal. This no-wound might never heal. Their relationship might remain fetteringly ambiguous. They would never be free to move on.

Would it be possible for them just to come together again without going over an itemized list of grievances? Or suppose they went over the whole list? Was it any of those problems? His client said his marriage had "just died." When they got to the end of the list, settled all the problems, mightn't they still just sit here and look at each other and realize, "It wasn't those things at all"?

After the movie they walked to the car with their arms around each other and, without saying anything significant, went home and made love.

As he was holding her after, he finally said, "Let's not do this thing. Let's stay together. Let's try again."

Tears came to her eyes, but she shook her head.

"But it's been so good."

"I know. But maybe it will be a period of growth. Good for both of us. We should at least try it."

He went to sleep holding her. He could have protested, argued. She wouldn't have thrown him out of the house. But he didn't. He felt sad and bewildered, but at least he had tried. And he had meant it. It hadn't been to put the responsibility on her.

13

Wednesday Jack was about to call Kim when she called him. "Do you have a lunch date?"

"No."

"It's a beautiful day. Will you drive me to the Cloisters?"

"Sure."

"Pick me up on the northeast corner of Park and Seventy-second at twelve-thirty. I'm sure they serve some kind of food up there. I took Colin once."

She arrived in a cab at twelve-forty-five. Jack had been double-parked waiting for her. As she got in the car, she smiled. "You know it's infuriating that you're always on time."

"I know. Nothing I can do about it." He leaned over and kissed her. "How are you?"

She sat back in mock exhaustion. "I had to drag Colin to the doctor's this morning because he woke up with a sore throat. On the way out, Scott yelled down the stairs that he couldn't find his favorite shirt. I've been wrangling all morning with my company about a marvelous show they don't want to produce, and here I am all cheerfulness and joy and eager to get away from it all for a couple of hours. Thanks for obliging me."

As they drove up the West Side Highway, she went on with what he had come to call "Kim's overture." She talked brightly and interestingly about her work, about the "marvelous" show her company didn't want to do, about Colin's plans for the summer, his victories in the school field day. He kept her talking about herself and her work by asking questions, wanting to put off till later what he had to tell her.

Finally, they turned up the drive to the Cloisters and parked. As she got out of the car, she looked out over the Hudson River. "What a beautiful day!" She quickly cased the grounds for familiar faces. The place was practically empty. "Let's walk a little or sit on the grass over there."

As they sat down, she said, "I'm sorry I've been a bore. Why do you egg me on to talk about myself and my work?"

"I enjoy hearing about it."

"How are you?"

He shrugged. "All right."

"When is Cat coming home?"

"She's home."

"Oh. And?"

He looked at her a moment. "In a week or so I'm going to Cambridge. I've rented a one-room apartment up there. I don't know for how long, but we're definitely separating."

She looked at him, stunned. "Why Cambridge?"

"I have friends up there. I know it and Boston. I might take a writing course in the Summer School, or work on a book on copyright I've been asked to do, or maybe do something at the Law School, if I stay." She was studying his face. "It's no good here." He shook his head. There were tears starting in his eyes. "It doesn't work."

"I've been terrible, I know."

"I can't handle it." He looked at her, then moved quickly to her and embraced her and kissed her, "I love you so."

"Then why do you go away?"

"I can't stay here. You can't see me as I want to see you. I can't live alone. I have to . . . I have to have someone. Does that make me weak, to need someone?" He shook his head. "The whole thing is ridiculous. I love you. I love her, and I'm supposed to go out and find someone else."

"If I'd been able to see you more."

"Perhaps, but how could you?"

"I could have. If I'd tried. When will you go?"

"I don't know. Maybe a week or so."

"You talked to Cat then?"

"I said I thought we should try again. She didn't want to. She wants this trial separation."

"Well . . ." She turned her head, and he could tell she was fighting back tears.

He moved to her and held her. "Oh, Kim, Kim. What else can I do?"

"I don't know. What you're doing, I guess. It's been terrible for you." She tried to smile.

"You love Scott. This simultaneous time doesn't work. If you've learned nothing else from this, remember that. Don't try it again."

She looked at him, angry for a moment. "You think I'm just going out and find someone else and—"

"No. No."

"It could work if you and Cat had stayed together and if I had tried hard enough. You always wanted me to say I didn't love Scott, and I couldn't say that, because I do. But I love you differently. I've been terribly disloyal to him, when we've made love, telling you, letting you know

114

how different it is with us. I've been ashamed, not of making love, but of letting you know." She shook her head. "But I've been terrible for you. It's my fault, I know."

"Kim, stop it!"

"You think I'm withdrawing from you to be with him. But that's not so. He's complaining, too. I'm withdrawing into myself."

"It couldn't work, no matter what. I want someone for my own. You'd never leave Scott. I wouldn't let you leave Scott."

"Why?"

"Because it's a very good marriage. You've always said so."

"Oh, I'm not so sure."

"Kim, don't tease. Don't hold out hopes."

"I don't mean to." They were quiet for a few moments. "Well, I don't feel like eating, but I'd like a cup of coffee, and then I must get back." They rose and moved up the hill. "Can I have your address and phone in Cambridge?"

"No. I don't think we should write or call." She stopped and looked at him. "It's going to be hard enough getting over you. I don't think I could manage it if we were in touch." He felt the need for some break, something clear and definite, a little bitter, not lingering hopes.

She walked ahead up the slope. He caught up with her and stopped her and kissed her and held her. "You've never understood how much I've loved you. You've not bled as I've bled. You could go on because it hasn't meant as much to you. You wanted me to love you that way. That first night when I said I wasn't sure that I loved you, you were shocked, hurt. Well, now I love you the way you wanted and needed me to love you. But it doesn't work."

"It could have if . . ."

• •

They took their coffee to the car, and he drove her back down into the city. She asked him about his pad and what Cat was going to do. Then he told her about his annual physical checkup. He thought it might amuse her. "When the doctor learned that I was separating, he gave me a prescription and said. 'You may find yourself sleeping around. If you have any suspicions, take one of these an hour before intercourse.' I asked the doctor what to do if I didn't know an hour ahead of time. And he said, 'Extended foreplay.'" She didn't react. "I'm sorry. I thought you might find it funny."

"It's all right. Of course there will be women."

He reached for her hand. "And I hate the idea."

She smiled at him as though not believing.

14

Cat and Jack had not been as close in years as they were the days before he left. Was it the sense that they were going to be free? Or did the other person become more dear because of the imminent loss, like someone dying? Or was there an excitement that had been lacking in their lives? They knew they were being talked about.

The few friends who knew were shocked and wanted to discuss it with Jack. He simply shrugged, sometimes smiling sadly, and said, "It's something we're going to try. It's crazy, but . . ." As far as he could tell, nobody discussed it with Cat or she with them. To acquaintances they simply said that Jack was going to Cambridge to work at the Summer School. Of course, when Cat moved out of the house, when she found a place she wanted, there would be more questions.

He had talked with Rich and Barbara, who were saddened, but since they shared their generation's scepticism about marriage, they were not surprised. Though Jack had never tried to influence them with their own problem of whether or not they should get married, he had always talked to them about the joys and satisfactions of marriage. He was aware that his analogies were trite. "It's a kind of gyroscope that keeps things more or less in bal-

117

ance." Or he would say, "There are days when I hate coming home, and days when I want to rush home. If I stayed away when I felt like it, there would be no home there when I wanted it. So, on balance . . ."

But mostly he was silent when Rich and Barbara looked at him with troubled concern after he had told them. It did not occur to them to ask, "Why?" Rich had perhaps been even more aware of the erosion than Jack had been. He said later, "Well, I never want Barbara and me to be away from each other as much as you and Mom were." Just as more than twenty-five years before, Jack had said, "I never want my marriage to be like Mother and Dad's," and Cat had said, "I never want to be a beautiful parasite like my mother."

And what would Rich and Barbara's soon-to-be-born child say twenty-odd years hence? Jack thought of Claudel's "Woman is a promise that cannot be kept." And he wondered if marriage too was a promise that could not be kept.

But it had been kept for him and Cat for a long time.

Up to the weekend of his leaving, Jack had made no preparations other than at his office. He had taken Oliver to lunch at the King Cole Bar of the St. Regis. "This afternoon I intend to tell the partners I want to take a sabbatical."

"I'm glad to hear it. Buckminster?"

"No, Cambridge. And the circumstances are a little different. Cat and I are separating. A trial separation."

Oliver looked pained. "I'm sorry to hear that."

Jack looked at his drink and shook his head. "It's complex."

"Of course."

"Maybe it's just all part of the churning." He looked up and smiled.

118

"I don't know what to say. Virginia and I have always liked Cat."

"She's a terrific woman. It was her idea. To be fair, I guess it really ended up our idea."

Oliver cleared his throat. "I used to hope that my divorcing clients and friends got back together again. Now I don't know. If it's any help, you know that Virginia and I . . . I was about your age when Harriet and I divorced . . . Virginia and I have had a wonderful marriage for twenty-five years."

Jack smiled. "One of the best."

"Of course, I was lucky."

"You were both lucky. If it comes to that, I'll try to remember." He buttered a breadstick. "I'll work on the copyright book, I've signed a contract for it, and I'll stay up there. I feel at home up there. . . . How long, I don't know." He smiled. "How long do trial separations last?"

"Well. . . ." He cleared his throat again. "In my experience, most marriages that are not intolerable, people stay together."

"My marriage is far from intolerable. I thought it was very good. I don't know." He smiled and shook his head. "I can't go into it all. . . ."

"No, of course not."

"I could stay here, but I think it would be difficult, awkward. The same friends . . ."

"And you need a change of place anyway. It's too bad it's under these circumstances. But who knows? You know the Chinese symbol for crisis is a combination of danger and opportunity."

Though he had rented his place in Cambridge from July 1, he had not actually decided on the day of his departure until one day late in June, when the phone rang and Cat had answered it and had turned to him after a moment and, smiling, said, "This is Marge Brownstein. She wants to know if we can come to her bash on the twenty-eighth. Will you still be here?"

They looked at each other and smiled. The Brownstein summer party was always one of the best. He said, "Yes."

When Cat hung up, she said, "Someone should write a story about a couple who want to separate, but they can't because parties they want to go to keep cropping up." They both laughed.

It was all that casual. The afternoon before he left they spent in the garden, weeding, cultivating, fertilizing the roses. "This must be done at least every six weeks."

That night she didn't want to go out for dinner but cooked him some of his favorite foods. They chatted idly during dinner, trying to conceal their tension. "I know you won't want to spend your time with children, but don't forget Penny is up there in Boston." Penny was his goddaughter, whom he hadn't seen in several years. "I'll give you her phone number. She had a great crush on you when she was fourteen." Jack smiled, remembering. The crush had annoyed Cat.

After dinner they did the dishes together in the soft summer evening light. Several times he put his arm around her and kissed her hair. It was as though they had nothing to do with what was happening. Someone else had sentenced them to separation. It was all happening to someone else up on a movie screen.

Later she went into her study at one end of the house, and he could hear her typing. The washing machine was humming. She was sending him off neat and clean. It was almost as though she were sending him off to a boys' summer camp.

He went to the attic and brought down several beat-up old suitcases and packed. He hated packing. He hated change. He gathered together his summer clothes. He left his fall and winter clothes. He took only what he would take on summer vacation. He was just going away for a while. He left the clutter on top of his bureau, only tearing up memos to himself which were no longer pertinent. He felt numb as he scooped up underclothes, shirts, socks, bathing suit. There was a beach at Ipswich. He should get a new suit.

He was more or less finished. The rest he would pick up tomorrow morning and just throw it into the station wagon. Tennis racket, cameras, typewriter.

Making sure that Cat was still in her study, he took his suitcases and garment bags down the back stairs and out to the garage. He felt like a thief in the night. Then he went to his study and paid all the current bills and gathered together the things he would need, bankbooks, tax records, a few books he wanted to take along. He started to write a long letter to Jorie in Holland, explaining his feelings, but he found he couldn't say anything. He would write from Cambridge.

He lugged his briefcase and attaché cases and a cardboard box filled with papers to the station wagon. As he returned to the house, he heard Cat running her bath.

He turned out the lights in the living room, noticing as he did the warm and cozy colors, the casual, comfortable air of the room. So many great parties. He went upstairs and undressed and took a shower in Jorie's bedroom. Since he was going, he wished he were gone.

When he came back to their bedroom, Cat was already in bed. She smiled as he slid under the covers. For a moment she lay on her back and looked over at him, then turned out the light on her side. He turned out his light and moved quickly to her, and they held each other, and she cried softly. If she had said, "Let's try again," he would have said, "Yes. Yes." but he could not bring himself to say it again.

They did not make love but fell asleep curled around each other.

The next morning when he awoke, she was already out in the garden. Before he shaved and bathed, he stood at the window looking at her figure, kneeling in the earth, pulling away at tough weeds, cultivating with a trowel. He could tell nothing about her mood, but her being up and out told him that she wanted to be out of the way.

She had already eaten breakfast, her cup and saucer washed and draining on the sink. There was nothing left to say except "Goodbye."

Jack ate breakfast quickly, returned upstairs to pack his last-minute things. When he came down, ready to go, she was in the kitchen, washing her hands.

"Good morning."

"Good morning." He came up to her at the sink and kissed her.

"All packed?"

"Yes."

"Did you get the clean laundry I left in the bathroom?"

"Yes. Thank you." He sat at the kitchen table. "We haven't talked about money or anything." It was always awkward for them when they discussed money. "Forward all the bills to me. And I've left this check for other things, to cover rent on a house you get. I have no idea how much things are going to cost you, but I want to take care of everything."

"I've got money."

"I know. But for my sake, at least until I get used to the idea, let me send you a check. And if it isn't enough, tell me." He prayed that she wouldn't argue about this. He wanted everything to be just the same. Except he would be away.

She looked at the check on the table. "Thank you."

"Here are phone numbers and addresses. . . . My apartment, the department I'll be involved with . . . other information you might want."

She picked up the list and, moving her glasses down from her hair, studied these details with conspicuous attention. "Yes, I see."

He stood. "Well . . ." He reached out and embraced Cat, feeling sick and close to tears. "Let's see what happens."

She put her arms around him. "Yes." And they kissed. He shook his head and picked up his small suitcase and his raincoat and looked at her.

"I put a shopping bag in the car with some things for your place . . . apples, nuts, some cheese and crackers. Also Debbie's dishes."

"Thanks. Let's keep in touch."

"Yes."

"Will you see somebody tonight?"

"I don't know."

He saw that he had better get out. "I think you should. Bye-bye." And he left.

Debbie was standing by the door of the station wagon, ready. As he started the car, he realized he had forgotten his dark glasses, but he wouldn't go back for them. He knew Cat did not want to see him now. For a moment before he moved away, he pictured her sitting at the table, crying. He knew he could not leave her if he saw her crying. His instinct was to go back, to hold and comfort her. It killed him to drive off and leave her crying.

As he drove through the village, where yesterday they

had bought the fertilizer for the roses and the new trowel and mole traps, he shook his head, near tears himself. She felt he didn't love her. His driving away like this would only confirm for her this feeling. He wished that she had found a place and were going to it, too. He did not like the impression that he was leaving her. They were leaving each other.

15

For the first two weeks in Cambridge, Jack lived in a confused state of shock and excitement. Part of him wanted
to withdraw into a deep sleep to avoid all the conflicting
feelings. Part of him was alive with some vague sense of
expectancy.

It was the first time in his life that he had "departed for
the unknown." He was free. But he had never liked being
free. He liked the boundaries of his life. They were re-
assuring, and he felt they engendered a kind of creativity.
In a poetry course Jack had taken, Robert Frost had said
that he didn't write free verse because he didn't like
"playing tennis with the net down." The net made it
more difficult but more interesting.

He had forgotten how stinking hot Cambridge could
be in the summer.

"The air conditioner is a little erratic." Julia Stevenson,
from whom he was subletting the apartment, was packing
the last of her things for a summer abroad. He was staring
out the bank of windows at the maples and the back
lawns of houses. "Are you batching it?"

He turned. "Yes. My wife and I are separated."

"Christ, it's an epidemic. How long?"

"This morning."

"Oh, my God! You should be in an incubator. The first three months of my separation I put on twenty pounds. Some people eat, some people—" She stopped. "Security blankets. Did the super tell you this bed is really two mattresses? If you have company, just slide one off and shove them together." She smiled. "You'll find lots of company here. Cambridge is loaded with transients, separated, divorced. Bright, attractive people trying to cope with the burden of their new freedom."

He watched her pack her things, sweaters, blouses, slips. He turned away. He felt lonely and homesick. He wished that she hadn't been here, leaving behind the feeling of a woman for him to cope with. He had wanted this place to be a pad, starkly neuter, for thinking and work.

"Get yourself an engagement book, and for a couple of weeks keep it filled. Especially nights and weekends."

"I've got a list of names and numbers. A Security List. But I'm not very good at calling up and saying, 'Hello, I'm here.'"

"Well, get good at it. It's called survival."

He helped her carry her bags to the car. She looked at him for a moment, smiling sympathetically. "Please don't kill yourself in my apartment." He laughed. "All kidding aside, you'll find the number for the Crisis Center on the kitchen wall next to the refrigerator. They'll talk to you all night if you want them to. I know."

After a shower he looked at his Security List, names and numbers of former teachers, widows of classmates, classmates now practicing law in Boston. Penny. He frowned, realizing that Penny was really the only one he wanted to call.

She had had a crush on him when she was fourteen, a beautiful gazelle that summer she and her parents had

126

vacationed near them in Vermont. A girl of fourteen can be shameless in her attentions to a man of thirty-five. And innocent. Always managing to sit next to him when they would all troop over to the neighboring town for a movie. His almost equal as a tennis partner. Rich had had no feelings for her, so the family had just teased Jack all summer. And later, in her third year in college, when her father had suddenly come upon temporary bad times, Jack had arranged for Penny to have a full scholarship without anyone's knowing about it. Not even Cat.

But he just couldn't call and say, "I arrived a half hour ago. Cat and I are separated. Can I see you?" He was embarrassed at his urge to call her. He thought of his father, who always wanted to be with young people, and his mother, who said, "Why should they want to be with us?" And the stream of young schoolteachers who had been invited to dinner because, as his father said, the president of the school board had to keep in touch. His father had not seemed to have felt the need to keep in touch with the problems of older teachers. Jack had often been embarrassed by his father's flirting with younger women. "She seemed to take a shine to me." Now he understood his father a little better but was embarrassed for himself.

Harvard Square hadn't changed. Still one of the great traffic bottlenecks of the world. Cars coming from all directions, wanting to go in all directions and all at once. Policemen frantically trying to keep the hordes of pedestrians who poured out of the subway station from crossing against the lights like broken-field runners. He remembered the ancient bearded English professor who had always crossed fearlessly simply by holding up both hands to stop the traffic, likes Moses crossing the Red Sea.

He bought a newspaper to read at supper. As he moved down Brattle Street, it didn't seem possible that it was

127

thirty years ago that he had first come there. He looked at the people sauntering, eddying past the shops. Young men and women (boys and girls to him). Girls in blue cut-offs and T-shirts, no bras (variously endowed). Boys in cut-offs, work shirts or no shirts and sandals or barefoot.

The sidewalk seemed awash with rumps, breasts, sun-burned legs, arrogantly bulging crotches, long and shaggy hair and arms indolently draped around waists and hips. It was hot, and the sensuous mood of summer was upon the Square.

Jack took off his tie and jammed it in the pocket of his seersucker jacket and opened the top button on his shirt.

At Zum Zum he ordered frankfurters and sauerkraut and potato salad and beer and noticed a lovely brown-haired girl across from him. She was laughing and kidding with the boys on either side of her, her large dark nipples erect and clearly visible under her T-shirt, which bore the inscription "LOVE." He quickly looked away, remember-ing the time he had kiddingly boasted to Kim about how he could make her nipples erect, and she had laughed and said, "They do that when it's cold, too."

God, how he missed her! Like the night he had sat in the Faculty Club and had written her the silly letter "WHERE ARE YOU?" And unconsciously he began to repeat to himself her telephone number.

He looked around. Why had he picked this town to come to? Was it some instinct to return to his youth or to the memory of his youth with Cat? To begin all over again, to take "the road not taken"? People were all the time flocking back to their colleges, weren't they? Retiring there. Settling there. Chapel Hill, Princeton, New Haven. Young people were taking longer and longer now to leave the universities and their congenial no-class environs.

Drop out, come back, drop out, drift back. Graduate courses, odd jobs. Working toward a degree, sometime. No rush. Coffeehouses, bookstores, bring-your-own-bottle parties, bars. Good talk. Improvised living quarters and living arrangements.

Where else could he have gone? And he had had to go, to leave.

He looked again at the girl across the way. If she had been alone, could he have talked to her? He rarely talked to strangers on trains or planes, in elevators or lunch counters. And he had never picked up a girl.

The girl's breasts made him suddenly miserably lonely, and he got up and left without finishing his meal.

He crossed the street and bought a yogurt cone, then stood with a group in the growing darkness and listened to a girl play the guitar and sing on the steps of the Brattle Theater, where he had once acted in a play.

He was filled with a longing which disturbed and embarrassed him. It seemed so banal. He was up here, not eight hours since leaving home and marriage, presumably to think, to make some vital decision about his life, and at the moment all he wanted was to touch and hold, not be in love, yes, that too. But mostly to hold and be held.

Almost trembling, almost afraid that he would reach out and touch someone, he turned away from the group and crossed the street to a bookstore. He felt less lonely there, had always felt at home in bookstores anywhere in the world. For half an hour he browsed, picking out five or six paperbacks he had meant to read, great books he had missed. He would read and work and think, and the longing would pass.

Entering the elevator in his building, a young couple in cut-offs and T-shirts held the door for him. She was

Shirley Colman, who lived next to him. He was "my friend Herb." As they walked down the dimly lighted hall to their apartments, she warned him about the cockroaches. As they both fumbled in the dark to get keys in locks, she suggested baking soda as a remedy, while Herb ran his hand affectionately up and down her spine. When the doors were opened, Herb, impatient with this neighborly chatter, practically shoved Shirley into the apartment.

After a few moments the stereo started. Jack could feel the rock bass coming up through the soles of his feet. Then Shirley squealed, "Hey, Herb, don't!" Jack stood there looking at the wall. Another half-protesting squeal. He had tortured himself by visualizing the couples in the Square ending the evening like this. He hadn't realized he was going to be treated to the sounds right next door.

Debbie lumbered in from the bathroom. The music didn't bother her. She was getting deaf. There had been a time when the children had amused themselves by singing a certain high note and roaring with laughter as Debbie raised her head and howled, until they all had decided that she was perhaps howling in pain, and they stopped.

He fiddled with the air conditioner, moved the lamps around and settled into a wicker chair with the books he had bought stacked on the floor next to him. He looked around the room. He liked the picture. One extension-arm reading lamp creating a pool of light by the bed with its orange-colored spread; one lamp swung away from the large worktable, shining on his book. The rest, shadows, bare floors, a few "found" pieces of furniture. It was a stripped-down existence, something he had often craved in his cluttered life.

He looked at the stack of books with satisfaction, yet

with some amusement. How many times before had he bought these same books to read on trips, summer vacations, voyages? *War and Peace*. *Don Quixote*. *The Brothers Karamazov*. *Remembrance of Things Past*.

He started *War and Peace* but couldn't concentrate. He found himself unconsciously listening for the sounds next door, the giggles and grunts of appreciation.

"Hey, Herb, that hurt."

He rose from his chair, put Debbie back in the bathroom and left the apartment.

On the way back to the Square, walking along the streets under trees in full leaf, he looked into houses and saw darkened rooms and the faint ghostly light of television screens. He never would have thought that the light from a distant television screen would make him feel homesick. Then he checked himself. Why did he imagine a happy scene of husband and wife nestled on a couch watching the tube? In his house it had most often been Cat watching alone, and he reading in some distant room away from the sound of the "box."

He had never been a pub crawler, but he found himself strolling by the cellar bars on Mount Auburn Street. He didn't really want to go in, but there were the sounds of life and people enjoying themselves. He hovered self-consciously, feeling that the young people loitering outside were watching him.

He opened the door and stepped down into the bar. It was freezing, jammed, noisy and smoky, and he could see at once it was filled with students. A few glanced up at him briefly. "Who the hell is that?" He looked around as if he were expecting someone. He even checked his watch. Forty-nine years old, and he still couldn't enter a bar without these ruses to indicate that he was not alone!

He edged his way toward the horseshoe bar, where young men were standing two and three deep, laughing, topping each other's stories, calling to the bartender over the blare of the music. He noticed one middle-aged man sitting at the bar, staring at his beer. He looked up and across at Jack with wistful eyes. There was something obscene about the searching, longing look in a man that age.

Jack remembered the last time he'd been in a pub, with one of his hard-drinking older authors, who had looked up sadly and said, "Jesus, Jack. You know there was a time, not so goddamned long ago either, when I'd go into a bar and I'd know there wasn't a man there I couldn't lick or a girl I couldn't have."

Jack stood for a minute, wondering what the hell he was doing there. Did he really want to strike up a conversation with any of these men? He knew that he had always been something of a snob in his relations with people, had disliked superficial chitchat, treasured warm and intimate (and rare) friendships. Would he have to change all that to survive? He smiled. There was no man here he wanted to "lick" or girl he could have. They were all children, such beautiful children, and he'd be goddamned if he'd sit like that sad-eyed man . . .

As he walked back to his apartment through the Radcliffe Yard, he dodged a rotating sprinkler on the lawn under the elms in front of the Agassiz Theater. He saw a boy and girl embracing against a pillar, the boy grinding his pelvis against the girl, both grinning.

Christ, I hope those kids are through with their fucking when I get back! He wanted someone to be there, in his bed, with him, holding close, fucking. Fucking was life and living and being young, and he suddenly felt very old and frightened.

• •

The apartment was quiet now. He poured out what was left of Julia's vodka, added some ice and sat on the edge of his bed, staring at the phone and his Security List.

But he was thinking of Cat. What was she doing? He had always called her when he was away. Are you all right? Would she want to hear from him? After all, they didn't hate each other, were still concerned about each other. Which would be kindest, to call or not to call? What the hell was the protocol of this separation business?

He called. "Hi, it's Jack. How are you?"

"Oh, hi. All right. How are you?"

"Hot."

"Yes, it's hot here, too. Which man do you use to fix the air conditioner?"

"Schullstrom."

"I knew you used him for the freezer . . ."

"He does the air conditioner, too." He paused. "I'd forgotten how hot Cambridge could be in the summer."

"Well, you remember that summer we went to Summer School."

"Yes. I just had dinner in the Square. It doesn't seem possible that it was thirty years ago I first came here."

"My God, it was. Longer for me."

He paused. He shouldn't have called. "I forgot my dark glasses. Would you send them to me?"

"I already did."

"Thanks." He felt awkward. He almost started to talk about his feelings in the bar and walking around the Square, but he stopped himself. He realized that probably for the first time in his life there was nobody to whom he could tell his feelings. Except Kim. There had always been a girl, a woman, at the other end of a phone, at some address to which he could write a letter. "Well, I just wanted to check with you."

"Thanks for calling. Have you called people yet?"

"No, but I have my list."

"Don't forget Penny."

"I won't. The number I gave you for me is correct."

"All right."

"Have you got some Valium?"

"Yes. Have you?"

"Yes. Well, take care."

"And you too."

"Have the air conditioner fixed."

"Yes, I'll do that. I have it on my list."

"Well, good night."

"Good night."

Around three o'clock he woke up wringing wet and shivering, terrified. He had seen himself lying on a flatcar moving slowly through a subway station, and his friends were lined up on the platforms on each side, staring down at him as he passed by and into the dark tunnel.

His sheets were soaking wet. He reached down and found his blue terry-cloth robe and mopped himself; then, putting on the robe, he scurried across the room to turn off the air conditioner.

Back in bed, huddled in the robe, he looked into the shadows and wondered, "What the hell would I do if I had a heart attack?" Whom could he call? He had never felt so alone in his life. He could call the police. Jesus, the police! A wave of self-pity came over him. He wanted someone there. Where was everybody? Bitterly he thought that all his life he had taken care of people, sick wife, sick children, sick and dying parents and aunts and uncles. Now where the hell was everybody?

Then he realized that everybody was where they should be. At home. And if he were at home . . .

He had no more nightmares, but the early mornings continued to be terrible, as he woke up around four and lay there semiconscious, defenseless against waves of fears and doubts. One morning he saw himself as a revolting creature, longing for contact with the curving, swelling young bodies he saw all day, but ludicrously impotent. Half-asleep, in a sweating panic, he brought himself off for reassurance. But he was not reassured. It left him feeling cold and alienated.

Or he would stare across the room at Kim's mottoes, which he had scrawled on a shirt cardboard and taped to the wall on his third day there. "BLAME NOBODY . . . EXPECT NOTHING . . . DO SOMETHING."

He *had* done something. He had carefully laid out his material for his book on copyright and had worked on it in the mornings. Religiously. It gave him some small sense of worth. But it was in the afternoons and evenings when the panic set in, and he had tried to rid himself of it by sculling for miles up the Charles, or jogging till exhausted, or going to the movies.

Two evenings he had gone out with couples he didn't really want to see, and as it turned out, they didn't really want to see him, because in some way as a separated man, someone actually "doing it," not just talking about it, he seemed to present an unwanted challenge to their perhaps shaky marriages. And he had come to look on the Security List as some kind of insult. He had not yet called Penny. But why should a man be so afraid to be alone? To call people he didn't really want to see because he was afraid to sit alone in his room at night!

Friday, terrified of the coming weekend, he considered

calling Cat and asking her to meet him in some neutral motel halfway between Cambridge and home. They would hold each other and make love like two disinspirited bodies. They were always great in hotel rooms. But he mustn't panic, rush back in panic. He had left for a reason, hadn't he? A hotel room would be too easy . . . and yet too complicated.

Instead, he went to the Indoor Athletic Building on Saturday afternoon to swim himself to exhaustion. There he saw Ted Aronson, a young assistant professor with whom he had served on several committees, teaching his four-year-old son how to swim. Ted had custody of Sam over the weekends.

Grateful for their company, Jack took them out for a hamburger supper and accompanied them to the Boston Aquarium, where he was suddenly seized with a wild urge to rush to New York to Kim's bedroom and snatch away the two little black fish he had given her.

Later in the evening, in Ted's book-lined suite in Eliot House, drinking beers, with Sam curled up asleep in Ted's lap, they had an old-fashioned bull session about marriage and divorce. He told Ted his feelings of failure in the marriage. "My father used to say, 'Anything worth doing at all is worth doing well.'"

Ted stroked Sam's hair. "Of course the present view of marriage is that it *can't* be done well, as it is now understood."

Jack mentioned Dr. Raskin's having said in the radio interview with Cat that it might not be the fault of the people involved but of the institution itself. Ted smiled. "Well, Cambridge is full of separated and divorced *and* married people trying to figure it all out. Graduates of ten or twenty years ago are flocking back to alma mater to ask questions, find new answers. But this time there are no teachers, just a symposium of bewildered experts." He shook his head and laughed. "There was a girl in this house who got married last spring vacation. She came back embarrassed at what she'd done and went around the whole term trying to explain herself."

Sunday was almost unbearable. In the morning he narcotized himself by plowing through the *Times*. In the afternoon he jogged along deserted upper Brattle Street and over to the Charles and back. Showered, he lay on top of his bed and enjoyed the after exercise sleep, but he awakened realizing that he was about to burst.

He was a man of feelings, and all his feelings were blocked, except for his overwhelming longing. But for Cat . . . for Kim. When he started to think about Cat, he was in the squirrel cage again, and he would finally escape exhausted and still paralyzed. As for Kim, he could write to her, pour out his loneliness, his need, his bewilderment. But then he would be back in another squirrel cage of if onlys and whys.

Each day when he had gone down for his mail, he had hoped that Kim had disobeyed him and had written a letter. And each day he was both disappointed and glad that she hadn't.

Then Monday morning, along with the handful of oil, electric, telephone and grocery bills, there was a letter from Kim. As he took the elevator back upstairs, the letter still unopened, he said, "Why? Why did she write?" And he hurried into his room to read it.

My dearest, dearest Jack:
I am showing enormous self-control in not calling you. But I can't resist a note. Your office gave me your address.
How are you? I couldn't bear it if you thought I didn't care how you are, even though there's nothing I can do

137

about it. And I know under the circumstances, it's not much comfort.

Perhaps you don't need comfort. And that's all right. As it should be. As we knew it would be.

But I feel, selfishly, that I must explain myself, how I felt those last terrible weeks when I seemed to be so awful to you.

I felt somehow cold at home and at work. I felt Scott's need and your need, and my inability to respond. I wanted to be alone, to have nothing expected of me, to be lonely. I really seek loneliness because somehow out of it I find strength. I have felt so empty and worthless, incapable of giving and without the sense of joy that has been my life. Without it I seem to occupy space, yet give nothing, and for me that is no life at all.

I could not spend time with you when I could not give. Without a sense of myself, I cannot help or love anyone, and being present without giving, as I have been the past weeks, is unbearable.

I wanted to inhabit my own body in peace until I was filled again. Can you understand?

Forgive me for writing. I expect no answer. But I wanted you (again selfishly) to know.

Love,
Kim

As always with her letters, he was deeply touched. Flip and assured and almost cool on the surface, underneath so needful. And that was always the part that appealed to him. She had once murmured, "How do you know my body so much better than I do?" But he had felt it was not only her body. She seemed to be so unaware of the forces acting in her life, the pressure. So demanding of herself, so full of contempt for not measuring up to her impossible demands.

He longed to open up the channel of communication

138

with her again, to write her that he understood, that she must stop running herself down.

But he must not write. He would only write himself back into loving her. As if that had ever stopped!

And yet, just as he had had to call Cat, he could not leave Kim's letter unanswered. It was not a letter. It was an appeal. But he must write about her, not pour out his anguish. He must not burden her with his loneliness nor find release for his loneliness in writing her. He must recognize that his longing could be a creative force, leading him, possibly, to some realizable relationship, not the beautiful hopelessness of his love for her.

Monday afternoon Penny called him. She had been away on a trip and had stopped off in Ridgefield to see her parents, and they had given her his number.

He took her to Locke-Ober, where she had never been and where Cat and he had not been able to afford to eat when they lived in Boston. Over the first perfectly chilled martini she looked at him and, smiling warmly, said, "Did you know, dear godfather, that I had a terrible crush on you when I was fourteen?"

He smiled, embarrassed, yet moved that she had remembered. She was so beautiful sitting across from him. That lustrous short, black hair. Deeply tanned skin, pink sleeveless dress. He shouldn't have come. She aroused in him emotions about the past and inappropriate hopes for the future. "That summer in Vermont."

"You knew then."

"Yes."

She covered her face with her hands in mock horror. "How embarrassing!"

"Why?"

"I don't know." She blushed.

"It was very important to me." She looked at him,

139

questioning. "It was a time of life, of marriage. I don't know. You were very beautiful." He stopped himself from saying, "You are very beautiful."

"I don't see how it could have possibly mattered to you, a gawky fourteen-year-old girl."

"You were never gawky. Catherine kidded me about it."

"She knew?" Penny frowned.

He smiled. "I'm afraid everyone knew."

"Oh, God!" She shook her head, then looked at him and smiled. "Well, that's all right."

"We'd play softball in the field behind your house, and I'd hit some miserable dribble off the end of my bat, and you'd cheer as though I'd hit a home run." She laughed and blushed. "It was very exciting for me."

"Really?"

It was also exciting and yet painful to be sitting across from this lovely young woman, talking about a time when she had been in love with him. "Catherine and I had a big fight over it."

"Oh, come on! Why?"

"She was jealous, irked in some way. You were showing me an affection, a kind of completely uncritical love she no longer felt for me. Never felt for me. She'd say things like, 'You're silly if you think it means anything.'"

She looked at him a moment, took a sip of her drink and blushed. "It meant a great deal. I went around looking for an acceptable substitute for you for years." He smiled, embarrassed. "I think I've finally found one."

He sat back. "I hope for your sake he isn't too much like me." He caught a glimpse of himself in the mirror behind Penny.

"Well, he's thirteen years older than I am, and he's married with three children." They both smiled and shook their heads. "I tried not to fall in love with him, but what

140

are you going to do?" Jack shrugged, agreeing. "I don't think Hal wants to marry. He'd be happy just living as we do, separated from his wife. But he's going ahead with the divorce. I know nobody's marrying these days, but somehow I want to. Very daring! I think you'll like him. He'll be back in town tomorrow."

Jack suddenly felt lonely again. She seemed to sense this and smiled at him affectionately, as though she understood his feelings. "We'll have to find you someone. Would that be all right?"

"I understand it never works."

And it didn't work. Penny and Hal invited Jack to their "love nest" for dinner to meet Caroline, a recent divorcée, forty-six, with two children. She was attractive, beautifully dressed, had just had her hair done, but the moment they said "Hello," he knew (and she probably knew, too) that it was impossible. He had rarely been more uncomfortable. In addition, he loathed Hal each time he touched Penny or kissed her playfully, which he did often.

Later he drove Caroline home to Brookline, and when she asked him in for a nightcap, he felt he had to accept because he was never going to see her again. He spent half an hour admiring her large house (which she had won in the divorce), her dog and the pictures of her children. He wished they could have relaxed and laughed and told each other how silly and uncomfortable they felt.

He said he would be in touch, but as he started the car, he realized he hadn't taken her phone number. He must never put anyone through that again. Or himself.

Back in his apartment he had a stiff drink to try to get rid of the strain of the evening. He sat on the edge of the bed, staring at the wall, utterly depressed. He was suddenly overwhelmed by the seeming futility of what he was doing. He seemed simply to have exchanged one kind of loneliness for another. His room, which he had pictured as a stripped-down launching pad for a new, uncluttered, uncompromising life, now seemed to him a prison.

16

Then he met Janet. Ted Aronson had invited him to join him at a large Summer School cocktail party at one of the University museums, then to go to a dinner party and finally to a jazz concert at Sanders Theater. The cocktail party had not added up to much. The surroundings were interesting, but it was hot and the air conditioner was not working, and they were about to leave for their dinner engagement when Janet sauntered in.

As he told her later, he took one look at her and groaned. There was something about her. The first effect was of a small child-woman with long blond hair and a warm and slightly mischievous smile. "I'll try anything once." She was dressed in a striking outfit of wide, long black silk pants and a pink and rose and lavender blouse with a short Chinese rose-colored jacket. There was something sensuous and slightly decadent in the small, round face, a look in the eye that seemed to say, "What's up? Where's the fun?"

Ted smiled. "Her name is Janet."

"Who is she?"

"She's quite a girl."

"What else?"

"She's in the midst of an ugly divorce. Custody fight.

143

Her husband's a very bright man in the administration down at M.I.T. I never would have thought of her for you."

She turned from talking to some people and moved toward Jack and Ted. She smiled. "Hi." There was an interesting catch in her voice.

"Janet. How are you?" Ted took her hand and kissed her cheek.

"What a great place for a party!"

"You're looking lovely."

"My summer rags." She looked at Jack, who was staring at her.

"I'd like you to meet Jack Montgomery. Janet Bentley."

"Hello." She took Jack's hand. She had a way of looking directly at you as though to say, "What do we do next?"

"Jack's spending the summer in Cambridge. When he's in New York, he's a very distinguished lawyer."

"I need a distinguished lawyer." Jack wondered if she had been a tomboy.

"What do you need a lawyer for?"

Ted disappeared to get Janet a drink. "I'm in the midst of an unpleasant divorce, and my lawyer seems to be helpless."

"That's too bad."

"I'm surrounded by nothing but incompetents. I went to a psychiatrist, and he seduced me. Then a lawyer, and he immediately lost me the custody of my children. But I'm going to get them back."

"How come you lost custody of the children?"

"Well . . . it's very complicated. My life tends to get complicated." She laughed. "Our marriage was on the rocks, but my husband didn't want to break it up. Imagine. So he said I should find a lover. Which I did. And then when I finally couldn't take it anymore and wanted to

144

leave, he's got this adultery thing hanging over my head. Unfit mother."

Jack smiled and shook his head, already smitten. She went on. "He claims I had four lovers. Actually, it was three, and one of them was impotent, so he shouldn't count, should he?" Jack burst out laughing. "Do you want to take the case?"

"I'd have to take the Massachusetts Bar exam."

"I've got a good lawyer now, but he's very much taken up with his own divorce. You've discovered, I'm sure, that Cambridge is a nest of divorced and separated people."

"I'm afraid I'm adding to the number."

She laughed. "Oh, I'm sorry. I shouldn't laugh. At what stage are you?"

"About two weeks."

She reached out both hands and took his, making cooing sounds. "Oh . . . Have another drink. That's a terrible time."

He felt foolish hanging onto her hands. "Do you live in Cambridge?"

"No. I have a shack out in Concord with some mattresses. One for me, on loan, and one for each of my children when they come for weekends."

"How many children do you have?"

"A boy and a girl. They're with their father for the summer, except some weekends."

"Are you taking a course here this summer?"

"Yes. Music 199. I hope to get a job teaching music in a small private school here in the fall. It doesn't look as though I'm going to get any money from my husband. I taught music once, before the children were born."

Ted arrived with Janet's drink and announced they would have to leave at once. Jack wanted to forget the dinner and the concert, but he didn't know how to go about it. Had Janet come with someone? There was a tall, attractive young man who had come in with her. Perhaps it was just coincidental. He felt awkward. He just stood there, looking at her and smiling like a Cheshire cat.

"I'm sorry I got here late. Nice to have met you. Good luck. Really." She squeezed his hand, "Good luck."

"Good luck to you."

"I'm afraid luck won't do me much good. This is Massachusetts, the home of the scarlet letter." She drew a large *A* across her breast and turned away, smiling.

As they left the museum, Ted said, "Stop grinning."

Jack laughed. "She's crazy, but . . ." He shook his head.

At the buffet dinner, held in a large rambling brown-shingled house, he met a number of interesting and delightful people; at least he was sure they must be, but he couldn't remember anything about them the next day.

What was there about this jaunty little "character" that delighted him? Was it the catch in her voice or the pink and gold face with the woman's eyes, the quietly amused air as though she were saying her mantra with her eyes open? The gaiety and sense of humor in the face of disaster? Her sympathy for him, as she reached out and took both his hands when he said, "Two weeks"? The obvious sophistication ("my four lovers") in the small girl's body?

The next morning at ten o'clock he found himself wandering around the hallway of the Music Building, checking his watch, nonchalantly studying the notices on the bulletin board and keeping his eye out for Janet.

She appeared at the end of the hall with two men, laughing and talking together. Jack felt slightly silly. What was the next step? He had hoped she would arrive alone. She saw him and waved a small greeting as she entered the classroom.

He looked through the glass panels of the classroom

146

door. Students were moving around, checking one another's notes. One young man was sitting at the piano, illustrating a musical point to a girl. There was only one thing to do.

He entered and hovered, feeling conspicuous. Janet looked over at him and smiled and in a few moments sauntered over to him. She was wearing a colorful sleeveless Marimekko jumper. "Are you taking this class?"

"No." Never in his life had he asked a girl for a phone number. He blurted out. "Could I give you a ring sometime? See you perhaps?" He blushed.

She seemed to blush too. Then: "Sure. Have you got something to write on?" He didn't. And he didn't have a pen or pencil. She ripped off a corner of a newspaper lying on a table and wrote the number. He felt that everyone was looking at him.

"Thank you." He stood there, smiling foolishly. "I'd like to call you."

"Fine."

"Would that be all right?"

"Yes."

"Maybe we could have dinner, or go to a movie, or . . ."

"Sure."

"It's all right to call you at night? I mean, you're not involved?" He surprised himself with these questions. His hands were sweating.

"God, no."

"None of your four lovers hanging around?"

She smiled and blushed. "No."

The teacher came in. They had met the night before at the dinner and concert. "Do you mind if I sit in this morning?"

"Of course not."

Janet moved off and sat across the room with the two

young men she had arrived with. Jack sat and wondered if that meant anything. Why hadn't she sat with him? During the class he looked over at her frequently, watching her frown as she concentrated or squint as she tried to read some notes on the board. She needed glasses. She never looked at him. He had barged ahead too fast.

He thanked the teacher for letting him sit in and said that he might like to drop in from time to time. As he turned away toward the door, Janet was waiting for him. "I think I gave you the wrong last number. It should be a six." He found the slip of paper and checked it.

"You said six."

"Good. It's a new number, and I haven't got it down yet." They walked out of the room together. "Did you enjoy the lecture?"

"Yes."

"Did you ever study music?"

"Yes. I even used to compose some songs for things here at college." They paused in the hall. "May I walk along with you wherever you're going? Carry your books?" He smiled.

"I'm just going down the hall to practice."

"Could I come listen to you?" He didn't want to let her out of his sight. Wanted to stay close.

"God, no. I'd be self-conscious."

"Would you have lunch with me?"

She looked up at him and tilted her head as though wondering what this was all about. "I have to pick up my kids at three. It's my weekend."

"Then maybe you shouldn't." That was more like him.

"No, I'd like to." She blushed and smiled. "But I've got to tell you something."

"What?" He was now going to hear of an involvement.

"I don't remember your name."

148

They ate lunch at the Bistro, a small but cool and airy restaurant in a converted house on the Square. There was nobody else there. Janet laughed and said, "It must be some kind of front." The veal piccata was delicious, and the wine. Within moments they were leaning forward, intimate, rushing to share confidences, to brief each other on their emotional states, to shake their heads, smiling in bewilderment over what had happened to them. "I met Dick here when I was studying music."

"I met Catherine here about the time you were being born, I imagine."

"I was on the rebound. Bad place for a girl to be. Dick was, well, very strong, persuasive. It was a strength that appealed to me but finally strangled me. My fault for marrying without being really in love."

"I was really in love."

"And still, here you are."

"Yes."

"Marriage."

"No. Not necessarily."

"I told you about my lovers." She smiled. "When I could no longer stand being told exactly what to do and how to do it, and I said I was leaving, he wanted me to go to my last lover. For him, in some way, this was more face-saving than just leaving the marriage. I just wanted to leave the marriage. And I did."

"Our leaving each other was much different. I don't know really what it was." He shook his head. "Maybe we resented each other for something neither of us could help. We both wanted to be deeply in love again. It's a strangely loving separation." For a few moments he felt very close to Cat, talking of her like this.

She looked at him. "It got so, this was before the lovers, he never touched me except when he wanted sex." She sat

149

back. "I mustn't talk like this. It's very unattractive. You'll find that nobody talks much about their divorces or separations. Everyone is kind of ashamed of having failed or having made the wrong choice, and they want to forget it. Only a few go over and over it, trying to justify themselves or to learn from the experience." They looked at each other for a moment. "It's nice being able to talk like this."

"Yes." It was a summer Friday afternoon, and he wanted to take her back to his pad and shove the mattress off and lie with her and hold her and make love to her.

"What are you doing up here except being separated?"

"Not much. I'm working on a legal book on copyright and sitting in on a writing course." He smiled. "People used to tell me I wrote good letters." He fidgeted with the spoon. "Trying to change my life, I guess. It goes with my age."

"You keep talking about your age. How old are you?"

"Forty-nine. How old are you?"

"Thirty-one. So what do you think you'll do?"

"I don't know. All my life I've done what other people wanted me to do, expected me to do. I've taken a leave of absence from my law office. We'll see. I'm in limbo. I've never been very comfortable in limbo. Unstructured time has been known to panic me."

"Where are you living here?"

He told her. "It's more like a pad, really. Mattresses on the floor. Two mattresses, one on top of the other. My landlady, who's off to Europe, told me one could be slipped off to make room for another person, when, as and if. A couple of white wicker chairs and a huge worktable. That's it. In the midst of my sometimes rather complicated life, I've often dreamed of such simplicity. Now I have it."

"I'm not much better off. I lived with friends at first.

150

Dick has the children for the summer. But I see them every other weekend. So I wanted a house of some sort they could come to. I have this little house, almost a shack, the cheapest rent I could find, and, like you, a few mattresses until I know if I'm going to get the children and some money and some of the furniture from the house."

"How old are your children?"

"A boy seven and a girl nine. Eric and Karen. Dick is Swedish. And yours?"

"A son twenty-one and a daughter twenty-three." He almost said he was about to become a grandfather but didn't.

She looked at him. "I'm sorry I have to go away this weekend with the kids."

"I could do something with you all. I'm very good at aquariums."

She smiled. "No. We've been invited down to the Cape. Maybe if I get back at a decent hour on Sunday night, I'll call you."

"That would be nice." He scribbled his number for her.

"I might call Saturday night, just to say hello. What will you do this weekend?"

"Oh, swim, jog, read. Look forward to seeing you again." He looked at her. "I'm very glad we met."

"Mmmmm." She touched his hand.

"What about Monday night?"

"Monday I have classes, an afternoon piano lesson and exercise class."

"You keep yourself very busy."

"It's the only way. Monday night there's a departmental party. Do you know the Allinsons by any chance?"

"Yes. I've served on a committee with him."

"Well enough to get invited to their party? I think it's a big bash."

"I'll send flowers and bring wine."

"If you could arrange it, then I could change in your apartment and save going all the way out to Concord and back."

"Of course." He tried to sound cool.

He walked her to her car, a slightly banged-up light-blue Fiat. He was carrying her canvas tote bag, bulging with bathing suit and whatever she would need for the weekend. He breathed deeply. "I feel very good."

She took his arm. "That's nice." She opened her car door. "I'll call Sunday if I get back in time."

"Good."

"Otherwise, Monday around five-thirty. Okay?"

"Okay." They looked at each other. It was obvious that they were both "charged" from the two hours they had spent together. He thought to kiss her cheek, but it would be too casual. He would wait hopefully.

She reached out her hand. "Thanks for lunch."

"Thank you."

She got in and started the car and moved smartly away from the curb, waving her hand at him out the window.

He felt marvelous. Once again it was all a cliché. He felt like one of those romantic men in perfume advertisements. He had the sense to know he didn't look like one, but he felt like one. Of course, she might return Monday from the weekend and have changed her mind. Or she might have met someone else, her own age. After all, twenty-four hours ago he hadn't known her.

And she had said that it was all very tricky because she had to be careful about her image in order to stand any chance of getting custody of the children. People were living one kind of life, but the courts were still playing by the old rules.

17

Monday morning Jack was beginning to wonder. She hadn't called Saturday night or Sunday. He had found himself again sitting home, waiting for phone calls. He could call her, but he felt she should call. If she had changed her mind, he didn't want to seem to be pressing.

Saturday he had looked at himself in the mirror in the bathroom and decided that he should get some color on his body. His face was tanned, but his body was white. He had gone to the beach at Ipswich and had hurried back in the evening for the phone call.

Sunday he had holed up with the *Times*.

The phone rang. "I'm sorry I didn't call last night, but it was too late when I got in. Is five-thirty still okay?"

He tried to do some writing on his book, but he couldn't concentrate. It had always been this way. With Cat. With Kim. The excitement, the anticipation were too much.

He should get a haircut. No, he shouldn't. No telling what a strange barber might do, and she had seemed to like him the way he was Friday.

He dashed down to the Square and bought gin, vodka, scotch, vermouth, wine, tonic, soda, cheese, crackers. He paused in front of the cashew nuts. He bought Janet's brand of cigarettes and some lemons. At lunch she had had wine and soda and lemon peel. He wondered for a moment if she liked to rub the lemon peel on her hands as Cat did. Was there ever anything that wasn't in some way associated with someone else? Was everything after a certain age double and triple exposure?

He bought flowers, avoiding Cat's carnations and Kim's white daisies. In the hardware store, buying light bulbs, he watched a man making keys. He had him make a key to his apartment for Janet. The presumption of it delighted him. Completely out of character.

On his way back he couldn't help smiling. For a man who had always hated and avoided the obvious, he was playing this very out of character. A woman was coming to his room to change her clothes for a party, and he was getting up a seduction scene. She might very well just want to change her clothes.

But he welcomed his impulsiveness. For too much of his life he had checked his impulses, conditioned as he was as a lawyer and as a man to examine all sides of a question before doing anything.

It seemed that five o'clock would never come. He had taken care of Debbie, shaved, bathed, napped, dressed (blue shirt, tan slacks, no socks or shoes) and was impatient. Yet he felt an almost overwhelming desire to go to sleep. He had felt this way before final exams and the few times he had appeared in court to try a case. He was brushing his teeth once more when the buzzer sounded.

"It's me."

"Come on up. Four B." He went out into the hall and down to the elevators and waited. The doors opened, and she came out jauntily. "Hi."

"Hi." She was wearing another A-shaped Marimekko cotton dress with splashes of orange and green, and sandals. He took her large tote bag. He wanted to take her in his arms and kiss her, but it was not time. She must have also been aware of how fast they were moving. She played it cool, moving along beside him.

"Where's your dress?"

"In that bag, along with the rest of my worldly possessions." She looked at him. "You look terrific."

"I went to the beach."

"I just get red. God, I hope your apartment's air-conditioned."

"It is."

"I bathed after exercise class, but I'm sticky again." They entered the apartment. "Oh, this is nice!"

"Very primitive. Back to nature."

"Just like mine. Only you've got more furniture."

"I saw some places that were more attractive. But I thought I'd get homesick in them."

Debbie ambled out of the bathroom. "This is Debbie."

"Oh. You didn't tell me."

"Do you mind dogs?"

"I love them." She petted and stroked Debbie.

"She's an old lady. We got her for the children."

"My kids are clamoring for a dog." She dived into her tote bag and drew out from the tangle a full-length knit dress, red with white discs. Debbie ambled back to the bathroom. "Have you got a hanger for my dress?"

"Sure." He went to the closet.

"I hope to God I don't bulge in all the wrong places. I haven't been to exercise class in weeks. I looked at myself today. Ugh."

"You look great to me."

"You can't tell because I'm wearing this tent. But right there, feel." She pulled the dress tight and indicated her belly. He put his palm against her belly. It was going to be all right. It was just a question of when. And they both knew it.

"Feels lovely to me. I like your clothes."

"They're kooky. I'm technically a suburban matron. But all my adult life I've fought like a tiger to stay out of Peck and Peck."

"Sometimes they're nice. Sweaters, skirts, polo coats."

"Well, since I've got to reconcile myself to being a pauper, it's cheaper to dress kooky."

"You have beautiful hair."

She blushed. "Not really." She nervously hunted for a cigarette in her bag. "You don't smoke, do you?"

"No, but I got you some."

"Thanks, but what I need now is a match."

He found the matches in the kitchen. "Success."

"Ah, ten more minutes off my life." He lighted her cigarette, and they looked at each other. Suddenly she sat down in the white wicker chair, and he was standing there, looking at the top of her head. She took a few puffs, then looked up at him. "Could I have a glass of water or something?"

He moved toward the kitchen. "Would you like a vodka and tonic? Or wine?"

"Wine and soda. That would be nice. Do you have any soda?" She came to the kitchen.

"Yes."

"Glasses?" She opened one of the cupboards. "She didn't leave you much equipment, did she?"

"I don't intend to entertain much."

Janet opened the refrigerator for the ice while Jack started on the cork. "Nice new refrigerator, at least. I've got a secondhand horror. I have to keep a pan under it. I find that refrigerators do not necessarily come with rented

156

houses." She looked at him struggling with the cork. "You need a better corkscrew. One of those with wings."

He finally put the bottle on the floor between his feet and pulled. He got red in the face. They both started to laugh. He finally succeeded in getting the cork out and stood up. They looked at each other, laughing. Their laughs faded, and he took a step toward her and kissed her lightly. She closed her eyes and made a purring sound of pleasure. He kissed her cheek, her ear and finally her mouth, moving close to her and holding her with his left hand, while still holding the wine bottle in his right.

After a moment she moved away, eyes still closed. "Slower, Slower."

"I wanted to kiss you the moment you stepped off the elevator."

"I know. I know." She leaned against the doorjamb, eyes still closed and frowning. He kept close to her, kissing her cheek. She took a puff on her cigarette. "Pour the wine."

With one hand he poured the wine and added the soda and handed it to her, then moved against her body. "When you came into the room at the party the other night, I groaned. I just groaned."

She opened her eyes wide. "Did you?"

"I did."

"I purr."

"I know. I heard it just now."

"You groan." She moved into the room and sat again in the chair. He crouched beside her. "Slower. Slower." He kissed her cheek, her neck, light, glancing kisses. She closed her eyes and purred again. "Mmmmm." Then she gently moved his face and hands away and looked at him very severely. "I don't want to fall in love with you."

"You won't." He had said it without thinking. He would have said anything at that moment. He kissed her again, lightly, and touched her breast. She sat there with her eyes closed as though she could feel the sensations better that way or as though she were waiting for some signal in her body. Then she opened her eyes and looked at him, and, with a long sighing "Oh . . ." as though of resignation, put her arms around him and gave herself over completely.

As they held and touched and stroked and kissed, there was the usual excitement of strangeness and of the first time and the usual awkwardness. After some moments they made it the few feet to the bed, and as she lay down, he turned back the brightly colored tent she was wearing and kissed the large, hard nipples of her small breasts. She lay there with her eyes closed, savoring what he was doing, her dress bunched around her neck. She smiled without opening her eyes. "We should get all undressed, but let's not."

Keeping contact, he slipped off his slacks and shorts. She arched her back, and he removed her gaily flowered panties, and as his mouth moved down her body, tasting the salt, he swung his legs up onto the narrow bed and his knee grazed her head. He laughed. "Sorry."

"Don't knock my teeth out. I need them to bite." She made a mock biting motion and edged her face toward him.

When it was over, they lay in each other's arms, a messy tangle of bodies and clothes, and opened their eyes and smiled. They had survived. They had dived in, all urgency and apprehension, and they had survived. They had shown and found their bodies to be accessible, responsive, eager and generous. Next time they could make love.

Now the sweaty clothes came off, and the bed was quickly opened and a sheet pulled over them, and they could touch and look and enjoy each other's bodies quietly. They smiled contentedly, numb with happiness

158

and sensuousness and the prospect of all the loving that lay ahead of them.

She smiled. "Were you surprised?"

"About our being together?"

"No. About my being . . . prepared."

"It was very exciting, knowing you had come here wanting me."

He kissed her and began to get excited again as he had been when he felt the edge of the diaphragm on entering her.

"The Pill does funny things to me. I thought you might be shocked."

"I was delighted. The world is full of men complaining because they never know if their women really want them or not. Promise you'll call day or night and say, 'Hey, get over here. I want to be fucked.'" She frowned. "I'm sorry. You don't like that word."

"It's okay."

"I never used to like it, but now I think it's nice." He snuggled close to her, gathering her small body into his. God, God, wasn't it lovely!

They kicked Debbie out of the bathroom and showered together, soaping and rubbing and getting excited again, but ceasing and desisting because they had a party to go to.

As they were dressing and sharing another drink, he gave her the key to his apartment, casually. "Here's something for you."

"What's that?"

"The key to this place." She looked at him. "You may want to change here again, or . . . I don't know. I like the idea of your having it." She just looked at the key in his hand. "I had it made this afternoon."

She smiled. "You did?"

159

"Yes."

"You were pretty sure of yourself. But then, I should talk."

"I just liked the idea of your having the key to this place. I was going to give it to you no matter what happened. It just makes it seem a . . . pleasanter place. The idea that you might drop in. Use it."

She looked at it for another moment, frowned. "You're too much."

"You don't want it?"

She paused, then snatched it from his hand. "Yes." And she kissed him and put it in her purse.

At the party, in a large house said to have been designed by Stanford White, they did not stay together. Soon after they arrived, he got involved in a policy discussion with an older professor, and Janet drifted off to mingle with the other music students, her age and younger. During the buffet she made no effort to come back to him, and he felt awkward about joining her and her young friends.

Later in the evening records were played, and the young people started dancing on a large porch overlooking the back lawn. Though Janet was thirty-one she looked twenty and soon was in the midst of the dancing, arms raised, hips and bare feet moving to the beat. Jack loved to dance. Some nights when he was alone in his apartment in New York, he would have a couple of drinks and put on records and dance. As a boy he had spent hours in the living room of his home pretending he was Fred Astaire. And in his twenties, when he got high at parties, he would do an imitation of Ray Bolger doing "Once in Love with Amy."

But in this group only the young were dancing, and he felt awkward and old. Dancing was a kind of barrier one generation raised against another. He remembered his father at country club dances where everyone was jitter-bugging, wondering, "Whatever happened to the waltz?"

Much later, when people were leaving, Janet rejoined him in the large high-ceilinged living room, flushed and exhilarated. "Why didn't you dance?" He shrugged. "Do you like to dance?"

"Yes, but—"

"You should have." She took his hand, and they said their goodbyes and left.

Jack followed Janet out Route 2 to her little house in Concord. He had a hard time keeping up with her. She drove fast and took every chance. Finally, she pulled off the main road and then down a secondary road and into a short drive. The house was pretty much of a nothing ex-cept house, shelter. One-storey, white clapboard small side porch. A couple of nice maples, a small lawn. As he joined her at the steps, she said, "You see, I didn't exaggerate. But I just couldn't go on living with friends, and this was all that I could afford. More than I can afford, actually. Sometime, when I know Dick is away, I'll have to take you over and show you our house in Lexington, so you won't think I'm a complete slob."

As they entered, the radio was playing. "It's less lonely to come home to that way. I have a beautiful stereo, but I know I won't get that."

"I'll get you one."

"God, no. If you want to get me something, get me a steam iron." She laughed. "I'm just kidding. I don't want you getting me anything."

The rooms were bare except for a few chairs and a table, the mattresses and, incongruously, two large oils of a man and a woman, painted sometime in the mid-nineteenth

161

century. "My great-grandmother and great-grandfather. Dick couldn't claim those were his."

They moved into the kitchen. She turned on the overhead light and immediately went to remove the drip pan from under the refrigerator. "Look at this horror. I've got my eye on a secondhand one . . ."

He shook his head. "It's funny. Both of us living like this. Yesterday I paid about twenty-five bills for our big house, the apartment in New York."

"Does it depress you? Do you want to run away?"

"No. I just hate the thought of your being treated like this." He put his arm around her protectively.

"If I get the children, I'll get some child support. If not . . . Anyway, I wanted out. Stupid letting you come here. He's probably got the house staked out so he can prove I'm an unfit mother."

She went to the cupboard and brought out two beautiful Waterford glasses. "I stole a few things." They made drinks and went back into the living room. "You didn't have a good time at the party."

"Yes, I did. I just felt a little awkward."

"I shouldn't have left you. I don't know why I did." She put her arm around his waist.

"I love to dance. But I didn't want to look foolish in your eyes."

"That's silly." She began to move in time to the music, and he watched her for a moment, taking a sip of his drink. "Come on." And at first, embarrassed, he took a few steps, made a few moves; then, putting his glass on the window ledge, he let himself go. Then he put his arm around her and led her through a few intricate steps, which she had difficulty following. She stopped. "Now it's my turn to feel silly."

"Why?"

162

"I never learned to dance like that, to follow."

"You mean nice little girls in Wilmington, Delaware, didn't have to go to dancing school?"

"Never. Will you teach me?"

"Yes."

They danced for a few moments, and then they stopped and just held each other. "I hear your groaning."

"I hear your purring."

For what seemed like hours they made slow, sensuous love on the mattress on the floor of her bedroom, the only light the glow from her electric clock-radio and the head-lights of an occasional passing car. He learned what she liked and didn't like, what she hadn't tried. "Dick always wanted to do that."

"How was it with Dick?"

"Very physical. Everything was a workout for him. It was just another workout. I shouldn't say that. It was all my fault for marrying him when I didn't love him."

She moved her body gracefully in bed, sometimes stretching and performing exercises from the morning's class. She lay spread-eagled and sighed contentedly. He moved down on the bed and nuzzled his face between her legs. She complained. "Let me do you, too."

"No."

"I feel so self-conscious, just lying here."

"Feel self-conscious then."

"Do you really like that?"

"Yes."

"I can't understand why."

"You're not a man."

"Dick didn't like it."

"That's his problem."

"He couldn't come when I did that to him."

"He had a lot of problems."

"Can you?"

"Yes."

"Don't you want to come again?"

"No. I just like the feeling of wanting you all night."

"All night?"

He laughed. "Don't worry. Just to be close to you."

"But doesn't that hurt?"

"Not at my age."

"I like your age very much." She snickered.

"It's not always reliable."

"I'll take my chances. Does it panic you when . . .it's not reliable?"

"Yes."

"It panicked Dick."

"I sympathize with him. About four days ago, afraid that I'd lost it all, I jerked off."

"Do you do that?"

"Sometimes." She laughed. "What about you?"

There was a moment's pause, then quietly: "Yes."

He reached up and took her hand and brought it down her body.

"No, not now. Not with you."

"If you ever want to . . ."

"Yes, all right."

"And now, if we can be quiet for a few minutes, I'll get on with my work."

She laughed. Then: "Mmmm."

Later he was asleep, pressing himself against Janet's bottom. She woke him. "It's three o'clock." He looked around, wondering what she meant. "It doesn't make any sense, but suddenly I'm scared. I think you should go home. I don't think your car should be in the drive in the morning."

"All right." He kissed her lightly.

164

"It's terrible, but I don't want to lose my children."

"I understand." He found his shorts and put them on over his semiengorged cock.

"Poor baby." She touched it through the cloth.

"It'll be all right."

"Call me in the morning. Or I'll call you."

"Yes." He knelt on the bed and kissed her. "Thank you."

"Mmmm. Thank you. I'm sorry, making you get up and go like this."

"It's been a great night."

"Me too."

18

The next morning Jack went to Sears in Cambridge and bought Janet a refrigerator. As he remembered, hers opened on the left. Icemaker? Freezer alongside refrigerator, above or below? He should consult Janet, but it would spoil the surprise. Delivery by Thursday for sure.

In the afternoon he learned all there was to know about the Electrolux vacuum cleaner.

"Go ahead, sir. Try it yourself."

"Yes, I see. Very good."

"And for the drapes . . ."

He allowed himself to be "sold" every gadget and "option."

Janet was overwhelmed and embarrassed. She blushed "I've never had a new refrigerator."

They assembled the Electrolux. "This is for curtains."

"Only I have no curtains."

He took her into Cambridge to show her her refrigerator. "Would you rather have another kind?" She just stared at it and shook her head. Over her protests he bought a steam iron.

"Too much! Too much! Please."

"Don't stop me. I'm having a great time." He suddenly

knew why he had come to Cambridge. He had really known all along.

They spent their nights either at her house or in his air-conditioned apartment, sliding around the cork floor on the two mattresses, sleeping, waking, sleeping. When they were at her house, he parked his car at the depot, and she taxied him back and forth so that his car would not be seen in her driveway overnight.

One night when they both awoke and started fondling each other again, he laughed. " 'How I Spent My Summer' by Jack Montgomery." She laughed. "Do I bore you with it?"

"Hadn't you noticed?"

"You must understand I skipped my adolescence completely. I'm living my life backwards."

But more important than the almost continual feeling of sensuousness were the feelings of closeness and connection. The wholeness. They pushed carts in supermarkets, weeded her scruffy patch of garden, hung India prints at the windows. And after, he would sit in the kitchen, stripped to his T-shirt and blue boxer shorts, and watch her make supper. It pleased her to see him lounging around barefoot. "Dick would never have done that." They had already done a number of things that Dick would never have done.

But Dick's influence was still very much with her, and he found he had to go easy on making suggestions as to what they might do or in giving opinions. She had been so completely smothered by Dick's discipline and control that she was rawly sensitive to even the smallest suggestion.

They went to the movies and strolled through Harvard Square with their arms draped loosely around each other and eating yogurt cones. He saw young couples looking at them and smiling. "Does it embarrass you to be seen with a graying elder?"

"Stop talking like that. You're the only one who notices."

"Watch them smiling."

"They're smiling appreciatively."

"Shall I get some cut-offs?"

"If you want. You've got nice legs."

They talked about themselves. How quick it had been with them. "I knew Cat for six months before we made love."

"Believe it or not, I was a virgin on my wedding night. Now people tumble into bed and get to know each other later."

"Oh, I think you know a person, a lot about them, right off. I knew about you." She smiled.

At the Harvest they got onto the subject of marriage. "It seems to ruin everything."

"It doesn't have to."

"I heard from my roommate at Wellesley. *She's* getting a divorce. God!"

"Well . . ." And they would shake their heads.

They would discuss the alternatives. Jack had lent her Carl Rogers' *Becoming Partners*. All his life, when he had encountered problems, he had gone to books. As an educated man he had been taught that most problems give way to rational analysis.

She said, "Having a lover on the side is a romantic idea, but a great strain, and very difficult emotionally and physically. One of my girlfriends said, 'You've got it made.' Ridiculous. I finally wanted out of it all and to be alone. And to be involved with two men at the same time—" She shrugged her distaste. "Of course, sometimes you find yourself in transition from one person to another. Uncomfortable but inevitable. But then, I didn't love any of my lovers." She blushed and laughed.

When he wasn't working on his book, he came to the practice room and listened to her play. And she persuaded him to sing in his now-husky baritone a couple of the songs he had sung in operettas in college. "You should have gone on with it."

They decided they wanted to get out of Cambridge one weekend. She suggested Tanglewood. Ozawa was conducting Schoenberg and Brahms. He asked Shirley to look in on Debbie and feed and walk her, called Ticketron at Sears to see if they could get seats, made reservations at the Red Lion Inn in Stockbridge and took off, stopping by Janet's house to leave her car and pick up some clothes.

As they drove along the Massachusetts Turnpike, they talked about their usual subject, the "Cambridge" subject, marriage, divorce, love, separation. Jack talked about her children and the paradox of a woman's getting her freedom from her husband, from her marriage, but not from the responsibility of the children. "I would have thought there would have been moments when you might not have wanted them, wanted to be absolutely free."

"There are such moments, of course. I felt it the first night I stayed with you in your apartment. But later that night I awoke, afraid."

"Of what?"

"Suddenly I was afraid that something might have happened to the children and they wouldn't know where to reach me. I knew they were with their father, but I had that feeling."

As they drove into Stockbridge, they both were laughing over their early problems with masturbation and how she was dealing with it with her children. He was suggesting that *je m'abuse* should be *je m'amuse*.

She wandered into the gift shop off the lobby as he registered them as Mr. and Mrs. John Montgomery. She looked like such a child he was always expecting some bartender to ask for her identification.

They both were a little shy with the new circumstances of sharing a hotel room. After they had hung up their clothes, they had lunch in the bar and then walked in and out of the few shops on Main Street. Over her protests ("Nothing more, for God's sake!") he bought her a striking photograph by Clemens Kalischer and, in the same store, an antique ring with a semiprecious stone that turned out to be her birthstone.

Back in the room they were content with just lying beside each other and napping. Then they felt very domestic showering and changing and having a pre-party drink while they got ready for the evening. She was even slightly behind schedule.

During dinner at Orpheus Descending, a quaint and colorful bar and restaurant in an old house out of town, she talked to him about the Schoenberg they were going to hear. He knew the Brahms. Everyone knew the Brahms First. He had studied it motif by motif in Music I. She talked about her music and how it had given her an identity. She had been the shy, retiring member of her Wilmington family until she discovered music. Then she had been a music counselor at a girls' camp and then accompanist for the choral group at college.

He told her it reminded him of something his headmaster had said to the class when he had been graduated from prep school. "My wish is that each of you will find something in which you excel. It will make your lives."

He talked about his wanting to be a writer, and she had asked him why he hadn't gone ahead with it. He smiled. "You've heard that saying 'Life is what happens while you're making other plans'?"

The Schoenberg impressed him but left him cold. He was more fascinated by the spectacle of the huge music shell, the dark lawns beyond where people had finished their picnic suppers and were lying on blankets in the twilight, the distant thunder and flashes of lightning possibly threatening a storm.

During intermission Janet saw someone she knew from Cambridge and steered Jack away and out onto the lawns. "It's just that I'm frightened. I know it's ridiculous, but Dick's likely to use anything to get the children." She was immediately annoyed with herself for feeling like this. "It makes no sense. He's living openly with a girl, even when the children are there. But I'm frightened. It's not fair, but that's the way it is."

Though Jack wanted Janet to have her children, he could sympathize with her husband for wanting them, too. He could not have given up Jorie and Rich.

The orchestra started to play the Brahms like the warhorse it is. Musicians grabbed for flies and mosquitoes, surveyed the audience when they were not playing and reacted to the claps of thunder with raised eyebrows, perhaps wondering if they would get home before the storm broke.

But then suddenly, a few moments into the first movement, that all stopped, and it became excitingly apparent that tonight Ozawa meant to play the Brahms First as it had rarely been played before. Eyes stopped wandering; violinists sat straight and ignored the thunder, their attention glued to the small, vigorous man in the black suit and white turtleneck sweater who was challenging them to exceed their own limits, to extract every ounce of dark pathos from this brooding music.

Everyone, including the audience, "took hold," began to realize that this was to be an extraordinary experience in which all must play a part.

Almost simultaneously Jack and Janet reached for each other's hands. His eyes filled with tears, and he hardly dared breathe as the tension mounted, the perfection built. It didn't seem possible that it could be happening on this very evening. And they were there!

He remembered that this symphony had been called "a soaring Gothic cathedral," but it had never seemed like that before. It went on and on, through the gentler, more subdued tracery of the second and third movements. Even through the pauses the audience remained hushed, no coughs, no stirring, not wanting to release any of the charge that was building in them.

Then, finally, toward the end, with the kettledrums pounding and the whole orchestra moving into the broad, sweeping hymn of triumph and joy, the audience could hardly contain themselves, and almost before the final notes, everyone was up and applauding and cheering.

Janet and Jack looked at each other finally, tears streaming down their faces, choked, unable to speak, just shaking their heads in wonder that such excellence and beauty still existed and pounding their hands together as Ozawa returned again and again, beaming, knowing he had pulled it off, had stunned everyone, including his magnificent orchestra. The applause went on and on and on until everyone was gloriously exhausted.

They finally moved out across the lawns, unable to speak. On this hot and humid night they were chilled by the excitement and the tension and by the honor of having been asked, in a sense, to perform, to be participants in this incredible event they would remember all their lives.

Driving back to the inn, they tried to speak, to express their feelings about what had happened, but whatever they managed to say seemed to diminish the experience, and they were still.

They went to the bar for a drink, but before they sat down, they knew it was wrong, the chatter, the music on the radio, and they left and went to their room and quickly undressed in the dark and lay on the bed and held each other. He was afraid he would hurt her, he crushed her so hard against his body, as though he wanted their bodies to become one.

Finally, releasing her but still holding her, he almost moaned, "Oh, how I love you!"

She put her fingers to his lips. "No. No."

"Yes!"

"You mustn't say that."

He kissed her and touched her lightly, somewhat relaxed, almost as if he had experienced a kind of emotional orgasm by saying the words. "I know you say I mustn't . . . and probably you're right. But I'm so full of love and loving, and not to say the words leaves me . . ." He shook his head. "At such moments to be cautious, to be honest, long-term honest, to hear some voice saying, 'You mustn't use those words because they mean things you feel now but might not feel sometime later . . .'"

"Yes."

"I can't make love that way, holding back, qualifying. I have to love each time as though it were forever. And yet I'm not so naïve as not to know . . . that it might not be."

"I understand."

He lay there a moment, his hand moving almost absentmindedly over her body. "I don't know where I am."

"I know. Neither do I."

"And at this moment I don't want to think back, and I don't want to think forward. I don't want to be a responsible man." He looked over at her and smiled. "I just know that I groaned when I first saw you, and I groan each time I see you."

"I like that."

They moved toward each other, feeling released in their understanding that everything was here and now and not necessarily tomorrow.

Sunday they drove slowly home, leaving the turnpike and taking back roads, stopping to investigate tag sales and barn sales, and finally loading up on fresh corn and lettuce and tomatoes and going to Janet's house and cooking in the twilight and gorging themselves, and then just lying on the bed and watching it grow dark and finally making love quietly, almost not believing that it could be possible after the night before. He was overwhelmed by the peacefulness. Somehow he was also frightened by it. But as he drifted off to sleep that night with the cool breezes coming in gently through the window, nothing was wrong.

19

When he awoke the next morning, he was alone in the bed. He listened. No sounds in the bathroom. After a few minutes, he wandered out of the bedroom. He found Janet asleep in the children's bedroom on one of the mattresses, with a sheet pulled up over her shoulders. With her long blond hair spread out on the pillow, her small body curled up in a ball, she looked like little more than a child herself. He went back to the bedroom and lay there, half-dozing, until an hour or so later, when he heard her in the kitchen.

"I was restless. I thought I was disturbing you." She looked at him. "I suddenly wanted to be alone."

He put his arm around her and kissed the top of her head. "Okay."

They had orange juice and toast and coffee and sat and looked at each other. "It was a great weekend."

"Yes." But her smile was troubled.

"I must try to get a recording of the Brahms. And something to play it on."

"No. Please!" She looked stern.

"Okay."

She took a shower, and he wanted to go in with her, but knew this morning he mustn't. She had drawn into herself.

As she drove him to the depot, he said, "Do you want to make any plans for tonight?"

"I'm going to see some friends tonight. I haven't seen my friends in ages."

"I should work on my book."

There was a stillness between them. When they arrived at the depot, he sat there for a moment. "Give me a ring when you want to see me."

"Yes. I will." She smiled.

"It was an incredible weekend."

"Yes." She shook her head.

"You know if you'd just like to spend an evening talking, I can talk too." He smiled.

She laughed. "I know."

Obviously it was something she wanted to work out for herself. He kissed her and drew back a few inches and looked at her and smiled. "Thanks."

"Thank you."

As he drove back into Cambridge, the stillness stayed with him. It had been an almost too perfect weekend. He was drained emotionally and sexually. And then the extraordinary music, which he would never forget. And the picture of her at dawn, curled up within herself on the mattress.

He took Debbie for a long walk. Shirley had come in and tended her over the weekend. Debbie kept running out to the end of the long leash, then rushing back and jumping up on him as though to say, "I thought I'd never see you again."

He took a shower, then sat at his desk to write in his diary and then get going on his work. Friday, Saturday, Sunday. He turned the page to Monday and realized it was his anniversary.

Twenty-six years ago, about three hundred yards from

176

where he was sitting, Cat and he had said goodbye to his father and mother and her mother and had taken off on their honeymoon in Williamstown.

He stared at the wall. He felt a dull ache. How would she feel if he sent her flowers? If he didn't send her flowers? He had never missed an anniversary. He could call, but what could they say to each other that wouldn't depress them?

At the florist's he lingered over the mottled red and white carnations which had been "their" flower. That would be too cruel. She never liked store-bought roses. Too stiff. Reluctantly he settled for a "mixed bouquet" to be left to the discretion of the local florist. He rebelled at this. Gifts, flowers, had always been carefully selected. The one large red camellia for the full black velvet dress, which swirled around the floor when she danced. The green orchid for the chartreuse chiffon dress.

He worked on the message. "Dear Cat, It is pointless to wish you a Happy Anniversary, but . . ." He tore it up. He looked around the store, trying to think. There were Kim's daisies. He shook his head and stared at the empty paper. Finally, he wrote, "Dear Cat . . . Love on this day . . . Jack." Christ, he might as well have sent a card with a printed "sentiment."

In the evening he stayed in his apartment, hoping that Janet would call before going out with her friends. He sensed she wouldn't. He wondered if she was really going out with "friends."

There was a knock on the door. He looked up from his books, surprised. He drew his robe around him and went to the door. "Yes?"

"Hi. It's Shirley."

"Oh." He opened the door.

"I took some flowers for you this afternoon. The guy

177

didn't want to come back and asked if he could leave them with me." She held out the plant.

"Thanks." He wondered who had sent the flowers. Debbie had wandered in from the bathroom. "Thanks also for taking care of Debbie."

"We got along fine." She scratched Debbie behind the ears.

"She's an old lady. Not long for this world."

"I had a cat, only Herbie's allergic to cats. My mother's keeping the cat until we see if Herbie works out." She laughed. "How are the cockroaches?"

"Under control."

"Anytime you want to, leave Debbie with me. Herbie likes dogs."

"Thanks. And thanks for taking in this." He raised the plant.

He put the plant on the counter in the kitchen and unwrapped it. There was a notice saying that it was a Rieger begonia and it should be watered with water at room temperature. He opened the card.

Dear Jack:
    I will be thinking of all the happy years.

Love,
Cat

Oh, Christ! He closed his eyes.

Then he felt the earth. It was dry. He ran the water, testing the temperature with his finger. He wished she hadn't sent the flowers. But he had sent flowers. He'd call her after supper.

He had nothing in the apartment to eat. He didn't feel like eating alone. He had been spoiled by Janet. He waited till there was no possibility of her calling, then went to the Square and sat at the counter at the Wursthaus with the *Times*.

As he entered his room, the phone was ringing. He ran to answer it without turning on a lamp. It was Cat. Damn, he should have called before he went to supper.

"How are you?"

"I'm okay. Thanks for the plant. It's beautiful."

"Thank you for the flowers."

"What did they send? 'Mixed bouquet' you never know."

"Oh, a little of everything. Enough for two arrangements."

"How close does this water have to be to room temperature?"

"Oh, just not cold. They said it would go on blooming most of the summer."

"It's nice. How are things?"

"All right. I hope you got out and enjoyed this beautiful weekend."

"I did."

"I hope you didn't get too much sun. Remember you're not supposed to get too much sun."

"I know, but I'm vain."

There was a pause. "I'm going into my house tomorrow."

"Oh?"

"Yes. It's a darling house. A woman who goes to Florida for the winter and spring. Let me give you the address and phone."

Then she reported on the children, Barbara's joy over the expected baby, Jorie's happiness in her new house in Holland. Rich might have a small show of his work.

He listened and responded, but his mind wasn't on it.

179

He somehow felt sick that she was moving out. He realized how important it was for her to move, too, not to be seen as the "left" wife. She wasn't. They had left each other.

Had he expected life just to stand still "back there"?

20

Janet did not call. And he did not call. It had been left that she would call. He wondered what was going on in her head, but he somehow understood that it was something she had to work out for herself.

He found himself hurrying home from dinner in the Square. He could no longer make himself dinner in his place. It was too lonely. He waited for her call. He had done the same thing with Kim. He missed Janet. Not in the same way he had missed Kim. It was not a question of loving either one more or less. There was a darkness in his feeling for Kim. With Janet, at least so far, there was only an extraordinary pleasure and sunny delight and contentment.

In college there had been a girl like Kim before he met Catherine. At the end of the brief and stormy romance she had returned his agonizing and passionate letters, and he had foolishly kept them. In clearing out the attic in the midst of one of their moves, Cat had come across the letters, and though he had left the girl to go to Cat, she had been hurt. "You never wrote me letters like that."

He hadn't. It was true. But he had left the girl for her, loved her and married her. But he hadn't written her of the darker side of his soul, his longings and frustrations and bitterness. With Cat he had not agonized over his love. He had simply loved her, enjoyed being with her, talking to her, making love with her, wanted to spend his life with her. But she had sensed, in coming across those letters, that she had been cheated. Would she rather he had written her those letters and left her behind for someone else? Would she rather have been someone's "hopeless love"?

Who had written that way to Catherine? She must have been somebody's dark lady. Ned, of course. He had been her "great love." Did she again want to be somebody's dark lady?

It was finally Kim who called. "Jack Montgomery?"

"Hello." It was good to hear her voice.

She spoke rapidly. "I'm calling you under tricky circumstances. Listen carefully. Neatness will count. I have to go up to Dartmouth or the area of Dartmouth tomorrow. Scott has an old maiden aunt up there who was once a crack law stenographer in New York City, but who always hankered to live in a shack in the woods by herself. Well, she does. With a dozen cats. She didn't show up at the village store two days running, and it developed she'd collapsed in her shack. Anyway, a neighbor has managed to get her into a hospital, no mean trick since she's a Christian Scientist, and I'm coming up to see what's going on. Are you following me?"

"Yes." He saw what was coming.

"I arrive in Lebanon, which is relatively close to Dartmouth, at four-fifty. Air New England flight from Boston. The neighbor's son is going to pick me up, take me to see Scott's aunt and then bring me back to the Holiday Inn in White River Junction, which is also near Dartmouth." She paused. "Do you feel like meeting me there Saturday

182

night and driving me back to the Boston airport Sunday afternoon?"

He smiled. How like Kim to have everything worked out.

"You don't want to."

"Yes, I do," he blurted out. Her daring and sense of adventure delighted and excited him. Somehow she had always seemed like a twenties girl who might suddenly stand up in a party and say, "We're all going to jump off the Brooklyn Bridge. Coming?"

"You don't sound very enthusiastic. I don't blame you." He was silent for a moment. She went on. "I'd like to see you."

"I'd like to see you."

Kim was giving him the details again when he heard a key turn in the lock, and Janet came in. He broke out in a sweat. In three seconds he felt anger that he should be in this position, embarrassment and shame. In a split-second decision, not really a decision but a compulsion to be as honest as he could be, instead of just waving at Janet, he said, "Hi." She waved back without saying anything.

"Did someone just come in?"

"Yes. Look, that sounds good. I'll go up tomorrow morning and be there when you arrive."

"You can't talk. Are you sure you want to come?"

"Yes."

"You're anxious to get off."

"Well, have a good trip."

"See you tomorrow. Bye."

He hung up and turned to Janet, who put her arms around him and kissed him. "Sorry. Making plans for the weekend. I'm driving to New Hampshire."

She smiled. "That's nice." He put his arm around her

183

waist and held her. His head began to ache, and he felt suddenly cold.

She looked at him and kissed him, then drew back. "All right?"

"All right." Apparently nothing more was to be said about the past week.

"I'm off to pick up the kids, but on my way I wanted to bring you this." She handed him a brown paper bag on which she had drawn flowers and birds and trees.

"What is it?"

"Something vital to your life."

"I hate to open it. The wrapping is so pretty."

"The wrapping is more elegant than the present. Go on. Open it. I have to leave."

He untied the brightly colored yarn bows and opened the bag. It was a corkscrew. "That's terrific. Thank you."

"Now we're even." She roared with laughter. "For your next seduction scene." He kissed her but felt sick inside. "I've got to get to the kids. I'm taking them to a party tonight, and tomorrow we're going to Cohasset for the weekend." She stepped away from him and smiled. "Do you want to stop by on your way out tomorrow for a cup of coffee?"

She was ready for this. It took him by surprise. "And meet the kids?"

"I think they can take it."

"Okay. But early."

"I'm glad you're getting away. Maybe later we can do things with the kids. But not yet."

"Can I bring anything for breakfast?"

"For God's sake, no! Just yourself."

When Janet left, he took the corkscrew into the kitchen

184

and put it in a drawer, then leaned against the counter, staring at the dripping faucet.

A few minutes later he went to the phone and dialed New Hampshire Information.

21

Eric and Karen were on the floor of the living room playing with Noah's Ark and some animals, and they elabo-
rately ignored Jack as Janet introduced him. Janet didn't
press the matter. He said, "Hello," and watched them for
a few moments, then followed Janet into the kitchen. They
were younger then Kim's son, Colin, and both towheaded.

Janet was slightly distraught trying to make breakfast,
put together a picnic lunch, get the children to eat something and see that they were packed and ready to leave.
"Eric, are you packed for the beach?" A vague murmur
for an answer. "Come on, now. You can do that another
time. If we don't get off, there's no sense in going. Drink
your juice." Her tone was mother-petulant. "Karen, come
and eat your cereal."

"I ate it."

"No, you didn't. Now come on!"

"I'm not hungry."

"The minute we get on the road, you'll want to stop and
eat."

Jack came close up behind Janet and whispered. "Perhaps I'm upsetting them."

"They're very aware of you." He reached out to touch

186

her shoulder, and she drew away quickly, frowning. Then she yelled, "Karen, now come on!"

Karen came in and sat at the other end of the kitchen table and, eyeing Jack, messed her cereal around in the bowl. "Are you going with us?"

"No. I'm going in the opposite direction. To New Hampshire."

"Where's New Hampshire?"

"It's up north. In that direction." He pointed. He wondered if Karen would ever run to him and beg to be swung around and tossed in the air and given a piggyback ride. "Maybe someday I'll be going in your direction."

"Why?"

Janet gave him a quick look and a frown. Then she yelled, "Eric, come in here right now. Either get your things together and eat your breakfast or we don't go."

Karen sang out, "I want some more sugar."

Without turning from the counter, Janet said, "Right in front of you on the table."

"It's empty."

"I'll fill it." Jack rose automatically with the sugar bowl and started to move to the cupboard where the sugar was kept. Then he stopped. "Where do you keep the sugar?"

Janet looked at him and smiled. "In that cupboard."

When he sat down again, Karen studied his face. "Do you have any children?"

"Yes, two."

"How old are they?"

"Oh, much older than you and Eric."

"How much older?"

"Karen, stop asking questions and finish your cereal."

"Oh, about twenty years older."

"That's not children."

187

He smiled. "Well, they're my children." He was about to tell them that he would soon be a grandfather but decided against it.

Eric had come into the room and grabbed a piece of bread and was munching on it reluctantly while clutching his mother's waist lovingly and staring at Jack. Janet hugged him a moment. "All right, lover boy. Work to be done. Let's get the show on the road."

Jack finished his coffee while they wrangled back and forth. Finally, he got up. "I'd better get my show on the road." He washed his cup at the sink. "Good-bye, Karen. Bye, Eric." They just looked at him.

"Say goodbye to Mr. Montgomery."

Some murmurs as Jack and Janet left the kitchen and went through the living room to the front hall. "I'll call you when I get back. Sunday or Monday."

She looked up at him. "Are you sure you want to?"

"Why not?"

She nodded her head toward the kitchen. "I'm sorry everything is in such confusion. And me nagging. But I'm in a foul mood. Dick played one of his usual charming tricks. Just before the kids are to take off for their weekend with me, he gives them some terrific present that they don't want to leave. Lousy bastard!"

"Maybe we could have something even more interesting waiting for them here."

"No. I'm not going to play that game." He put his hands on her shoulders and leaned forward to kiss her. She dodged. "Little eyes may be watching."

Eric called from the kitchen. "Let's get the show on the road!"

Janet smiled. "They're very jealous. Particularly Eric."

"I don't blame them. It's a rough time for them."

"Their father keeps telling them I don't want them. Well, bye-bye. Have a good time."

He drove away from the little house with confused feelings. A new view of Janet, with her children. He had always found young mothers and their children immensely appealing. Kim and Colin, so different. He was touched by the "package." He could move into their lives and set everything right. Not just refrigerators and steam irons, but the whole deal. He could take this small family in out of the storm.

But he also felt a little cheap, like a man sneaking off from his home on some bogus excuse, on his way to cheat in some motel on the outskirts of town. Was there still such a word as "cheating," such a concept?

22

As he approached White River Junction, he saw the inevitable tall yellow, blue and orange gas station signs reaching up against the dark green of the tree-covered hills. It was a complicated interchange with Routes 91 and 89 coming together, and he took the wrong turn and ended up down in the city itself. As he stopped to ask directions, he remembered vaguely that he had been here before, many, many years ago, when his father would drive them up to the cool mountains of Vermont or New Hampshire for the summer. It now seemed to be a small city capitalizing on its quaintness for the summer people. Still, it was charming.

He checked into his room and had a late lunch, then decided to scout the area for some inn outside the city where he and Kim could have dinner. He drove over to Hanover and walked through the Hanover Inn, and stood and watched the summer-school boys and girls playing softball on the green. He decided the inn was too crowded. There might be people there who knew Kim. A clerk in the bookstore told him about the inn over in Lyme, not too far away.

Before he left Hanover, he stopped in at the state

liquor store and bought the vodka, then lemons and the nuts at a grocery store and a candle and an inexpensive candlestick at a gift shop. But somehow getting these things, and a small bottle of her perfume, did not arouse him as he had thought they would, as they had in the past.

The Lyme Inn was just what he was looking for. Too bad they couldn't stay there for the night. Lyme itself he found a quiet, graceful little village by the Connecticut River with a long green, and at one end the inn, cater-corner across from the white Congregational Church, which was also shared by the Baptists.

The inn, built in 1809, was the perfect place for a love affair. Cool and dark inside, decorated with fine antiques (all for sale), and with white wicker furniture on the large screened porch, it practically cried out for lovers. The wide board floors, the fireplaces everywhere, the dark, cool tavern and the small dining room with antique tools and objects hanging on the walls. Loving almost anybody here would be easy.

He found that they served dinner until eight, and not on Tuesdays. He said that he would not be spending the night this time but inquired about the rooms. He found himself also asking about the beds and was surprised and pleased when the man announced that they had almost all double beds. Jack smiled and said that that was as it should be, that so many times he and his wife had gone away for a holiday together, especially in Europe, and had found nothing but single beds. They exchanged understanding smiles, and he made a reservation for dinner. He walked back to his car feeling better about seeing Kim, but also a little ashamed at all this talk about "my wife and I."

He suddenly decided that he would like to go to the

Lebanon Airport and watch Kim arrive. It would appeal to her sense of risk. It would amuse him to see her handle it.

He drove up the road to the airport, which was located on a large plateau among the hills. He parked his car along with maybe ten other cars by the chain-link fence which separated the field from the parking lot and went into the small low red building to inquire if Flight 522 from Boston was on time. It was. He went out to the parking lot again and noticed a beat-up old Chevy parked in the number one spot with a middle-aged man sitting in it reading a newspaper. There didn't seem to be anyone else waiting for Flight 522, which was due in ten minutes.

Jack sat on the bench outside the terminal building and looked at the runway and the mountains beyond and the cloudless blue sky above it all. The man in the Chevy looked up from his newspaper and looked across at him, then back at his paper.

Then, in a few minutes, over the loudspeaker: "Air New England announces the arrival of Flight Five-twenty-two from Boston." A man opened a large gate in the chain-link fence and rolled a baggage cart through and closed the gate.

The small two-engine plane came in low over the hills and landed, ran the full course of the runway and taxied back to the terminal. The man who had wheeled out the baggage rack now moved the steps up to the plane, and the door to the plane opened. The man left the Chevy and Jack stood up and lingered near the gate. Two or three businessmen carrying small suitcases left the plane and headed for the gate, which they pushed open, and went to their cars. Finally, Kim stepped down, carrying a small overnight case. The man from the Chevy ambled out toward her. Jack smiled. What style! Tan pleated skirt which flipped from side to side as she strode away from the plane. Blue double-breasted flannel jacket. The toss of her head. She'd had her hair cut shorter—it was jaunty and glossy. He shook his head in admiration. A beautiful racehorse. She was cordial to the man who took her bag and chatted animatedly to him, probably about Scott's aunt, as they came toward the gate.

Then she looked up and saw him. He smiled slightly. She looked away immediately and asked the man another question as they turned toward the car. He put her bag in the back seat, and as she was opening the car door for herself, she looked quickly over at Jack but didn't smile. She didn't look at him again. Jack was delighted he had come. Something like that had been needed.

It was seven o'clock when Kim called. "My God, I'm finally here."

"Hi. What room are you in?"

"Twenty-seven."

"You're practically next door. I'll be right there."

"I have some calls to make, and I want to take a quick bath—"

"We have dinner reservations about a half hour away from here in a half hour."

"Oh, dear."

"I'll be right there." He gathered together the vodka, nuts, candle and candlestick and left his room. He knocked on her door. He had to wait. She was on the phone. She opened the door and rushed back to the phone.

He deposited the bottle and the lemon and the rest of the things on one of the bureaus, then came over to her and sat across from her and watched her on the phone.

"I think it would be a disastrous mistake to take on that project. I left you my report on it. The budget is completely unrealistic. Harry is notorious for never bring-

193

ing a project in on time, and . . ." She listened and made faces at Jack. "Well, look, I'm up here checking up on a sick maiden aunt. I've got a terrible headache from a bumpy flight from Boston, and the whole thing will have to wait. I'll be back in the city on Monday. He's not in such great demand that we'll lose him between now and then. . . . Please. I have to hang up now. I'm due back at the hospital in ten minutes." She smiled at Jack and ducked because she had lied. "All right. Monday morning I'll come straight to you and we can discuss it. Bye-bye." She hung up and sighed. "I'm sorry, but that's my life." She stood up and opened her arms. "How are you?"

He stood and embraced her and kissed her. She felt strange to him. "I'm fine."

"I almost lost ten years of my life when I saw you standing there."

"You saw me then?"

"Saw you? My God!"

"Didn't it please you?"

She looked at him. Kissed him. "Yes. It was exciting seeing you there. Made me feel you really wanted to see me." She looked at him with her wide, wondering eyes as though to ask, "Do you really want to see me?" Then she said, "Look, I have to make a call home to Scott. He's on the Island. Then I want a quick tub, and I'll be with you."

"Okay. This restaurant closes at eight."

"Couldn't we go to one in town?"

"No. This is very special. An old country inn. Perfect. I spent the afternoon finding it."

"Did you? All right then. I'll hurry." And she picked up the phone and gave her number on the Island. Jack left. He never liked listening to her talk to Scott.

In a remarkably short time, Kim knocked on his door

194

and came in. "What a lovely room!" And they both laughed.

"You were very quick."

"A special present for you." She looked beautiful and fresh and cool in a pink sleeveless linen dress, as though she had done nothing all day but get ready for the evening.

"You're fantastic." And he kissed her lightly.

"I know it." She beamed.

He led her to the car, and they started their drive out into the country. There was a hazy sunset. For a while they jabbered nervously. "How's your headache?"

"All gone." She couldn't stand people, herself or others, who were ailing. Her mother had declared herself an invalid ten years ago and was eating up the family resources with her hypochondria.

She discussed the "crazy" aunt who was stubborn as hell and wouldn't move into a nice, neat, tidy apartment in Hanover. She wanted to stay in the shack with the cats and walk in her sneakers three miles round trip to the local store each day. She had a bad case of pneumonia, but she wouldn't let the doctors give her any medicine.

Then they were quiet for a few minutes. It was getting on toward dusk. "I'm sorry to take you driving after your long trip, but I wanted it to be nice."

"It's beautiful. So lovely and cool. It's been murderous in the city."

"Cambridge has been no joy."

There was a pause. "I promised myself I wouldn't ask."

"What?" But he knew.

"When I called yesterday. Who came in?"

Somehow he was unprepared for the question. Wished she hadn't asked it right then. He frowned.

"It was a girl."

"Yes."

"With a key."

"Yes."

Kim turned her head to the window and leaned against it. "I'm sorry. But you knew there would be." He felt sick. Oh, Christ. He looked at her and heard a sniffle. He pulled quickly to the side of the road and stopped and moved across the seat to her. "I'm sorry."

"No. No. It's all right."

"It's not all right." He took her hand.

"No. It's just . . . I knew there would be . . . others. I just didn't know there would be *one* . . . with a key."

He just sat there, his eyes closed.

She blew her nose. "I'm sorry. It's silly for me to be upset."

"It's not silly. And I hate it. But—"

"But there it is. And perfectly understandable." The "reasonable" Kim was taking over.

"We knew this would happen. I stayed in New York. We tried."

"I know. It was a bad time." She turned away from the window at last. "Come on. We'd better get there before they close up."

He shifted into drive and pulled back on the road, and for the next few minutes before they arrived at the inn, they said nothing, their hands clasped on the seat between them.

As they entered the inn, aglow with candlelight and soft colors, Kim muttered, "I'm going to disappear for a moment. Go ahead to the table."

Jack sat at the table staring at the candle, feeling numb. He ordered two glasses of vodka on the rocks with a twist.

As she came to the table, all eyes were on her. She

was stunning and moved with such strength. He rose, and she smiled as she sat down. It was clear she had been crying. "I'm sorry. That was very sloppy of me." He shook his head, not taking his eyes from her. "Did you order me a drink?" The large goblets of vodka and ice arrived. "Oh, my, lovely!"

He held up his glass. "Well..."

"Cheers." They both sipped their drinks. "I feel terribly sad, but also a little bitchy."

"I don't blame you."

"You were always criticizing Scott about his girls. And now... But then I guess if it were just a girl, I wouldn't feel this way. But I know with you, it can't be just a girl."

He waited for a moment. "I feel sad, but also a little mad."

"I know. I treated you horribly, but I didn't intend to. It was just a bad time for me. I became a neuter. So where do I get off being hurt?"

"You were out of the picture..."

"Absolutely right. You were free. Are free." She took another sip. "Mmmmm. This is good."

"But I'm mad too, because I loved you so much, wanted you so much, bled for you so much. So I'm mad because you weren't there, and I guess I'm mad now because you're hurt. And I'm sad to be the one to hurt you. If you had been like this then, I wouldn't have gone away."

"I know. I'm very unreliable. You want someone constant and always there."

He didn't pick up the old argument as to what love is, expectations, counting on being "there." He accepted her needling. After a few moments he reached over and touched her hand. "It's so good to see you."

"Is it?" She smiled brightly.

"Yes."

"That's nice." She buttered a breadstick. "What's her name?"

He shook his head. He didn't want to discuss Janet. At that moment he wished he had never met her. He was sitting here in this beautiful place with his "great love," and somehow he couldn't love her because he had hurt her. And yet, it had all been inevitable because of the situation. The argument inside his head kept turning back on itself. One moment he felt guilty; the next, accusing. He wanted to reclaim Kim, to say that Janet was "just a girl," that she was "just there." But he couldn't say that because it wasn't true, and even if the words might make him feel whole again and able to love Kim, he knew he couldn't live with them.

"Please tell me her name."

"Janet. Two small children."

"How old is she?"

Uncomfortable, he reached for the menu. "Around thirty-two."

"That's nice."

"Stop it!"

The rest of the evening, during dinner and after, they talked about many things: Cat and Scott, her son and work and his writing. And from time to time each would stop and look into the other's eyes, and then they would try to define and redefine positions, going over and over the same ground until they were worn out.

Driving back through the dark summer night, she swung around and lay curled up on the seat with her head in his lap and slept.

At the motel she opened the door to her room and looked at him. He kissed her lightly on the cheek. "I'd like to stay with you tonight."

"Do you really want to?"

"Yes."

They shut the door, and without turning on the light or lighting the candle, they undressed quickly and got into bed. Impulsively they turned and kissed and held each other with a mixture of love and sorrow and bewilderment and exhaustion. He started to stroke her body, but it was with tenderness and not desire. He wanted to make love to her, in some way to make things right between them, but he sensed it wouldn't happen. In younger days just the closeness would have overcome all confusion and carried him through the physical act, which then might have ended up as deeply emotional.

She touched his face. "Let's just sleep. You're tired. I'm tired."

"All right."

She turned her back to him and pressed herself against his belly. "Do you want a Valium?"

"I think I'll sleep."

"If you want one during the night, they're on the bathroom shelf."

He hugged her. "I love you so."

"Do you?"

"But I know I can't have you the way I need you. So what am I to do?"

"What you *are* doing, I guess."

He reached over and down, and she opened her legs slightly, and he wedged his hand in between them, pressing hard, not moving, not trying to excite, just holding close, and went to sleep.

The next morning he awoke with the rising sun filtering through the drawn curtains. Kim was asleep. He came back from the bathroom and found her lying on her back, looking up at him and smiling. He leaned over and kissed her, and she drew him down to her, and for a long time

199

they made wordless, intense love. After she had come, he tried to hold her quietly, as he had so often done before when he had said he didn't want to come, wanted to prolong the sensuous tension. But now she insisted with a determination and almost a violence, driving on to claim her own. Once she had said that he had wanted to send her back to Scott a "ghost." Now it was her turn. When it was over, she looked down at him and smiled.

Later he lay sprawled on the bed watching her dress, bending over to cup her breasts in her bra. He had never seen anyone else do that. He always laughed when she did it. Watched her slithering into her panties. Always white. He had always liked to watch women dress and undress, brush their hair, put on their makeup with a craftsman's skill. He had never seen Kim in the morning. Usually he had left her in the middle of the night, or it had been in a hotel in the afternoon. He could understand why Scott did not let her "escape" often in the morning.

He rose and stood beside her and kissed her. She flashed a smile that made him sad. He touched her face. "I thought of you and that smile last week."

"Why?"

"I saw a student production of *A Doll's House*. There's a line Nora speaks. She says, 'I'm cheerful but not happy.'" She turned to the dresser. "When you used to cry in bed and yet insist on smiling at the same time . . ."

"Well, I don't like grouchy people. I don't like myself when I'm grouchy."

He stroked the back of her neck. "Sometimes people are entitled to be grouchy."

"Then they should go into the next room and shut the door."

Kim visited Scott's aunt once again, found her still adamant about leaving the hospital and left her in the care

200

of an old friend who was a reader in the Christian Science Church and who said that she should stay in the hospital.

On the way to Boston, Jack and Kim chattered away, laughing. She discussed the inanities of producing shows for television. He mostly listened, though occasionally he would talk about his being unable to write. Then she would throw in a barb like: "You don't have much time or energy left to write. You know Hemingway said something to the effect of 'Don't leave all your creative energy in bed.'" And he smiled, glad that she could joke about it.

But then she would be immediately sympathetic. "You're pushing yourself too hard, expecting too much too soon. You're under a terrible strain, whether you know it or not."

Farther along he saw her studying an airline schedule. "The shuttles to New York leave every hour."

"I know. But I have to know what plane I took from Lebanon to Boston. What time will we get to Boston?"

"Well, we should stop for lunch. Maybe the five o'clock shuttle."

"All right then." She studied the schedule. "I took the two-thirty-five from Lebanon." Very pleased with herself, she smiled and put away the schedule. "It's called organization."

Jack looked at her and shook his head, smiling. "How was the flight from Lebanon?"

"Beautiful." She laughed and put her head on his shoulder. "I wish we were going in the other direction, starting the weekend the way it should have been started. We've always needed a little time, a few jokes." He took her hand but said nothing.

They left the highway to find a pleasant place for lunch, confident that every small New England town would have a picturesque inn. It turned out to be more of

201

a tearoom than an inn, but it was a quaint old house. They sat across from each other, sipping Dubonnet on the rocks, looking and smiling. There was an elegiac feeling in the air, and strain. He looked up at the scrubby paintings by the local artists hanging on the walls. "You know these paintings are all for sale."

"Thanks a lot."

"I think I'll get you one as a souvenir of this weekend. Which one would you like?" He glanced around the room at the pictures, then back at her. She was looking at him. "You don't want a souvenir of this weekend. I don't blame you."

"I'm all right now."

"It's funny. I want you to be all right, and I don't want you to be all right. Last night in the car was the first time I really could believe you loved me." She shook her head. "For so long I've wanted you to bleed, as I bled. And you did bleed, a few drops. And I hate having done it to you."

"It was very sloppy." Then she looked at him seriously, almost with irritation. "I take incredible chances to be with you, to come to you, and you can't believe I love you."

After lunch they strolled around the village for a few minutes, their arms loosely around each other. He stretched his neck and shook his head and sighed, and she tightened her hold on his waist. Finally, she looked at her watch. "Well, the two-thirty-five from Lebanon is running behind schedule." He kissed the side of her head, and they turned back.

As they neared the airport, Jack was tense, had been tense for some time. After the strain of the night they had fallen easily into their old camaraderie, jokes, smiles, banter, chatter. And now the inevitable moment of parting. His face ached with tension. If they were going to talk, they could only say again what they had exhausted themselves saying last night.

"You can just drop me. You don't have to park."

He looked at her and smiled. "I'll just slow down, and you can jump out."

At the shuttle gate the line for New York was already forming. Kim filled out her form and started toward the security check. He held out her bag for her. "Well . . ."

"Aren't you coming through with me?"

"I don't think I'm supposed to, am I?"

"You run along. You're anxious to get back."

"No. I just don't think . . ." He looked around. "Let's see." He picked up her bag and put it on the conveyor, and they passed through the checkpoint. "I thought they didn't allow people who weren't boarding . . ."

"I'm being mean. Go ahead."

"No." He put his arm around her as they joined the line.

"Will you be coming to New York?"

He frowned. "Not for a while. It's funny. I drive out of Cambridge weekends, but always north. Never toward home. The pulls are very strong, and I guess I'm afraid of of them. I feel something like an exile. It's strange about Cat. I feel I've been meaner to her now, more thoughtless than when we were married."

"Well, that's what separations are for. To be separate."

"It just goes against my nature somehow. Anyway, I guess it's inevitable if I'm going to find out more about what I want. I know I don't want to live alone."

"I think I would love to, with Colin, of course."

"You have so many pressures on you from all sides. The complete modern woman." He smiled. "Husband, career, child, house . . . me."

"No longer you."

"Don't say that." He shook his head.

She looked at him. "You really didn't want to see me this weekend. That's not nice after you've tried so hard. Shut up, Kim!" He stopped and drew her out of line for a moment and held her and kissed her. "Come to New York with me. No one's at home."

"I can't."

"Is Janet waiting?"

"No."

She took her bag as the line started to move. "I know it sounds bitchy, but you wanted to be free and already you're tucking yourself in." She frowned. "That was nasty. I'm sorry. Run along. Thanks for staying with me. I'll call, or shouldn't I? I'll try not to be a nuisance."

Before she turned away, she smiled. That cheerful, unhappy smile. Then she was moving briskly toward the passageway, not looking back, her pleated tan skirt swinging jauntily from side to side.

All the time he had wanted to know that she loved him. And now he knew. And wished he didn't.

23

As he rode down on the escalator, he wanted to be alone, yet he dreaded returning alone to his pad. He did not feel he should get in touch with Janet that night. Some curious sense of delicacy and propriety dictated that decision. And yet he wanted to see her. He realized as he started his car that he was experiencing some sense of "going home." He was always leaving Kim and "going home." To Cat. Now to Janet. "Tucking himself in." Too soon, according to Kim. Someone else had advised him, "Don't do anything too soon. Be sure it's a choice and not a compulsion." But what is love, a cool intellectual decision? Would anyone marry if he didn't feel in some way he "had" to? There are always reasons not to marry. He could reason himself out of anything, and often had. He treasured the few feelings of passion he had had in his life that would not listen to reason.

He felt shabby about himself.

He realized he might never see Kim again. Rejected, he had run. She would do the same. Pride.

He walked into his apartment and immediately went to check Debbie in the bathroom. She barely got to her feet and shook her tail. Her newspapers were wet, and she was ashamed. Shirl hadn't done her job, or perhaps she had. There was no telling with Debbie. He scratched her head, gathered up the papers, put her on a leash and, after stopping by the incinerator, took her for a walk. She tried to prance once in a while, half jumping up on him to show she was happy he was back, but it was a sad and touching effort.

When he brought her back, he noticed the scroll tied with a light-blue yarn propped against his pillow. He picked it up and sat in the wicker chair and for a few moments just held it unopened, wondering what she had written. It could be anything. "We must move on." Or "It's all over." Or . . . He slipped the yarn from the scroll.

> Dearest Jack:
>   I don't like not knowing how to reach you. The phone was ringing, and I was just returning from a walk. But I couldn't find a key and open the door in time. So I'm still up, hoping the phone will ring again. It doesn't matter who phoned. To me it was you.
>   You're so incredibly rare and wonderful. There are so many feelings, thoughts and energies streaming through me. Of you. And me. Including conflicting ones threaded with fears and doubts, troubling things.

He stopped for a moment, embarrassed by her praise, feeling dishonest, wondering what she was leading up to.

> I care so much for you. You are so caring. An extra-ordinary caring that wants and allows someone to come within your being. I feel so close to you, or maybe it's a closeness that's just an intake of breath away. There's such an image of us, of what has happened between us, what we can have, and so much more that moves between those unmeasurable, always changing points. There's something so dear, so tender and at the same time almost violent in its rawness. . . .

These are some feelings this evening, dear Jack. I've also been hoping a lot that you are fine. That there's a strong stillness in the landscape, early morning sun, soft rain, bright winds, whatever is good for you as you roam around Jack and the many facts of his life.

He looked up from the scroll feeling ashamed.

I had a nice time with the children. There's always a gentle wrenching when I say goodbye. The terrible fear that I may lose them in this dreadful custody fight.

I feel very good (which is another paradox of my life). Good . . . but what about all those terrors and uncertainties? Anyway, I send you a warm, bright smile.

Love,
Janet

It was the perfect letter for his mood. And as he read it again, written in a girlish hand with a green felt pen, he was touched by her confusion and excited by her characterizing part of what they had as "violent rawness." He smiled as he dismissed "caring" and "dear" and "tender."

He dialed her number. She was not in. He had not said when he would be back. He wanted to be in touch with her. She seemed at the moment his "real life," and he was eager to resume it.

He sat at his table to write her a letter, which he would give her. It was the first letter he had written her. He had written Kim so many letters, right from the start. He paused, not knowing what to write. Could he express what he felt for her? Certainly a desire to be close to her, to be with her, not just in bed, but eating, going to the movies, shopping. He smiled, wondering if a girl would be flattered to know that he enjoyed going to a supermarket with her.

He went to the kitchen and made himself a drink,

looked in the refrigerator to see if there was anything to eat. There wasn't. He decided he would go to the Square and eat and come back and write the letter later. On the chance that she might drop by, he scribbled a note and left it on the floor.

On the way to the Square, he saw her car parked near the church where she and the chamber group sometimes rehearsed. He opened the door and found an old envelope in the litter of junk mail in the back seat and wrote. "Have gone to the Square for supper. Will be right back." He left it on the seat of the car.

When he returned to his place, he saw Debbie sitting in the middle of the room and heard the shower running. He also heard Janet whistling. He smiled. She was the only woman he had ever known who whistled. He took off his clothes and was about to pull back the shower curtain and come in with her when he decided it might frighten her to death. He stood in the door of the bathroom. "Hello!" he shouted.

"Hello," she called back. And he pulled back the shower curtain.

Later, as they lay on the two mattresses on the floor, he said, "Thank you for your great letter."

She burrowed her head against his neck, embarrassed. "I almost didn't bring it."

"I'm glad you did."

"I missed you so, and I didn't know where to call you, and I guess I didn't really want to call you. I wanted to say things I could only write. Does that make any sense?"

"Yes."

"I wanted to write the words. I wasn't sure I wanted you to read them, and I'm not sure I want you to say anything about them. It's like your wanting to say, 'I love you,' but not wanting me to hear or believe."

208

"I understand."

"I didn't want to frighten you. But at the moment I felt that way."

"I'm glad you wrote it, and I'm glad you left it for me."

"It's awfully serious. And it may be miles away from what you feel or what we are, really."

"I started to write you a letter before I got too hungry."

"I didn't want to force you into any 'statement of position.' I shouldn't have left it."

"I'll give it to you when I finish it. But I started out by saying, 'I still groan when you come into the room.'"

"All right. If that's all you said."

Then he felt he had to tell her something about Kim. He felt it somehow stood between them. When he was loving, he wanted to be open, naked. "We've talked a lot about your marriage and about how you're on the rebound. But we haven't talked much about where I am."

"I know. I've been selfish, tied up in my own problems." She drew away and looked at him, waiting.

"You're on a rebound. I'm on what you might call a ricochet. That's not exactly the way to describe it. But before I came up here, I was very much in love with a woman, a married woman. It's very complicated. There was never any idea of her leaving her husband, but . . . well, there were times she would see me and times she wouldn't. She just wanted me as her lover. And finally, it was too much for both of us. So when I came up here, I was in a kind of double shock with very confused feelings about my wife and this woman." He felt better after telling her this. It was not a confession, but it was the truth and more than she knew before.

She smiled. "After thirty, we all come in very complicated packages, don't we?" She didn't ask any questions. She turned and snuggled up to him and went to sleep. He

209

had never known anyone to go to sleep so quickly after lovemaking. There was something trusting about it.

A few minutes later the telephone rang. He looked at it and let it ring. Janet woke and raised her head and looked at him. "I forgot to tell you. It was ringing when I came in." He smiled at her and let it go on ringing. She looked at him for a moment, then turned and burrowed into the pillow again.

24

For the next weeks Jack lived in an emotional pressure cooker. The telephone had rung again several times during the night, and it rang again soon after Janet left in the morning. It was Kim.

"I called you all last night, at least till one. Then I knew where you were." Jack listened helplessly. "I tortured myself the way you used to torture yourself, looking at the clock. 'I looked at the clock hoping you were asleep. I looked at the clock knowing you weren't.' Did you look at the clock?"

"No."

"God, it was desolate here when I got back last night. Empty house. All I could think of was how anxious you were to leave me at the airport."

"Kim . . ."

"Just let me talk. There's nobody I can talk to. I know there's nothing you can say, and I know I have no right to talk like this because I wasn't there, or here, when you needed me. I had no idea I would feel this way if you went to someone else."

"Kim, we knew . . ."

"I know. I know. It's very poor form calling this way. Where's my famous pride? Vanished. You wanted me to bleed; well, I'm bleeding. But never again. Never as long as I goddamn live will I ever leave myself open like this again."

His head began to ache with tension. "Kim, you know how much I love you. But it's an impossible situation." It was unbelievable that cool Kim, who was usually so brisk and almost flip on the phone, was talking like this, the way he had wanted her to talk for months. Now he couldn't listen, couldn't respond.

"Am I making the situation worse? Sorry. I know you think it's just jealousy. I've tried to be honest with myself about that. But this is not jealousy. I know it isn't."

"Kim, what can we do? Wednesday afternoon from one to three are not enough. You're not going to leave Scott."

"Oh, I'm not so sure."

He felt miserable for her. "Kim, be honest. Anyway, I wouldn't let you leave because I know you don't really want to. You want simultaneous time, each one of us in our own compartments."

"Don't lecture me!" Her voice was strained.

"I'm sorry."

"Don't stay up there. Come home!" He didn't say anything. "Don't make me beg. Come down this weekend. Please!"

"I can't."

She hung up. Jack sat slumped, shaking his head. His instinct was to call her back, to go on talking, to try to comfort her. But he knew it would be no use. There was probably no question that she belonged more to his world than Janet did, that he loved her in that dark, consuming, unhappy way that was the essence of "a great love." He had never before been loved more than he had loved. It was a strange feeling. But there would be this weekend with her newly discovered passionate love for him. And then what?

Looking around his room, he realized that he would have to make some kind of decision soon because Julia would be back early in September to reclaim her apartment. Janet had told him about real estate agents who handled furnished rentals, but he had not called them.

He did not go to New York for the weekend. Instead, he was finally allowed to spend the day with Janet's children. Dick was off on a jaunt, and they switched weekends. It started out like the other Saturday. He dropped by for breakfast while Janet tried to feed Eric and Karen, pack a picnic and get them under way. The children seemed no more easy with him than they had been before, but he made no effort to push himself on them. He was available if they were interested.

As he watched them, he thought of what must be going on in their heads during this period. Until the court handed down its decision, presumably soon, they didn't know where or with whom they were going to live. Their father was living in a big house and already had a woman he was probably going to marry, so they were functioning in a family of sorts when they were with him. With Janet, they lived in this improvised way, mattresses on the floor, some games and toys, no real friends in the neighborhood. But it was obvious they both adored her, and she, them.

At the beach at Ipswich the children sat and played at a distance. Jack felt that they were very aware of his age and that by staying off like that, they were announcing to other children with young fathers that this was not their father.

When they all gathered on the same blanket for lunch, Eric suddenly opened up with enthusiasm about the "neat" things he had done with his father and how this fall his father would take him to the football games. Jack said that was great and mentioned in passing that he had been on the football squad for a year. Eric showed some mild interest and asked what position he played, and they discussed the team's chances this fall, and that was that. Jack asked him if he played any sports, but he didn't seem to want to talk about it.

Watching Karen, he wanted to take hold of her chubby little body and swing her in the air as he had swung Colin, and as he had swung his own children so many years ago. But they went back to their castle building some yards off.

In the water he struck out and swam far out by himself. As he turned and treaded water before swimming back, he noticed that Eric and Karen were watching him. Perhaps he had wanted them to watch him. He wondered if he swam as well as their father.

When he was standing in shallow water again, Eric swam vigorously parallel to the shore, clearly for Jack's benefit. "Hey, that's good."

"I swim a lot down on the Cape."

"You're good." Karen then began to paddle furiously near him. He ducked down and half crawled, half swam up to her. "You're good, too. It runs in the family."

She smiled and stopped and stood up and pushed some water in his face. He flicked some back at her with his finger, and she squealed and batted water back at him. He made mock-angry sounds and descended on her, scooping her up in the air as she laughed and squealed some more. For the next few minutes she wouldn't let him stop till Janet, smiling, said, "That's enough."

Afterward he and Eric found a clear spot down the beach and skimmed a Frisbee back and forth for a while, Jack enjoying having Eric show him some new tricks. Back

214

at the blanket Karen wanted to be swung around, then, after a nap and another dip, feeling dried out with the sun and salt water, they headed home. Jack knew that his shoulders would ache tomorrow, and his bad ear would be a little worse from the swim. So much for showing off.

While the children scrapped and wrangled in the back seat, Janet dozed in the seat next to him, that special "I am experiencing pleasure" smile on her face. Jack felt very "family," and it pleased and frightened him. He thought of the four letters he had received from Kim during the week, and the flowers and plant. (He had explained to Janet that he had bought the plant and that Cat had sent the flowers.)

> I know that you are doing all the things with her that you wanted to do with me, shopping and supermarkets, going to the movies, dining with friends, staying all night and making love again in the morning. And I hate it. And you. And her.
>
> It also saddens me to see you settling down so soon again. You wrote me you wanted to fly. Do you remember? Is this what you broke up your home for? All that courage it finally took you to leave? Was it for this . . . or at least so soon?
>
> I'm sorry. Don't listen to me. I'm a jealous bitch. But there is some truth in what I say. Please come home.

Jack suggested that they eat at a restaurant, but Janet said the children were too tired, and besides, they didn't really like restaurants.

While Janet prepared supper, fresh corn, native tomatoes, lettuce, watermelon, hamburger, Jack sat on the floor with his vodka and tonic and played Monopoly with the children, trying to mediate their arguments.

"You moved too many spaces."

"No, I didn't. You can't count."

Then Janet would yell from the kitchen.

She set a lovely table with her great-aunt's china and her mother's silver and candles and linen napkins. He was touched by the care she took with things, to make them nice.

Sitting across from him in the candlelight, Janet was infinitely desirable in her role as mother and housekeeper. Forget all her other attributes: lover, musician, sometime small pixie girl. He had again that sense of playing the show all over again, and he felt a pang for those days with Cat and his own children.

And while the children argued over who should have the last ear of corn, he thought of his own father and how he had been forty-two when he was born and, therefore, about in the same relation to him as he was to Eric and Karen. He had always thought of his father as an old man.

It was all seductive, oddly sensuous, the young mother and her young children. Through the door behind Janet he could see the big bed. Just to relax (the actual words he thought of were "to give up") and become part of this family.

Don't give up on us so easily. I need your love, to be adored by you. You are right. I didn't know how much I needed that until you left. I am overwhelmed by my own sense of longing and love for you. Can a relationship of a few weeks change so quickly all we have had?

After it was dark and the children were in bed, they sat on the couch. She stretched her neck, trying to ease the tension.

"It's been a lovely day. Thank you," he said quietly.

216

"Thank you. You were terrific with the kids."

"I'm not sure. It was fun to be with them, fun to see you with them. Very sexy." She snorted her disbelief. He reached over and started to rub her neck. She moved away quickly and looked at the open door to the children's bedroom.

"Can't we shut the door?"

"No. They've always slept that way. Especially here, I don't want them to feel I'm shutting them out."

"Okay. The feeling will hold." He smiled.

She looked around the room, keyed up in spite of her tiredness.

"I don't know what I'll do if I don't get them." And she started to cry, soundlessly.

He moved his hand along the couch and slid it under her thigh.

"You'll get them. They love you."

"I know, but he hates me. He's always gotten his way in everything, and it will kill him if he loses this time."

"When will you know?"

"God only knows. They keep postponing it. The investigation is not finished." She smiled. "I went and bought a nice conservative navy blue going-to-court outfit. I look like a good suburban mother."

Eric came out for a glass of water, but Jack sensed it was really to see if he was still there. He got up noisily and said loud enough for Eric to hear, "Well, I'd better be going. It's been a wonderful day. I'll call ˙ou."

On the porch she held him away from kissing her. Then to soften her move, she said, "He may have spies in the bushes."

Back in his apartment he took off his clothes and showered and lay on top of the bed.

It is unfair to say how much I love you now, when it should have been said before or not at all. Please don't go away. The pain I feel is no small twinge. It is destroying, and I know now what you described as being sick to your stomach. Have you left me for good? I am afraid the answer is yes, and I do not know what I will do if it is.

Soon after, there was a notice taped to the elevator wall.

FOR IMMEDIATE SALE (Apt. 6B)

1 double bed 40.00
1 large chair and ottoman 10.00
Drapes 10.00

It seemed to be some kind of sign. For sixty dollars he could have his own place.

He found the occupant of 6B, a sad middle-aged neuter of a man sprawled in the huge imitation leather armchair, his feet on a matching ottoman, holding a beer can in one hand and a girlie magazine in the other, watching TV. The rest of the room was empty except for the bed, an old bridge lamp and an expensive set of barbells. It was a depressing sight. Jack wondered how many other single men had owned the bed, the chair and the drapes.

The next morning he found he could rent an apartment the exact duplicate of the one he had been occupying, and he moved in. He bought bed linen and towels at Sears, and a few odds and ends of secondhand furniture at Goodwill.

When he told Janet about his decision to stay on, she smiled and said, "That's nice." When he told her it was a one room affair again on a month-to-month basis, she said, "Oh. Well, that's okay."

The next day, while he was cleaning up Julia's apartment, getting it ready for her return, Cat called to tell him he was a grandfather. He was moved by the obvious joy in her voice. All suddenly seemed right in the world for her. They congratulated each other. He talked with his son, whose main concern seemed to be that this would be the first night since he and Barbara had been living together that he would have to sleep alone.

"And we're going to get married!"

25

He had been gone a little more than two months, and now, on a brisk day, early in September, he was headed home to see his grandchild and, inevitably, Catherine. Before he had met Janet, the temptation to give up and go home had been almost overwhelming. It had been like the pull of gravity. He had resisted largely by trying to block it all out. Ted had said, "Remember the bad times." But that hadn't worked, because when he did, he began wondering why they had been bad, and he was once again on the merry-go-round. So he had tried blocking. He must see what kind of new life he could make for himself and then at some point let the past out of the box and make a decision, or a decision would become inevitable.

Years ago at prep-school graduation someone had given him a small book by Sir William Osler in which the great surgeon had written that we should live our lives in day-tight compartments. This summer he had done just that. He and Janet had another way of putting it. "I'm all right as long as I don't think about anything." And they would laugh, realizing how impossible it was to live one's life like that, not responsible for one day to the next. But for the first time in his rather rigidly disciplined life he had seemed incapable of thinking or reasoning.

He knew also that he would see Kim, would have to see Kim. No, that was not the way to put it. Wanted to see Kim. But he also dreaded it. It had been difficult enough trying to read her letters, not letting the agony in them sink in, because he could not bear it. He realized how flat and unsatisfactory his answers had been. "Be realistic." He had not known what else to say, had come to dread her once eagerly awaited letters, letters ironically now filled with a passion he had hoped for, longed for, three months ago.

He would stay a few days, see the baby, Cat, take Debbie to the vet, get his teeth cleaned, pick up a new suit, stop by the office. Then he would come back. He had agreed to give extracurricular lectures on copyright and literary and entertainment law at the Law School.

At the hospital Jack walked cautiously into the room Barbara shared with three other mothers. She had just finished feeding the baby. Rich got up and came toward him, and looking at the baby nestled against Barbara's breast, Jack hugged his son and kissed him on the cheek and smiled through his tears at Barbara and the baby. He knew he was overreacting. They were not just the tears of a happy grandfather but of a prodigal returned, even if briefly.

Of course, there was very little to say except to remark on every gurgle, every eye opening, each almost-smile, the perfectly formed fingers, and to hear in joyous detail how they had shared the birth. Cat had been in all morning but had had to go back to tape an interview and was going to be back in the afternoon. Also, she had forgotten to tell him that she was giving a small party at her rented house and he would be very welcome. All old friends.

Rich and Jack sat in the sunroom for a while, and with some embarrassment Rich asked how things were. He said that at first he had been hurt that Jack had not discussed the separation with him and Barbara, but then he realized that it didn't concern them since they were grown and away. But they *were* concerned. Jack found it impossible to go into the matter. He emphasized that it was a trial separation, to think things over and consider alternatives. One alternative, living alone, he knew was not for him.

"Nor for me either." And he said again, "I don't know how I'm going to get through tonight." He smiled and shook his head.

Jack asked about Cat. Rich told him that she hadn't discussed the separation with him or Barbara. He had asked her something once, and she had started to cry.

As he came around a curve in the road and looked down and saw his house, he felt a sense of dread. When the real estate agent had shown them the house, they both had fallen in love with it from this spot and had known that no matter what was wrong with it, they were going to buy it.

Debbie, of course, was excited and for once tumbled from the car herself and lumbered around to visit old haunts.

The grounds looked well kept. He was sure that the inside of the house was in order too. Cat was famous for that. But the place looked shut up, like a well-tended mausoleum. No wheelbarrows or watering cans or tangled hoses or trowels left carelessly about.

He picked up the notice of oil delivery wedged under the door and entered the house. It was chilly. He thought of Cat's always saying, "Why is it so impossible to keep the house warm the first days of fall?" He moved to the living room to turn up the thermostat and saw two dead mice caught in a trap on the hearth. As he looked around, his gut tightened. How often had they called each other in to notice the way the afternoon sun slanted into the living room. He poured himself a short shot of bourbon and went outside to let the house warm up.

He checked out the pool and the gardens. His roses were coming into a last September bloom, there were only a few Japanese beetles, and the mums were out. He found the clippers in the shed and picked a large bunch of mums for Cat. He thought of cutting a rosebud and putting it in a bud vase and taking that, too. But that carried too many connotations of happy days with breakfast trays and dressing tables.

He lugged the suitcases into the house and up to the bedroom. The top of Cat's dresser was bare. He knew before he looked that her closet would be empty. His closet was still full of his winter clothes, his bureau top the usual accumulation of notes and mementos and paraphernalia. He had taken only two suitcases with summer things, what he would have taken for a vacation. When he had driven out of the driveway a little more than two months ago, he had left a house with an unmade bed, dishes in the sink, squashed cushions on the couch, magazines and books on the floor next to chairs, the first roses in bowls throughout the house and Cat busying herself, infusing the whole with her energy.

He felt desolate. He unpacked his summer clothes and put them away and took out his winter suits and jackets and trousers and socks and sweaters and laid them on the bed in Jorie's room.

He called the vet, who said to drop by with Debbie. And then he called Cat. They went on and on about the baby. She was almost gurgling. He could remember the evening he had come into the house and she had beamed at him and said, "Mix me a stiff drink. I'm going to be a grandmother."

Later: "Was the house all right?"

"Yes. You certainly cleared out."

"Well . . ."

"There are two dead mice you forgot to take."

"Oh, I'm sorry. I meant to get over there today to check and get in things for breakfast for you, but it all just got too hectic."

He changed into his country clothes and drove Debbie to the vet's. She wagged her tail when she saw him. They were old friends. The vet and he stood on opposite sides of the high steel table while the vet probed her and asked questions. "Why don't you let me keep her here overnight, see what's going on?"

Jack drove into the village to pick up the second-class and junk mail and to buy a few things for breakfast. "How are you?" "How have you been?" "How was the summer?" "Are you back now?" He was like a child returned from a long summer vacation, running around the neighborhood, checking up on friends and dogs and old haunts.

Back at the house he put things in the refrigerator, then found a bushel basket and went out and picked some apples for Cat.

26

Catherine was renting her house from a woman of seventy, recently widowed, who had moved her furniture from an apartment in New York to this neat, attractive one-storey white house, beautifully set back from the country road on a ledge overlooking a pond through the trees. As Jack climbed the winding stone steps, bordered by pachysandra and myrtle, he thought, neat and trim, yet quaint.

He approached the half-open front door and heard the familiar voices of his friends. He was about to go in when he stopped. This wasn't his house. He put down the basket of apples and the mums and knocked. In a moment, Catherine, wearing a long black skirt and a blue blouse with a pretty apron he had given her one Christmas, pulled the door all the way open. She looked radiantly happy.

"You found it."

"No trouble." He put his arm around her and kissed her somewhere between the lips and the cheek. He picked up the mums. "These are for Grandmother."

"Aren't they beautiful!"

"From your own garden." He picked up the basket of apples and went in. Catherine made off to the kitchen with the flowers. Jack left the apples in the hall and went into the living room to greet his old friends.

It was awkward. They, of course, knew of the separation, and as he shook hands with the three men and kissed the women, they seemed to look at him with uneasy grins. "How's school?" Todd asked and smiled.

"Fine. I'm going to be giving some extracurricular lectures this semester at the Law School." And he went on around. "Hello, Mary, Hi, Phil. I had a nice dinner with Penny a couple of months ago in Boston." And then they all just looked at him for a moment.

Mary raised her glass. "Congratulations."

"Thank you. Did you hear they're going to get married?" Mary smiled. "Yes."

"I haven't been in touch with Penny for a long time. Has she set the date for her wedding?"

"There isn't going to be a wedding. Hal called off the divorce and went back to his wife a week ago."

"Oh, I'm sorry."

"We're not. He was charming, but to start a marriage like that . . . anyway—" She stopped, possibly embarrassed to be talking about divorce and separation and remarriage. Before, they all had talked freely about the subject, speculating, giving their feelings: "I'd never marry again," or "It's easy for men . . ." or "No, it's easier for women." But now . . .

Catherine came from the kitchen with the mums in a vase. "They called from the hospital just a few moments ago. They've decided to call the baby Catherine." She stood there beaming, tears coming to her eyes.

Jack choked up at her delight. "That's great." He put his arm around her and kissed the side of her head. "With a C?"

"With a C. I told them they should name it after Barbara's mother if they were going to name it after anyone, but they liked the name Catherine."

Jack smiled. "It's a nice name." Cat hurried into the kitchen. "Where's the bar in this house?"

Roger sprang from his chair. "I'm doing the honors. What will you have?"

Jack followed him into the dining room, where Catherine had set up a bar. It was strange being served. He had to remind himself again that he was just a guest in this house. Several of his friends had seemed uncomfortable watching him embrace and kiss Cat. Roger handed him his drink. He looked at Jack, genuinely concerned. "How's it going?"

"Some days good, some days bad."

"Well, that's the way it is anyway, isn't it?"

"You and Doris see anything of Cat?"

"Yes, but not much. She seems pretty occupied. She doesn't seem to be talking to anyone. I mean, really talking. Lots of class."

"No question about that." He took his drink and went into the kitchen and kissed Cat on the cheek. She had been crying with pleasure. "I think that's lovely, calling her Catherine."

"It's nice, isn't it?" She turned and started fussing with the pots steaming on the stove.

"May I poke around the house?"

"Yes. Go ahead. I have to watch the dinner."

The house was pretty. He walked through the dining room to a study, where there was a fire burning, and then to Catherine's bedroom. A single bed with a dainty pink and blue bedspread, a reading light and on a table Cat's usual stack of books. Somehow it gave him a chill. He sipped his drink and looked at the pictures on the dresser. The children, her mother and father. None of him. He felt a pang of hurt. He studied the room again. It might have been just the accident of Cat's finding this widow-lady house, living in her furniture, but he seemed to sense something more than that. He sauntered back to the kitchen. "It's a nice house."

"I just love it."

"It has the slight feel of a maiden lady. I never saw a smaller bed."

"Well . . ." She blushed. She lifted a lid and stirred.

"You look great."

"The baby's a big shot in the arm. Isn't she adorable? New grandmothers should be locked up." She lowered her voice. "Doris is furiously jealous. Her daughter has been living with a succession of men and no grandchildren. Someone should do a study on the effect of the new lifestyle on mothers longing to be grandmothers."

Jack sniffed the dinner. "Mmmm. My favorite. I tried cooking chicken this way for . . . friends, and made a mess of it."

"I'll send you the recipe."

He wanted to stay on in the kitchen with Cat. He felt at home there. Their pre-dinner kitchen time had always been a good time. Drinks, he making the salad or cutting up fruit for dessert or feeding her cheese and crackers. "Can I help?"

"No. You go in and be with your friends."

Dinner was awkward. Cat had put him at the head of the table opposite her, but he did not feel comfortable there. He had been away for more than two months, and while they all talked of their summer experiences at Truro or Naushon or the Vineyard, he could say nothing of his summer. He had spent his summer largely in bed making love. He sensed they were aware of this and that he made them uncomfortable.

Jack wondered if these people would still be his friends after a divorce. Would they welcome Janet or anyone else into their group? They would say they would, but he doubted it. The thought made him sad. These friends were very much part of the textures of his life. He was Penny's godfather. They had lived in Roger and Doris' barn for a month when they had a fire in their own house. They were in and out of each other's houses and lives. Tennis, poker, bridge, car pools, even a European trip once together with Todd and Grace. (And they had still been friends after it!)

Catherine seemed to feel no strain and was buoyant throughout. "You know it took me a year to try to decide what to call Barbara. I couldn't say she was my daughter-in-law, so I finally thought of calling her my daughter-in-love. I think I'm going to go on calling her that even after they get married."

After dinner he began to wonder. Should he leave with the others or wait to be with Cat alone? Help her clean up and wash the dishes. Talk. About what? She had said that even though they were separated, they might be lovers. She looked beautiful, flushed with grandmother-hood. She had changed so little over the years. He could still see the girl in her. He had read a line of poetry some-where to the effect that "Men are only boys grown tall." In spite of her white hair, Cat was in many ways a girl grown tall. He had kept wanting to touch her and hold her during the evening. She seemed very dear to him.

He did let the others leave first. Again, it had been awkward, and they all had joked about it. Doris had said, "These schizophrenic separations make me uncomfortable. I much prefer it when people really hate each other." Jack and Cat stood at the door saying, "Good night," as though nothing had ever happened.

She wouldn't let him help with the dishes. They sat at either end of a rather stiff sofa and talked about where she was going to hang some pictures she had stacked against the wall, what kind of gift they should give the new mother and father and what the news was from Jorie in Holland. There was still so much "we" and "us" in their lives. And he imagined there always would be. A friend of his had married a divorcée and finally left her because her former husband was always very much "there" in their marriage, advising on the education of the children, showing up for birthdays and anniversaries, even stopping by at hospitals when she was ill.

Among other things, she talked about her radio program and how it might be syndicated and about a new public relations business she was starting in a small way. She had not had time for any poetry recently, though she had spoken at a writers' workshop. She didn't ask him any questions. At first he was hurt at what seemed like a total lack of interest. Then he decided she was being discreet and thoughtful in not asking.

He felt the growing strain and returned to the subject of the furniture. "There are some nice pieces here. That's a nice chair." He rose and went to a small antique chair.

"That's mine. I bought that." She said proudly.

He touched it, and it swayed. "I know. You wouldn't have let me get it." And immediately she seemed sorry to have said that.

He felt a certain sickening, a probing of an old dull ache. "It's very pretty. Goes nicely there." They looked at each other.

"It's really a lovely place."

"Yes."

"Well," he drew it out, "I guess I'd better run along."

She rose. "Will you be seeing the baby again before you go back?"

"I'm not sure. I left Debbie at the vet's. She been having a rough time."

230

Cat frowned sympathetically. "Oh . . ." He knew she left an unspoken "You should have her put away" hanging in the air.

"Then I'm going into New York. Perhaps see the dentist."

"That same tooth?"

"Yes."

"I wish you'd see my dentist."

He smiled. It was an old argument. She would not go to his doctors or dentists. She had found (through constant searching) "miracle" men of her own.

He looked at her and put his arms around her and held her tight, and she put her arms around his waist. They stood like that a long time, as though waiting for something to happen. If they could just silently go to bed, not the little bed in there, but the big bed at home, and hold each other and try to grow back together through their bodies. But if they tried to talk . . . He kissed her forehead. "I miss you."

"I miss you, too, but . . ." She smiled sadly. They just looked at each other.

"Well, good night."

"Good night. Think about what we should give the kids."

"Yes. It was a lovely party."

"Yes, it was. I'm glad you could make it."

"Take care."

"You too. Thanks for the mums and the apples."

"There are a lot more over there."

"Yes. All right."

He turned and waved again and went down the steps to his car.

As he came within sight of their house, he saw it was dark. He had forgotten to leave the lights on, and the automatic timers were obviously not working. He had the

231

impulse to drive right on by and go into New York. The New York apartment had always seemed more his than theirs, and he wouldn't feel so dismally lonely there.

But he drove into the garage and went into the empty house and straight to the bedroom and went to bed. As he lay there, naked, curled up on his side, his hands tucked between his knees, he was cold and felt he might cry. After a few moments he turned on the light and rummaged through his bureau drawer. He had always kept a pair of pajamas in case he had to go to the hospital. He found a white top and a blue bottom and got back into bed and went to sleep.

27

Before he started into the city, he called the vet. "I'd like to keep her here awhile longer. See if I can do anything with medications. She's in pretty rough shape."

"I'll be in New York a few days. I'll call you and pick her up on my way back to Cambridge."

At the hospital he had a look at the baby through the window in the nursery and then chatted with Barbara. Finally, she looked at him a moment, frowned and said, "How are you? Are you all right?"

Her concern touched him. There was a special relationship between them, as though somehow they both existed outside the family proper. "I'm all right."

"Is it interesting up there?"

"Yes. Complex."

"I can imagine. Rich told you we're going to be married."

"Yes. I think it's great."

"I'm not so sure. Rich wants it. And for the baby, I suppose . . ."

Jack took her hand. "I approve of marriage. I love it. I know that sounds funny at the moment, but Cat and I had some marvelous times together. And who knows? This is just a trial separation."

"Rich is worried about you. So am I. Catherine is here with her family, in a sense, and her various jobs and projects. You just seem to be up there in exile." Then she asked shyly, "Is there someone?"

"Yes."

"That's good."

"I'm not so sure. Two small children. That's maybe not such a good idea. We'll see. And I miss Cat."

"Complex."

"Yes."

As he crossed the Triboro Bridge, he felt his usual "charge" on entering the city after an absence. And now in the fall with the streets full of purposeful New Yorkers, revved up by their summer vacations, starting their lives all over again, it was at its best. Ever since his schooldays, the year had begun for Jack, not in January, but in September. His forwarded mail had been full of notices and invitations for previews, publication parties, concerts and talks at the Century, opening of exhibits at galleries. "We're going to have a party for X. Will you be back home by then?"

He changed into city clothes at the apartment, where the closets and drawers were still full of Cat's clothes, and breezed over to Park Avenue and into his office. As he moved along the corridors, he shook hands right and left like a victorious politician. "You look great." "How long you back for?"

His secretary rose and held out both hands in greeting, and he glided into his office as though he were about to tackle a day's work. But, of course, there was no work. He stared at his empty desk and for a few moments panicked. He looked out his door down the richly carpeted, discreetly lit corridors, the wood paneling, the modern art along the walls. His Cambridge "pad" seemed very far away. As remote as those stark, summer beach houses had seemed the day after Labor Day.

He found some paper and started to make a list. He had the dentist at eleven. Haircut. Suit. He paused then wrote, "Kim." He was almost afraid to see her. He did not know if he could take the emotions of her letters face to face.

"Hi, it's Jack. I'm in New York."

"You are!"

"I became a grandfather a couple of days ago, and I came down to see the baby in Connecticut."

"Congratulations!"

"How are you?"

"I'm okay." She sounded chipper.

"I'm going to have my teeth cleaned in an hour. I thought you might like to look at them over lunch."

"Lunch is booked. What about dinner?"

"Dinner?"

"Yes. That's the meal one generally eats in the evening around seven, but I suggest you come around nine, because I'm going to be working late with a director." He was about to ask where Scott was. She went on. "Scott is still on the Island soaking up the last of the summer sun. Colin's there too."

He hadn't expected this. "Can I bring anything besides cashews?"

She laughed. "No." Then in answer to his unasked question, "Scott's giving a party out there tonight. He's taken up cooking. I bought him a wok, and he's going crazy in the kitchen. He wants a Cuisinart for his birthday."

As he made his rounds, he was touched and pleased with the way people remembered him. The dental hygienist: "Is that place still sensitive?" At the coffee shop:

235

"Black, right?" The barber: "Watch it over the ears." The captain at lunch: "Dubonnet with a twist." The tailor: "High right hip. One half inch."

At five he was at the Tavern on the Green for a publication party. There were three women in their forties who had been married the last time he had seen them but were divorced. He listened to the views on separation and loneliness of an editor recently cut adrift from his wife. "I don't seem to be lonely. You know there was a sexual revolution going on out there while you and I were otherwise engaged, and I'm just catching up."

He went home and took a nap and a shower and then was off for Kim's. As he sat in the taxi, it was almost as though summer had never happened.

He was about to let himself in with his key, but then he stopped and rang the bell. Kim came to the door wearing his favorite outfit, the rose-colored turtleneck sweater and the snug black pants. "Hi. Why didn't you let yourself in?"

"I don't know."

They kissed, and she said, "Come along. You can wash the lettuce and fix the drinks. I'm behind in my schedule. This director didn't leave until a half hour ago."

"And you had to wash your hair."

"Yes." She laughed.

All during dinner and for long after, Kim was all bright smiles and darting looks as she chattered on about her work, her problems with her associates, the house they might buy on Long Island, how Colin had grown over the summer. It was a lively but somewhat nervous performance. He listened to her and watched her. This was not the bleeding Kim who had written the letters he could not read, who had pleaded with him to "come back."

After dinner, when they were sitting on the couch, she ran out of chatter, and for a moment they just looked at each other, smiling.

"Are you going back?"

"Yes." Then quickly: "I'm giving a couple of extracurricular lectures on literary and entertainment law. And I'm going to be sitting in on a couple of classes as a kind of visiting expert on copyright." He was embarrassed that he had given all the reasons except Janet.

She smiled as though noting the omission. "Did you see Cat?"

"Yes."

"How was it?"

"Difficult. Complicated."

She looked at him for a moment. "I can't tell you the number of times I've selfishly wished that you hadn't left her." She smiled. "Do you think you might come back to her?"

He knew she meant "to us." He shook his head. "I don't know."

"I apologize for all my clutching and grasping. The letters and phone calls and flowers. Very unbecoming and unfair. Nobody should be grasping for you now. You should give yourself time. Hang loose. Don't run for cover." She sipped her drink. "Still, it must have been exhilarating to have two women pining for you."

He smiled. "Not really. I tried to tell you that night in New Hampshire. When I fell in love with you, it was, of course, fantastic. But I felt a sense of loss. Some image of myself as a husband, a man. And as I tried to tell you, I felt another loss when I fell in love with Janet. Exhilarating, but . . . More is less for me. It seems to violate some principle I'm stuck with."

She looked at him, smiling sadly. He was tempted to move to her, to kiss her and hold her. They should have met in some public place.

The phone rang. It was Scott reporting on the success of his wok dinner. Jack got up to leave the room, to go upstairs, but she motioned him to stay. "I've got two messages for you. Hold on while I go to the other phone." She pushed the hold button. "I'll be right back. Get yourself another drink."

He resented her cheery greeting to Scott; he had always left the room when he called. He couldn't stand listening to their loving husband and wife exchanges. They made him actively sick and, since his separation, homesick. He had never realized how much he would miss the "Don't forget to get the car fixed" aspect of his life.

As he sprawled on the couch, he realized he should be happy at Kim's cheerful tone with Scott. He should be relieved that she had not replayed the unbearable agony of her letters.

When she came back into the room, she was carrying a small lavender Bergdorf-Goodman box. She approached him solemnly, her beautiful light-blue eyes wide open, almost pleading.

"What's that?"

"Your letters." She put them on the coffee table and sat at the other end of the couch. He frowned and felt sick. "I'm not doing this out of bitchiness, but out of kindness. I'm not kicking you out. I'm removing myself for your sake as well as mine."

He stared at the box. Twenty? thirty letters, the unguarded outpourings of his heart. They seemed at that moment to have a separate existence of their own, and he felt a twinge of pity and embarrassment for them.

And for her. He was aware of the elements involved in

this almost ritual scene. He understood, sympathized. It was natural for her to want to dramatize the situation, bring it to some climax, not just let him drift back to Cambridge, the relationship ambiguous. In a way, it created an exciting, if sad, emotional tension. It was also her way of regaining position.

He looked at her and leaned over and kissed her cheek, feeling it necessary to keep some physical contact while her words were separating them. She went on. "I should have stayed away. Then you would have been all tucked in up there."

He smiled at her tone and shook his head. "I don't know."

"And I don't think we should call or write. Which should be something of a relief for you."

He really had nothing to say. This was the way it should be, if he were going back to Cambridge, to Janet. She was presumably making it easier for him. Taking him out of the pressure cooker. Removing one of his options. But somehow he did not feel like thanking her. He looked at her. "Do you want your letters back?"

"God, no!" Thus contemptuously dismissing all the love and anguish and joy she had poured into them. "*Yesterday you brought me a joy I have never known. Do you realize that, Jack Montgomery?*"

He sat there staring at the box. Somewhere he was crying.

"When will you go back to Cambridge?"

He looked over at her. "Maybe tomorrow. The next day. I'm not sure."

She had been unsuccessful in trying to get him to come back with her letters and phone calls and flowers. But here she was, sitting there, beautiful, sad, intriguingly complex, in *his* town where the barber knew about his hair and the tailor knew his measurements, returning his letters, which she knew were really the heart of their relationship; the love, the trust, the openness. . . . Trying to reach him one last time.

"Scott and Colin come home tomorrow. I'll have to buy Colin all new clothes for school. He's grown so." She talked on about the new school he was going to, the inadequacies of the old one. It was as though she were giving him time to think. Then she stopped, and they just looked at each other.

Finally, Jack reached over and picked up the box. "Well . . . I'd better be going." He stood up and moved from behind the coffee table. She rose and put an arm around him and walked with him. It seemed impossible that they were saying goodbye. He stopped in the hall near the door at the foot of the stairs. He looked at her, frowning. "Well . . ."

"I'll always be here. I just won't be pursuing you."

Touched, he put his arms around her and just held her, rocking her slightly from side to side. She pressed the side of her face to his chest and held him tightly. "Please stay." She drew back her head and looked up at him with her questioning, almost frightened look. He was frowning. "Please come upstairs."

He looked at her. He smiled and shook his head. "You want everything, don't you?"

"Yes. We'll just sleep."

She moved away, her hand sliding down his arm, and taking his hand, as she had done the first night, she led him up the stairs.

While she disappeared into the bathroom, he took off his clothes, feeling that he was acting out some role that had been written for him, some obligatory scene. He threw back the covers and lay naked on the bed.

240

He waited. He studied the two delicate black angelfish he had given her. He listened. Then he heard a sob. He hurried to the bathroom door and opened it. Kim, still fully dressed, was sitting on the edge of the tub, crying.

He went to her and held her, feeling awkward with his nakedness against her clothes. "I'm sorry. Please go home. This was a silly idea." He crouched next to her and kissed the side of her face. "You don't want to be here. Why did you come up? You don't owe me anything."

He continued to comfort her, to stroke her hair. Suddenly she blurted out, almost shouted, "I can't share you! I won't share you!"

He kissed her cheek. "I know. I know."

She calmed down and looked at him. "I'm sorry. This is so sloppy and undignified. How can you stand me?"

"Come to bed."

"No." She shook her head.

"Come on." He stood her up.

"I don't want to—" She stopped.

"I know. We won't. We'll just sleep." He started to undress her as he would a child. He reached for her nightdress on the bathroom door and slipped it over her head. Her closeness and her confusion and her dearness had excited him. But it must not be tonight. Painfully they had come to some kind of parting based on the reality of the situation. If he were with her, it would all be hopeless again.

They got into bed, and he pulled the covers up over them. She turned on her side, and he nestled against her back.

She looked at him over her shoulder. "Did you set the alarm?"

"No."

"Five?" She reached for the clock.

"Yes."

She turned slightly and looked at him. "Thank you for staying."

He smiled. "We don't thank."

She went to sleep almost immediately, and as he lay there, holding her, he knew that he would probably always love her, no matter what happened.

An hour later, unable to sleep, he got up and dressed in the dark. He thought to leave without waking her, but he couldn't do that, not this last time.

"Good night."

"Good night. Remember I'll always be here."

Downstairs he picked up his raincoat and the lavender box with his letters and let himself out and went home.

28

Jack stayed in the city for two days more, boning up in the firm's library for his lecture, going to the dentist, buying a dress for Janet and some music she couldn't find in Boston.

At noon on the third day he was holding Debbie on the vet's operating table. The time had come to put her away. "It's something we can do for animals we can't do for human beings." He wondered why he was putting himself through this, but he knew he had to. For years he had taken care of her, plunged his fingers deep into her throat to remove forked twigs that were choking her ("Watch out, she'll bite you!"), removed ticks ("Have you ever heard of Rocky Mountain spotted fever?"), cleaned her rear end like a baby and mopped up after her. Reasonably he could have had her put away a year ago. He knew he had a way of hanging onto things.

When the vet's assistant had carried her into the room (she could no longer move her hind legs), she had stretched her neck toward him to be petted. Sprawled on the table, she nuzzled him as though to say, "Where are we off to today?"

The vet left the room and took the assistant with him. Jack held her head and stroked her, running his hand over her flank, which was soaking wet from her own urine. He would have liked to have cleaned her up. She had always been so proud, had pranced so beautifully when she had been bathed. There were tears in his eyes. Christ, so trusting! She was panting with happy excitement now, her front feet slipping on the shiny steel surface of the table. Jack put his face to hers and nuzzled her back.

He thought of her chasing groundhogs in the country, always pretending to lose the scent just as she got dangerously close; in the city, pulling him in a mad dash around the block if it was raining; riding shotgun beside him in the car for those thousands and thousands of miles they had traveled together; getting her name from Jorie when she first came into the house and the four of them stood at four corners of the room and each called her by the name they wanted to give her. What had his choice been? She had always been good company, accepting all the love that any member of the family had to give when he or she couldn't find anyone else who wanted it at the moment. He remembered one Sunday morning, when everything in the family had just been too much and he had felt trapped, he had taken Debbie in the car and driven around the countryside for two or three hours till he had calmed down. She had accompanied each member of the family on lonely, brooding walks through the woods or across city blocks. She had been bought for the children as a friend and to teach them responsibility. With her loving nature she had taught them all a great deal more.

The vet came in with his assistant and started to prepare the syringe.

"So much of her seems to be still alive. If she's in no pain, I'd still be willing to take care of her."

The vet looked across the table. "Jack, it's time. Believe me. We've put it off as long as we should."

The assistant moved to the table to hold Debbie, but Jack almost jealously blocked him. He did not look at the vet, but at Debbie's head nestled in his arms. "It's amazing. She just sits there."

"Well, I've never hurt her. And you've never hurt her."

In a few moments Debbie's body relaxed, and Jack eased it down on the table. A leg twitched. "That's just muscle reflex." Jack bobbed his head, tears now streaming down his face. Why did he stay there? Why did he wait in airports till planes took off or on street corners till people vanished from sight?

For a few moments they just stood there staring at the body. Then Jack finally took his hands away, murmured, "Thank you," and hurried out through the waiting room, waving at the receptionist, whose eyes were red from crying.

In the car he leaned his head on the steering wheel and cried, realizing that somehow he was crying for more than Debbie.

29

He had meant to stop by his house and get the snow tires and a small scatter rug to put beside his bed. But he couldn't do it. He called at the post office and picked up his mail. There was a package with the three dozen Red Emperor tulip bulbs they had ordered from Holland. He left them for Cat.

As he drove out of the village, it started to rain, the car heater suddenly stopped working, and he felt cold.

He also had the sickening feeling that he was going in the wrong direction.

He thought of his first time away from home, when he was a boy, his first year at prep school, when he had gone home for Thanksgiving vacation, and how he had felt after going back alone on the train. It was too soon to have gone home.

The rain had splattered the bright fall leaves on the windshield and pavement. It would soon be time for fires and early evenings inside.

"I miss you."

"I miss you too. But—" Had she expected him to stay the night, be her lover? Had he again confirmed for her that he didn't love her?

He felt a terrible sense of loss. Cat and his home and

Kim. And Debbie was the only loss he had been able to react to with tears. He was responsible in part at least for the other losses. He felt no guilt for Debbie. As the vet had said, he had never hurt her, and so could cry.

He turned on the radio.

Later, looking in the rearview mirror, he saw the apples for Janet, the Bonwit box with the dress. In his briefcase was the sheet music she wanted. He didn't want to go to his place; as a matter of fact, he dreaded the spareness of it that he had cherished in the summer. He wanted to go to Janet's. To their bed, their refrigerator, their steam iron, their vacuum cleaner. It would be warm and cozy there. They would be together. Maybe everything would come clear and simple. He would be overwhelmed by the truth. Years ago, when he had been facing a crisis, a psychoanalyst at the club had told him that dreams never lie. They tell us the truth about our real desires. For weeks after, he had courted sleep and dreams, hoping they would tell him what he really wanted to do. But he had not dreamed.

He must stop at the first gas station and call Janet. He didn't know why he hadn't called her from New York. It had all been too complex. And again he had had that feeling that being with Cat and Kim, he shouldn't call Janet. He was aware that this nicety possibly spared him feelings of guilt but was really insensitive and thoughtless. He smiled as he remembered a friend's saying that when he was away from home, he called his wife every night, even if he were in some other woman's bed.

Janet sounded euphoric. She had won the custody of the children. Dick had just suddenly given up. "I meant to call you."

"I meant to call you, too."

The furniture had been moved in the day before. She

got the piano. Finally, she pulled herself up short. "Hey, how are *you*?"

"I'm okay. Anxious to see you."

"How's the baby?"

"Beautiful, naturally."

"Where are you?"

"I'm on the turnpike. Could I take you to dinner?"

"I have to take the kids to Dick's for the weekend."

"Well . . ."

"When would you arrive?"

"Oh, hour and a half."

"Come here and see the place, and then we can decide."

"I got the dress."

"Oh, you're too much."

As he drove in the short driveway and saw Janet's little car and the children's bicycles lying on their sides on the scrubby lawn near the porch steps and saw the lights in the living room, he could almost feel he was coming home from a day at work. He felt tender and loving toward this plain, squat house and the family within it. Everything would be all right.

He left the dress and the music in the car and lugged in the basket of apples. The house was not transformed, but there was a handsome Persian rug on the floor, some fine old chests and tables, attractive tole lamps and, dominating the living room, a small grand piano. The children immediately pulled him into their rooms to show him their bunk beds and their toys, and then they dragooned him into playing a game of Monopoly.

He kissed Janet discreetly while little eyes watched, made himself a drink and settled on the floor to play. Janet, barefoot in the long, clinging Marimekko cotton knit he had given her, came in to watch them. She looked smashing in the dress, had worn it to parties and to bed, and he had a strong impulse to run his hand up her leg. It would all be very simple.

While the children packed their bags, Jack went into the kitchen. "You seem in great form."

"I am. My God, I'm so glad I fought for them. We're going to have a ball together as they grow up."

"It's terrific to see you feeling so spunky." He ran his hand down her back. She drew away and looked toward the door, then smiled and kissed him quickly.

"I've got my kids and my job and a house, such as it is. I've waited so long for this, went through such crap from that man. For the first time in ten years I'm free. I'm not getting any alimony, just child support, so I don't know how I'm going to make it, but—" She shrugged and laughed.

Again he had the impulse to scoop up this little family, to make all things right and easy for them. In passing, he ran his hand quickly across her jaunty haunch. "Hurry back."

When she had gone to take the children to Dick's, Jack brought in the Bonwit box and his briefcase with the music and the pictures he had promised to bring her of the house and family.

For a few minutes he played the piano. He hadn't played in years. He poured himself another drink, carried it into the bathroom and took a shower. Looking up at the shower head, he laughed. It was *his* shower head too.

He started to dress again, then had an idea, went into the bedroom with his drink and got into bed. "Hurry home! Hurry home!" He took a sip of his drink and wondered if now that she had the children she would let him make love in here. Of course, he couldn't spend the night, except every other weekend. "Hurry home and make everything right!" He looked at the clock. She'd been gone almost an hour.

He got up. Maybe that wasn't such a good idea, lying naked in bed, waiting for her. He started putting on his clothes and was standing there in his boxer shorts and shirt when she came in, carrying a shopping bag full of groceries. She laughed. "What are you doing?"

"I took a shower, then had the cute idea of waiting for you in bed, and then as time passed, I decided it wasn't such a cute idea." He took the shopping bag.

"I stopped to buy some things. I decided we'd eat at home. Okay?"

"Okay."

The house was warm, and for a while he padded around in his shorts and shirt, the way he had done during the summer. Then he felt somehow strange and put on his trousers, and then later, his socks and shoes.

But he kept touching Janet now, and she purred her "mmmm" but was preoccupied with her cooking. Jack had his third drink now and didn't want to be out of touch with her, wanted them to go to bed.

During supper he told her about putting Debbie away, about New York. "It's beautiful there this time of year. Everyone zipping back to work." She asked about Catherine, and he told her briefly about the party. He kept reaching over and touching her, leaning over and kissing her. She asked to see the pictures of the house and family. He tried to put her off, but she insisted.

"Is that Catherine standing in the doorway?"

"Yes." He kissed the side of her head.

"I didn't know she had white hair."

"Yes."

"She's beautiful."

250

"Yes." He kissed her again.

"Very elegant. Very stylish."

"Yes." He ran his hand down her back, not looking at the picture.

"And the children. My God, he's handsome!"

"Let's look at them later, shall we?" He took the pictures from her and moved in on her, bringing her to her feet, kissing her passionately.

"Let's finish supper."

"Let's not. Please."

It was all rushed, with a kind of desperation, not like the long summer nights of loving they had known. Not the sensuous, often languorous pleasuring of each other. It was a striving, a blind driving, as though there would be an answer at the end. At first she hardly seemed to participate, but then, looking at him with what seemed like sudden understanding and sympathy, she clutched him to her, his face, his hips, finally almost wrapping herself around him as though to help him and protect him.

After, they lay in the dark for a long time without saying anything, his head resting face down on the pillow next to hers. She slowly stroked his shoulders and his back. He kissed her cheek, and at last he rolled away but still lay close, staring across her face at the light coming from the other room.

She turned a little on her side and looked down at him, smiling. "You're going home, aren't you?" He frowned. "To Catherine." He looked at her. "It's all right. Say it."

"I don't know."

"I've always known you would."

"Have you?"

"Yes."

His right hand drifted idly up and down her back. "I don't know."

251

"Yes." She smiled again. He shook his head. "Don't be embarrassed. You've always been honest with me." She lowered herself and rested her head on his shoulder. "We've been playing house here. You were homesick, wanted a house, a home, a wife. I loved it, and needed it, and you. But . . ." She traced lines on his chest. "I didn't know how you would come back, but I imagined. And when you didn't call—"

"I'm sorry. I don't know why—"

"No. No. It's all right." Then, after a moment: "There's no place for us to go from here, that either of us wanted to go. Getting custody of the kids, feeling free for the first time . . ." He waited. "I've been dependent for so long, I want to be independent for a while before I become dependent again." She laughed. "Does that make any sense?"

"Yes."

"It would have come to this even if I hadn't known that you would go back to Catherine, sooner or later. I mean totally independent. See who I want to see, when I want to see them, how I want to see them."

He smiled. "Men."

"Yes. I make it seem as though there were dozens waiting at the door. There are none. I've wondered if we couldn't make it more casual. Just be good for each other. But I knew I couldn't just be the girl you fucked when you weren't fucking someone else. Or vice versa."

There was something harsh in the way she said this. He drew her close to him as she went on. "The first night I said I didn't want to fall in love with you, and I meant it. But I did. There's so much I want to do. Get my head on straight. Get myself together. Be my own woman before I fall in love. I know you can't order it that way. What was it you said, 'Life is what happens while you're making other plans'? And I may end up with, I don't know. At least with my kids, thank God!"

She seemed to him at that moment infinitely dear and troubled and courageous. He kissed the top of her head, listening. "I seem to want to retreat into whatever is at the core of me and work myself out again, slowly." He thought of Kim. Janet had what Kim wanted. "I was okay, you know, before you came along. Missing all that, of course, but I was okay. I'm not sure I thank you for stirring up all those feelings again. Oh, yes, I do. Of course." She kissed his shoulder.

He lay there listening but not really concentrating as she went on about what she wanted her life to be. He felt a certain calm, a sad but kind of rushing calm. Was he going home? Had he known it all along, too? It was true that everything he had had with Janet, the house, the children, the kind of loving, somewhere he had wished it could have been with Cat. The nights with Kim, too. They were all special in themselves, of course, but they had contained the echo and the wish. Was it possible? Could his romantic soul and his Puritan will, trained to try and try again, join to bring this about? Tears came to his eyes at the thought, the possibility.

They dozed for a while; then they cleaned up the kitchen together. He stopped from time to time to kiss her affectionately, the back of her neck, her ear. She purred appreciatively. It was like that last night with Cat in the kitchen, drying dishes.

"You know anyway, it's going to be different around here. Dick goes away for a month of traveling for his job, and I'll have the children all the time. We couldn't be together here. It wouldn't be the 'enchanted cottage' it has been."

He smiled. "Then how are you going to handle your lovers?"

She blushed and looked at him. "Stop it!"

Later he asked, "May I stay tonight? I don't want to go back to the pad."

"Of course." And she put her arms around him and kissed him.

30

Four days later the phone rang as he was making a final outline for his lecture. Since the night with Janet, he had concentrated on getting ready for the lecture and on brushing up on his notes about the new Copyright Law for the lectures he was to sit in on the following week. He had testified before the committee in Washington considering the revised bill, so it was only a matter of going over points he knew well.

He had buried himself in his work. The calm that had settled on him with Janet that night had carried over. He ate alone with a newspaper without too great a feeling of loneliness. He could walk through the Square without feeling the need to reach out and touch, to gather to him for warmth and comfort. He did not actively think about what was happening. Whatever it was would announce itself to him in due time. He missed and did not miss the rich pain of his longing. He felt something of a neuter. He remembered one of his writers who had said to his analyst, "Please don't take my longing away from me."

He answered the phone. It was Cat. "How are you?"

"I'm okay. Did you give your lecture yet?"

"Day after tomorrow. I'm boning up on it."

"Good luck. Listen, I'm calling about the house. Tom

255

Stevens says he thinks he has a buyer for it, if we want to sell it." Jack froze and stared at the floor. "Jack?" She waited a moment, then went on. "You know we often talked about what we thought it was worth. And I told him what we'd figured. But I said you would have to give him a price." Still, Jack said nothing. "Tom said that if we waited longer, we'll miss the market, and nothing much will happen until spring."

He still said nothing; then suddenly he blurted out, "I don't want to sell. I'm coming home."

There was a pause. "Oh?"

"Yes." He waited. Over the telephone was obviously no place to bring up the subject of their getting back together.

"When will you be coming?"

"I have two commitments next week. I'll be packed and ready to leave after the last one. That's the twenty-third."

"Your birthday."

"Right. Can we have dinner that night?"

"Let me check my book. Yes, that's fine. I'm going to be away the week after that, but that's fine. It's your fiftieth, isn't it?"

"Yes, slightly terrifying."

"No. I didn't find mine terrifying. It's all in the mind. And you look great, when you stand up straight, and smile, and get your clothes pressed. . . ." She laughed.

"And my buttons sewn on, and my hair cut." Now they were both laughing. "How's the baby?"

"Great. Rich took some pictures. One of me holding her. He's captioned it, 'Catherine the Great and the Small.' "

"Did you pick up the tulips at the post office?"

"Yes, I planted them on the bank near the pool. Isn't that where you decided to put them?" And they chatted on easily and warmly.

When he hung up, he was excited. Scared but excited. He wanted to call Janet and tell her. He had dialed her number before he thought how inappropriate it was. She picked up on the first ring. She was happy for him, thought it was great. When was he going?

He took out his suitcase, then realized he wouldn't be going for a week and jammed it back in the closet.

He couldn't sit still. He put on his coat and went down to the Square. And now once again it was the Square he and Cat had known. The Cambridge they had known. The entrance to the Coop was not the place where he had stood lonely, watching the street musicians play on a hot summer night, but the place where he had waited for Cat, across the street from the subway. Sages was where he had shopped three afternoons a week the first year they had lived in Boston, and he had carried the groceries home on the subway. Agassiz Theater was where Cat had read her poetry, and the Wursthaus was where they had huddled over beers, figuring out how much it would cost them to live.

He took the subway and went into Boston. He had been afraid of Boston, had subconsciously avoided it in the months he had been in Cambridge, but now, getting off at Charles Street, he smiled, remembering the cold winter night when he had left Cat's apartment very late and had stood against the wall of the Charles Street Prison, waiting for the last bus to Cambridge. Suddenly two police cars had stopped, and four policemen had approached him with hands on revolvers.

He stood on Chestnut Street on Beacon Hill and looked at the house where he had met Cat at the poetry gathering and where he had first made love to her. He passed the florist's at the foot of the street, where he had arranged for her to pick up a pink and white carnation each morning for a month on her way to teach. Then up Beacon Street and down to Kings Chapel, where they had been married.

Back in his apartment, he wanted to call Cat and tell her about his pilgrimage. But he mustn't do this. He must not sneak back in.

But he wanted to be in touch with Cat. Sometimes when he had complicated things he wanted to say or when he wanted to say things without interruption, he had written letters to her, and she to him. What would he say to Cat? It would be nice if he just appeared in the door and she threw her arms around him. He smiled. That wasn't Cat. He reached for a piece of paper and a pen.

Dear Cat:

He had not thought what he would say, but as he sat there, the first thing he wanted to say was, "I love you." He needed to write it, to say it, but he had said, "I love you," too often in the last months. Still, he wanted to write it but didn't. Somehow he felt it would offend her as being too easy.

I will be home on the twenty-third, and I hope that we can talk about getting back together again. I have wanted to talk about it on the phone, but I realize that that's too casual. But perhaps you could hear the happiness in my voice at the idea of coming home.

I sit here and wonder, "What in God's name did we think we were doing?" How could we do it? I know that all the time it was happening, when I drove out the drive that day, I felt as though I were sitting in a theater watching someone else on the screen. I mean, my God, I can't believe that we just casually walked away from each other. People who are going to leave each other run out of the house, pack and take off in the middle of the night. They don't dawdle around making love, caring for gardens, going to parties. I know the fact that I was the one who drove off that morning gave the impression that it was I who left . . . when it was really that we left each other.

He started to write that he had several times asked her to "try again," but he decided not to. She would remember.

The whole thing has been unreal. I realize that the only way I have been able to stay up here has been by blocking out of my consciousness everything we are, everything we have . . . When I drove down for the baby, it all came rushing back to me. I don't know why I didn't stay then. There was something, I guess, too sentimental about it. Too cliché, rushing into each other's arms over the crib of a newborn child. We have always studiously avoided clichés, sometimes, perhaps, to our own detriment.

When I said, "I miss you," and you said, "I miss you, too, but—" I guess I didn't want to go into what was behind the "but" anymore than we wanted to go into it all that night in the kitchen. And I wish that now we could just come together again without examining the "but." My side of it seems so petty now, so out of proportion to the feeling I have of wanting us to be together again.

In spite of our problems, it seems inconceivable for us to be apart.

I have been living up here in what is virtually a colony of separated and divorced people. But when I listen to them, they all had *real problems*. By and large they are touchingly discreet, but when you get to know them, there is a lot of hatred for ex-husbands and ex-wives. And though I guess I have always realized it, I realize all over again exactly what it is that we have in our marriage.

I think that we have perhaps unwittingly been playing a dangerous game.

I know there are problems, but I feel that we can work at them better once we are back together, acknowledging that we want to be together, rather than trying to solve them as a prerequisite to our coming together again. So I do not want to mention them here . . .

Except to say I feel that *I* have made a great, great mistake in the way I have let our lives drift apart. I have always been proud of your work, your career. You know that. It was understood from the beginning that we would be a two-career family. AND I WANT IT THAT WAY! You are much more interesting to me that way.

That night I fell in love with you (I have just come back from looking at that apartment), I fell in love with your talent and your drive, along with your loveliness and kindness and beauty, and . . . But in urging you to take on more and more, I think you have sometimes had the impression I don't need you, don't want you. When people have said to you, "aren't you two apart a good deal?" you have said, "Oh, Jack's essentially a loner." I am not a loner. I love being with you. But I knew that if I protested too much (and you know I *have* protested. Remember our early shouting bouts about shifting priorities?), you would stop, and you would be resentful, and we would both be unhappy. So, when we get back together, I am going to say, "Well, I'll miss you terribly," but I will expect, will demand, that you go right on doing what you were going to do. But perhaps, knowing that I miss you, when you come back home, you will not look on me as someone who has done very well alone, but as someone who has missed you.

He stopped. The letter had gone off course. He had meant this last as an expression of his love, and it had come out perhaps petulant, argumentative. The only hope was to avoid this kind of thing, which would lead them into a 'round-and-'round discussion, which would leave them frazzled and apart. Well, he would not send the letter, but it had helped to write it. He would keep it. Perhaps give it to her. It would depend.

The next days he found every excuse to call Cat. He called to tell her how his lecture had gone, to thank her for the pictures of herself holding the baby, to ask her to have the storm windows put up, to have the oil burner checked and cleaned.

And then, a few days before he left, he had a farewell dinner with Janet. They did not go to one of their haunts, but to the Copley, where he and Cat had danced on Friday nights. It was a bittersweet evening for him and Janet, both of them shaking their heads and smiling over how quickly they had moved the night she had come to change her dress. She blushed. He had brought her a book of Cat's poems, for some reason, eager for Janet to know her. And he reminisced about their days in Boston, years ago, dragging Christmas trees home from Faneuil Hall Market, sailing in the boat basin, riding the swan boats in the Garden. He stopped, embarrassed. "It seems somehow indecent to talk to you like this."

She smiled. "No, go on."

"You're relieved that I'm going."

"No. Yes. No." They laughed.

"What a great time we had!" He took her hand.

"Mmmmm," she purred. "Totally unreal. A kind of time-out."

"Saved my life."

"Oh? Well, maybe. That's nice. I'll remember that. I won't have any trouble remembering you. My house is full of things you've given me. Every time I open the refrigerator . . ."

He smiled and shook his head. "It was certainly intense."

"Yes. You kept trying to commit yourself to me, but you couldn't make it. It was sweet and touching."

"I like being committed."

"I do too, I guess. Settled and secure. So you can concentrate on other things in life. It's less exhausting that way." She laughed. "Cat's a lucky woman. I hope she knows it."

"Ah, you've seen me under special circumstances. I can be a bastard, cool, detached, unloving, resentful. What's been good about it is I could be all the things I like to be. I've liked the image you've allowed me to project."

"And I've liked the image you've allowed me to have of myself. I've never been in love before, really. But wait! Wait!" She raised both her hands. "I still want what's happening to happen. Everything I said that night."

He drove her home, walked through the house with her again, arms around each other, looked in on the children asleep in their rooms. Then they kissed. Still holding her, he said, "Goodbye. Let me know how things are going. No, I guess you'd better not."

"Good luck at home. And thank you."

They held each other again for a long time, looking, shaking their heads, smiling, remembering; then he turned and left.

At the car he looked back, and she waved, and he waved, and then she turned quickly and went into the house.

As he drove away, seeing the lights of the little house finally disappear from the rearview mirror, he felt a pang. But he knew that he had made the right decision.

At five he woke in a sweat. There had been a dream. It had something to do with his being back with Catherine. They were in the kitchen, making supper and laughing,

262

but he had awakened in a sweat. He burrowed under the covers, his eyes open, frowning. He tried to sleep again, but he couldn't. "Dreams don't lie." But in the dream they had been laughing.

Obviously part of him was afraid to go back. Broke out in a sweat at the thought. Well, all right, he had broken out in a sweat years ago, the morning after he and Cat had definitely decided to marry. Both the decisions involved "giving up," responsibilities.

It would not be a movie scene with two lovers rushing at each other across a field, caught in a final stop-frame two feet from each other, arms stretched out, mouths open with joy.

It would be difficult, but the alternatives were unthinkable. His reasons were complex, but what should be written or spoken were words of love, of passion, of longing. This is what reuniting lovers wanted of each other. Certainly Cat would have to be convinced that he loved her. But he knew that he did not want to rush at her and sweep her off her feet and carry her off to the Caribbean and a deserted cottage on the beach for a week of passionate love. He wanted to embrace her lovingly and gratefully in their home as part of his home and his life and in many ways the maker of his home and his life, as the mother of his children, as the "rememberer" of twenty-five years, as the condition of his life.

Of course, he knew he would be lonely again with her, that special kind of married loneliness that makes you at once blaming and guilty. One is supposed to be lonely alone, but not married. Perhaps if he could bring himself to acknowledge that it was normal to sit at a candlelit dinner with your wife and occasionally feel lonely for something else, then there would not be the strain.

He must remember the sour taste of alone loneliness.

263

Could he remember it? It was as difficult to remember as sexual ecstasy. You could see yourself, but you couldn't remember the feeling. It would be easier for him to remember the pasty-faced man whose bed this had been. That image chilled him and would always chill him.

Cat had always admired people who tried. She had given him a silver shoehorn with the word "TRY" engraved on it. They would try, try to make the "poem" beautiful and effective "with the net up." Even the giving up, forsaking all others could be meaningful. He remembered one of his clients, a famous actress, told him that when she was doing a picture in Rome, an attractive priest had dogged her steps, and one day she had had a cappucino with him, and he had told her how much he loved her. She had said, "But, Father, you're a priest." And he had smiled and said, "Oh, I'm not going to do anything about it. That's my gift to God."

To judge the value of something by what you will give up for it. Was this a negative way of thinking? Kim wanted it all. But didn't she paradoxically lose something by "having it all"?

He looked over at his night table and saw a letter one of his playwright friends had written, inviting him and Cat to the opening of his new play in two weeks. He saw Cat and him going to their seats as they had so many times before as though nothing had happened, greeting friends, holding hands, going to the party after and hearing people say, with a special look in their eyes, "It's so nice to see you both." Three months ago there had been a kind of sad and strange excitement in saying, "Cat and I are separated." How much more exciting it had been to say, "I'm coming home." And the best would be standing there together among friends, not having to say anything.

31

At one o'clock on the twenty-third, his bags were in the station wagon, and he stood taking a last look at his place. In a burst of euphoria he had given all his furnishings to a young couple down the hall, everything, including pots and pans, dishes, glasses, pillows, blankets. They had removed it all while he was at the lecture, all except the bed, which they would come for later. And Kim's plant. The girl had left a note under the plant. "Were we supposed to take this, too?"

As he stood there, he felt it was somehow appropriate that all that was left was the stripped-down bed. He had spent much of the last three months in bed, this one and others.

He saw that his Security List, now augmented by the numbers of doctors, Janet, movie theaters and superintendent, was still taped to the wall by the phone. He peeled it off and wondered if he should keep it as a reminder.

"Penny." He hadn't called Penny since he'd been back, had felt awkward about calling after Hal had returned to his wife. He should have. He'd been selfish. He hoped other people would call him, help him at a bad time. He hadn't helped Penny. It wasn't much good to call now and say, "Goodbye," but it was better than nothing. He sat on the bed and dialed her number.

"Hi, Penny. Jack Montgomery."

"Oh, hello. How are you?"

Her voice sounded cool. She had a right to be hurt. "I'm okay. I'm on my way home."

"Oh."

"How are you? I was sorry to hear from your mother about Hal."

There was a pause, then a choked "I'll call you back."

He sat with the receiver in his hand, frowning. He shouldn't have mentioned Hal. He shouldn't have called. Now she was sitting there in her apartment in Boston, crying.

She called back in five minutes. "I'm sorry."

"No, I'm sorry. I shouldn't have brought it up."

"It's only that I just got a terrible letter from his father blaming me for the whole thing."

"I don't understand. He went back to his family, didn't he? Your mother said he'd gone back."

"Yes, but—" Then a flat "You haven't heard?"

"What?"

There was a pause. "Four days ago he shot himself." She started to cry.

"Oh, God!" He closed his eyes. "Oh, Penny! Can I come over?"

"I'm going away for a while. Perhaps later. Thanks for calling." And she hung up.

He sat staring at the wall. "Oh, Christ! Dear, lovely Christ!"

As he crossed the Charles River and swung back along the drive on the way to the expressway, he glanced over at the towers of Eliot, Lowell and Dunster houses and thought of Ted, who would be taking his four-year-old son

266

to the aquarium on Saturday, and of Ted's wife, who wanted a reconciliation, and of Penny, who had wanted to be married, and of Hal, who had been married and had just wanted a girl, of Janet, who had been crushed by marriage but who had salvaged two children from it, and of Kim, for whom one hundred percent was not enough, and of the agony the extra percentage points had cost her.

Kim didn't know he was coming home. He hadn't called. He was coming home to Cat.

Once in Connecticut, he left the interstate as soon as he could and drove down through the back roads, past antique shops where he and Cat had bought cupboards, chairs, bric-a-brac, past restaurants where they had eaten and riverside picnic spots where they had lunched, houses and acres they had thought of buying, the kennel where they had bought Debbie.

Last night he had packed Debbie's collar. The vet had sent it to him, thinking he might want it. Besides the license and the rabies shot tag, there was a copper disc which Rich had made for her years ago in shop class. "I am Debbie. I belong to the Montgomerys." He would have liked the collar to have gone with Debbie. She had always felt lost without it. Whenever he had taken it off to bathe her or remove ticks or brush her, she had kept straining toward it, sniffing at it, obviously uneasy without it. It was as though she would lose her identity without it.

Well, he would keep it now, not meaning really to keep it, but put it aside for the time being along with all the other mementos that he couldn't throw away "just yet" and that accumulated in drawers and on upper closet shelves. Cat always shook her head at the clutter, was much more interested in what was going to happen tomorrow than in what happened yesterday. The only thing she was sentimental about was birthdays. She rarely forgot the birthday of a friend. A card, a phone call, a single flower, a bottle. But old letters, champagne corks, children's drawings, keys to "memorable" hotel rooms, dog collars . . . No.

It was dusk as he turned the bend into his road and saw there were lights in the house. The garage door was open, welcoming, but Cat's car was not there.

On the kitchen table was a large pot of white mums and a note.

> Dear Jack:
> Welcome!!!
> Happy Birthday!!!
> Come over at six-thirty. I will be out and around doing errands till then.
>
> > Love,
> > Cat

The house was pleasantly warm; there was food in the refrigerator and a cup and saucer on the counter by the sink. One of Cat's sweaters was bunched up in a chair in the library. She had been reading or watching television. There was a cigarette butt in the ashtray. Upstairs there was a small vase of flowers on his dresser, another cigarette butt in an ashtray in the bathroom. He was like a detective looking for signs of her presence.

Turning into Catherine's driveway at six-twenty-five, he noticed five or six cars parked near the neighbor's garage, a hundred yards away. They must be giving a party.

But it was Cat who was having the party, a birthday party for him. When he walked in the door and saw a dozen of his friends, he stared at them in surprise. He had wanted to be alone with Cat, but her welcoming him back like this, into the family of his friends, augured well, and he moved in and greeted them all with warmth and affection.

People had brought joke birthday presents, which he was flustered opening and they were embarrassed giving. "Cat said 'something nutty,' and that's all I could find." There were toasts, and he responded by saying that he was glad to be back among them, that his tennis was rusty, but he hoped they would put him back on their list.

Since it was a weekday night, the party broke up early. The lady who had come in to help out had done all but the glasses, and after she left, Jack helped Cat with those as they talked on about the party. He was going to say how nice it was to see her cigarette butts in the ashtrays in their house, but this wasn't the way to go about it.

Finally, they sat on the sofa, and she lighted a cigarette. She seemed nervous. "That kind of party was probably not what you wanted at all, but—"

"No. It was great. A wonderful welcome home." He looked at her and slid his hand along the sofa and took her hand. She shifted her cigarette into her other hand. He wished they could go on talking about the party, watch the eleven o'clock news and just go to bed as though nothing had happened.

He started. "Cat, I'd like us to think about coming back together. It's inconceivable to me that we shouldn't be together." She looked at him with a small, fixed smile. "It was insanity for us to go through this separation thing. I don't know what we could have been thinking about. I've missed you so, our home, everything. Ever since I knew I was coming home, I've been walking around, shaking my head, wondering what in God's name got into us."

She took a puff on her cigarette and looked back at him, studying his face. "I know there may be problems. None of them seems that important to me now. We didn't

269

discuss them that strange night. I hoped we could get back together without going over them, that we could just come back together, easily, with the love I think we have for each other . . . and deal with the problems as we go along." He stopped and looked at her. "I love you. And I don't know what happened. Some craziness."

She bit her lip and shook her head as though she found it impossible to speak. Finally, haltingly: "I was hoping too, that we wouldn't have to go through it all. But—" She kept looking at him, opening her mouth to say something, then looking away, again shaking her head.

"What?" Gently. "Tell me."

"I just don't want to." And she started to cry. He felt sick, but instinctively he moved quickly along the couch and put his arm around her. Her tears subsided, and she blew her nose and reached for her cigarette. "We were doing so well, I thought. So many other couples tear each other to bits till there's nothing left of them." She looked at him.

"We won't tear each other to bits, I hope. But . . . tell me."

She shrugged. "I don't know. It's everything. No, not everything, of course. That's not very nice of me, but—" She stopped and blew her nose again. "If we go over all the little petty resentments, it will all sound so mean. And it's none of them. My God, it's not where we would or would not plant the tulips." She paused. "I don't know. It's time . . . everything. It must happen to everyone. Some people go on, and that's fine. But I don't want to."

"What is 'everything'?"

She looked at him, her eyes red from tears. She stroked his hand. "You feel it. You know it. We're . . . used up. That's not a nice way of putting it, but . . . you want something else"

270

"No, I don't."

"For a man so painfully honest you can be very dishonest about your deepest feelings. You left."

"We left each other. I don't know why. It was a bad period. I was . . . unhappy all around. Work." He was immediately ashamed for saying that, though it had been true. "I did say several times we shouldn't go through with it."

"Yes, I know."

"And the night before I left, you cried."

"I've cried now. It isn't easy. I cried for days after you left. And possibly if you'd come running back, or if I had called that night and had asked you to come back, we might have gone on for a while. As you know, the idea of marriage was never as important to me as it was to you. But I can still feel a sense of failure, of sadness. And, at the same time, resent that feeling. Why can't two people part when it's time to part without a feeling of failure? All these guilt feelings for not loving forever and ever."

"I love you."

"You want to love me. Oh, God, I was never going to say that. A woman of fifty-four should be grateful that her husband at least tries."

"Cat . . ."

"Watching you try to will it kills me. I want to be loved that way, want to love *you* that way. But you can't"—she paused and looked at him—"and I can't. Sometimes I've thought it would be better if we didn't try, if we just . . . I sound so ungenerous. You're a good lovemaker. Very considerate and . . ."

He sat there with his arm around her, comforting her but also trying to understand.

"But none of that is really it." She looked at his hand and stroked it. "I've thought so much about you, worried about you. I know that I get along by myself better than you do. I've thought of us back in Cambridge, you waiting for me outside classrooms where I was lecturing, rushing over from Law School to grab a quick lunch with me, waiting for me at bus stops with an umbrella if it had started to rain. I know how much you need someone, some one person. And I know sometimes I've failed you in that area. But I enjoy and get support from dozens of people. Maybe I'm more superficial than you. I kow the depth of your love and commitment. It's wonderful and frightening and demanding, though you don't see yourself as a demanding man. Even your kindness. Sometimes I've hated your giving and kindness because I couldn't permit myself my honest and legitimate anger because I felt like such a monster in the face of your kind attentions." She turned away and shook her head. "I don't know how I got on to all this. I'm sorry."

"I didn't mean my love to be demanding."

"I know. Of course not. You see, I knew if we started to talk . . ."

They were both quiet for a moment. It was already confusing. Cat went on. "You know I've suggested that we separate before. Then last spring I seemed to sense something in you, some brooding, more than your usual dissatisfaction, along with an almost violent lovemaking, touching attempts to find something that couldn't be found. And I thought you might be ready, too. And I mentioned it that night, and you *were* ready."

Jack closed his eyes. He had been trying to cope with her picture of him, and now added to that was the realization that he had brought home his anguish over Kim and Scott. Sitting there with his arm around her, he couldn't seem to come to grips with what was happening. It seemed like a room full of feathers. He kept trying to

272

come back to reality, to moments that were clear. "We made love the night before I left."

"I know."

"I wasn't 'trying' then."

"No. But that was a . . . strange night. Oh, I know you can go back point by point, night by night, and say, 'That was good, wasn't it?' " She stopped for a moment. "Our being good in bed meant so much to you. Oh, to me too. But it seemed to reassure you that things were all right. And they were, in a way. We were luckily very responsive to each other, and you were very . . ."

"Considerate." He wanted to go into what they would lose, if they parted, what might lie ahead in the way of loneliness and despair. But he knew that love and loving were the only acceptable topics now. Their pride would keep them from talking about any other reasons for going on together.

She shook her head. "I thought we had moved apart so easily in the spring, as though we both understood, were sad, but understood." Her voice started to break, and she stopped.

He resented her unwillingness to discuss it. He didn't know what they would discuss. She was right. He would bring up good times, happy times. But even those did not seem to have been good for her, happy for her, as she wanted them. She simply didn't want to be reached. She was Catherine the strong, whose ancestors had beaten across the plains with handcarts, who had declared her own father dead as far as she was concerned when he had crossed her, years before Jack had met her. He had been drawn to this strength, had depended on it often. And yet . . . and yet how often she had lain cradled in his arms, needing comforting and release from her strength. Kim had said that she did not dare to appear weak with Scott.

273

That is where he had come in. He had never felt himself especially strong, but he had been a refuge for two strong women exhausted by their own strength.

They had been quiet for a time. He felt sick. Then she started, hesitantly. "I had hoped that there would be someone up there, and that you would come here, full of awkward embarrassment, saying that you wanted to go through with the divorce because you wanted to marry her."

Perhaps she had intended to be generous, but he was angered by her tone. She had moved out and beyond "them" too easily and was showing a concern for his future he did not appreciate. Years ago, at college, saying she was too old for him, she had tried to shunt him off to other, younger women. He had resented it. He resented it now.

"There *was* a woman." He stopped. He shouldn't have said that. Well, it might just . . . his honesty might reach her. "But when it came to the point of thinking about marriage, I woke up. Somehow it had never dawned on me that it would mean leaving you. Idiotic, I know. Also, everything we did was too full of echoes of our life and made me want *us* again."

"But as we were."

Her dogged insistence made him angry. He blurted out, "You're my wife. I'll never marry again. If you marry again, you will still be my wife. I am not rushing back here full of illusions, that everything is going to be simple. You said it would be a period of growth. Well, I think I have grown. I love you, and I want us to be together, to try. What's wrong with trying? You've always admired people who tried. Can't we just be together and see what happens? When we got married, we backed into it, full of doubts. We said, 'Let's see what happens.'"

274

"I know, and I'm glad we did, and I thank you for all the happy years, but—" She started to cry again.

This time he did not try to comfort her. He rode over her tears. "You cry, and yet you say we are used up. How can we be used up when you cry like this?"

She fought for control. "I only cry when I see you."

"Doesn't that tell you something?"

"Not what you want it to tell me."

"What does it tell you?"

She quieted down and looked at him. "It tells me that we mustn't see each other."

He looked at her. She could not be reached. She had made up her mind a long time ago. He felt it had nothing to do with what they had talked about. Did she know about Kim and was not saying? Was her pride keeping her from talking about it? Had his telling her about Janet done just the reverse of what he had hoped it would do? Had it confirmed her idea that he didn't love her? But he had come back.

Restless, he got up and walked away and looked back at her. She sat there shut off from him, as though she knew something that only she knew, which made all the difference. He wanted to shout, "God damn it, tell me what it is. Make me understand so that I won't go around the rest of my life trying to figure out what happened."

She looked up at him. "Would your firm handle it for both of us?"

"Stop it!"

"Anything you want is agreeable to me."

"Stop it! For Christ's sake, stop it!" Suddenly his rage and bewilderment and a sense of utter desolation overcame him, and he started to cry. He put his hands to his face and turned away from her; then ashamed, he hurried to the hallway and grabbed his coat.

She followed, reaching for him, catching at his arm, looking at him, concerned. "Stay. Stay awhile."

He turned and clutched her to him, shaking his head.

"Don't go yet." But he couldn't stand her compassion, didn't want her comfort. He wanted to strike her, to beat on her. He felt he was going to be sick and turned and yanked open the door and left.

He rushed blindly down the garden steps and around the corner of the house and across the gravel drive to his car, as though eager to get out of her sight, to hide. As he opened the door, his stomach heaved, and he turned to throw up, but nothing came, just dry gasping. He leaned against the roof of the car, full of desolation and anger at Cat and himself.

He stayed that night in a motel on Route 7. He could not go back to their house. The room was chilly. The air conditioner–heater blew in only cold air. But he didn't care. He undressed, ripped the blanket off the second bed and wrapped himself in it. He remembered that he had two Valiums folded in tissue in his wallet. He got into bed and turned out the light and lay there, huddled, waiting for the Valium to take effect.

32

For two days he wandered aimlessly through the city, full of self-disgust and bitterness and bewilderment. What in God's name had he thought he was doing? That Friday night at the kitchen table, calmly talking about separation as if they were discussing taking separate vacations. Casually driving out the driveway that morning in July and eight hours later drifting around the Square, longing to touch firm, young breasts. And later that night: "By the way, I forgot my glasses."

The small charge he had felt in saying, "My wife and I are separated," feeling he was "with it," one of the walking wounded from the marriage wars, one of those "who dared." The looks of sympathy and envy. Jesus!

He looked around, sure that people could hear his screams or could see him suddenly drop to his knees and beat the pavement.

He had walked through Cambridge full of longing to hold and be held. Now he moved through the streets or sat unseeing in movies or lay on top of his bed, gutted, without desire, wanting no comfort, unable to imagine any comfort.

He stared and shook his head at his self-delusions. His whole joy in Janet and her children. His fantasy of their all being tucked away in a little house in the woods with him beneficently watching over them and sparing them the pain of life and living. Blocking out Cat completely. Blocking out, never realizing the anguish he would feel if he and Cat divorced, an anguish that would in one day burst the seams of that unreal little family nest, would, indeed, probably make it impossible for him ever to marry again. Cat was his wife, would remain his wife, even if they divorced.

Then he would irrationally curse the glibness of the times. Cool. The New Morality. Serious men on the Op-Ed page of the New York *Times* casually discussing how to arrange for mutual infidelity. "I found my lover in the *Times*." Or at least the idea it was A-okay to have one. Doesn't everyone?

Why had he gone home with Scott that night? He could have gone home with him and still not have fallen in love with his wife. What had there been about that night? The unconscious accumulation of some longing inside him, and then suddenly Kim there in the kitchen with Colin. Cat all over again. Janet had been Cat all over again. A man of forty-nine, now fifty, thinking he could play the game all over again.

He must have been insane. Why hadn't someone shouted, "Stop it!"? Who, for instance? His father was dead. And years ago his father *had* shouted no at his older brother, now also dead, when he had talked of divorce. His father had not entertained divorced people at his table. Had probably in his marriage lived a life of quiet desperation. Was it worse than a life of bewildering options?

He had had no options. He only thought he had had options. Cat's mind had been made up all along. Hadn't it? His bitterness shifted to Cat. She had never wanted the marriage. It had been *his* marriage. He had been the keeper of the marriage. But he had known that from the beginning, had accepted that as the challenge, known how she felt about her mother and her marriage. Ah, but he had thought that with his amazing power of love he could change that. And he had to an extent. After the abortion, soon after their marriage, she had gone ahead and had Rich and had cried out, "Why didn't someone tell me how wonderful it is!" And she had rushed on to repeat the wonderful experience with Jorie and had been lucky to find a nanny in the neighborhood so that she could go back to work. And she had written those beautiful poems about her surprise at her joy at having children.

They *had* made it work. Foolishly proud that they were so far ahead of their times. Smug. "We lived together while I was in college." . . . "Yes, way back then in the olden times." . . . "And we managed our two careers." (His one, Cat's five or six.)

But what the hell had happened? Something had just given way. Their marriage had been like a huge tent supported by the various stresses and strains of effort and trying. And then that Friday night they had stopped trying, and it had all collapsed.

Christ, he didn't want to live with someone who didn't want him. To keep trying. Never to be accepted as loving enough. Didn't his wanting to come back prove it? Or had she thought it was loneliness and guilt?

But he mustn't blame Cat. He had seen some of his divorced clients gradually moving out of their shock and bewilderment by arriving at an "account" of what had happened, self-serving, something they could live with, invariably blaming the other one.

The afternoon of the second day he got in his car to drive to Cat's house, to give her the letter he had written in Cambridge, to which he had added a few paragraphs. Halfway out, he remembered that she wasn't there. She had said at the party that she was going to the Midwest for a week's poetry workshop and reading. She was going to give him her address, but then they had talked, and he had run out.

He called Barbara and she gave him the address, and he sent the letter. The next morning there was a letter from Cat, mailed in Iowa. It had obviously crossed his letter.

Dear Jack:

I wanted to see you before I came out here, but when I couldn't reach you at the house or the apartment, I decided it might be better if I put it in a letter. We have sometimes done better in letters than face to face.

I left you with so many wrong impressions the other night, among them, that you were somehow to blame. And I am sorry. I would like to think that neither of us is to blame, that we are doing something to which no blame should be attached.

I believe it is possible for two people who love each other to want to separate. I know it might be easier if we hated each other, but we don't. Unless you hate me now.

We have been moving in different directions; I, inward toward myself, you toward wanting more closeness, almost desperately needing it. Bad timing, or is it age? A shift in needs. Of course, I have always been more "separate" than you. But now my sense of privacy has developed to the point I even resent the doctor's poking and probing. (I don't know what this has to do with it, but it seemed appropriate to mention.)

And your need . . . sometimes when you're with me now, I feel you literally want to fuse with me. And why not? It is a loving need. Normal. But you can see that it is threatening to my need . . .

280

We have accommodated each other for a very long time, lovingly and successfully, in many areas. I know I am grateful to you, because I know you were often lonely and said you weren't, to save me from guilt. (I still felt guilty.)

But I think we mustn't try to accommodate each other now. These drives are too basic, and I feel we would accommodate them at our peril. At this stage in our lives, I think we're entitled to what we want and need.

I know I said we should go through the trial separation "to learn." You think that you learned you wanted our marriage. I could argue with you, but won't. I learned what I already knew . . . that I wanted something else. Not someone else. I suppose it would have been a miracle if we had both learned the same thing.

You've always made a greater investment in the marriage than I have. Perhaps that's because you gave up doing what you really wanted to do, to be a writer, for the security of the law. I have felt guilty about that, too. You felt you wanted to be able to support a family, though I didn't want to be supported, as you found out, too late.

I think we have succeeded in a remarkable balancing act all these years, largely thanks to you, our "home-keeper." Completely different temperaments and needs. An incurable romantic, touchingly (and sometimes maddeningly) at war with the inevitable . . . and a New England pragmatist. I probably never should have let you persuade me, but I'm glad I did. I would be a much lesser person now if we hadn't married. For one thing, the unexpected joy of the children you insisted on . . .

Dear Jack, you have never wanted to let go when something is over and done. You have always felt that if you exerted just a little more effort . . . not recognizing that things sometimes just give out, *must* give out, can no longer be repaired. Cars, clothes, dogs, friendships. I will not say love, because I think we still love each other, and

281

maybe always will . . . unless, as I said, this makes you hate me.

Of course, we could get back together again. We could "settle" sensibly, and you could take your longing off to some love affair. I could accept this intellectually, but I couldn't take it if I found out about it, and a woman inevitably finds out about it, if only by the way her husband treats her. And anyway, it's just not you. And you deserve more than that.

Oh, Christ!—cold, white-haired, New England bitch, analyzing, neatly parsing my emotions. I will cry for a very long time. Because I am not entirely that woman who wants to be alone. Things don't happen that neatly. But in spite of my tears, I am sure of what I want to do.

Somewhere you want it too. You are afraid at the moment. You are lonely. You feel something you were given to do you did not do well.

Just know that it has nothing to do with love. I will probably love you always. I just want to live my own life now, to be removed from the tensions and frustrations that our different needs at this moment inflict on us.

I wish we could be happy for what we had and not let the unrealistic expectations of going on and on forever spoil that.

I write the next knowing you will want to tear it up and throw it in my face. But . . . you did fall in love in Cambridge. It will happen again. You're entitled to the kind of relationship you really want at this time of your life.

Know that I leave you with love and will always think of you and speak of you lovingly. People say, "Then why are you doing this?" I smile and shrug my shoulders and say, "I just want to." I don't feel I have to explain to them. I wish I could explain to you, but I know I can't. When we were married, people said, "Why are you marrying him? He's four years younger. You're complete opposites in temperament." I couldn't explain it then. I can't now. I know I am glad we married, and I hope (after the tears) that we will both be glad we parted.

Love,
Cat

P.S. I have just read this over, and I hate how it sounds, stiff, instructive, awful. It is my trade as a poet to try to make sense out of chaos, to express the inexpressible. I seem to have drained out all the blood and pain and love. Forgive me.

He was now sorry he had sent his letter. She would answer it, of course, would have to go through the anguish of trying to explain again to him. But he already has his answer.

That night Kim called. "I've heard your news from Scott. I'm terribly sorry."

"Thanks." (Scott had suggested he call Kim while he was away, take her to dinner. "She knows lots of attractive women.")

"I have instructions from Scott to ask you to dinner. You probably don't feel like coming here. Can I bring some dinner over there?"

Automatically he said, "What about the Maxwells?"

"I'll take the chance."

"No."

"Do you want to see me?"

He lay there on top of his bed, saying nothing. In the last few days he had sometimes included her in his sullen bitterness against himself.

"Jack?"

"Yes, I'd like to see you." He didn't really want to talk, but his morbid solitariness had begun to frighten him. At one moment of almost complete disorientation the day before, he had thought of checking himself into a hospital. "But I don't want you taking a chance."

They met for a late dinner at the Museum Café on Columbus Avenue. She did not lecture him on his desire for "wholeness" or tell him he had "had it made" before he left Cat. She did say, "I'm sorry. I know it was what you really wanted."

She listened to him castigate himself. He told her he did not believe it was just Cat's wanting to be alone. "If I had tried harder. If . . ."

She disagreed with him, said she understood Cat completely. She had gone to a party recently, and there was a stunning single woman there who arrived alone and left alone, and she had been green with envy. "But I would never do anything about it. It's my marriage. It was *your* marriage. It's always somebody's marriage."

She went on to say that she felt the marriage should serve the lives, not the lives serve the marriage. And he said, "What is a life? I'm one of the best damned lawyers in the world in my field, but my life was my emotional life. My marriage was the only really creative act of my life. My work was something I did. Back in Cambridge, I was a damned good student, but I had no life until I met Cat, what I call a life."

She said she didn't think she could take that demanding a marriage. "Scott's demanding, but not emotionally. It's more services." They looked at each other. She smiled and shrugged.

"You once wrote me about how undemanding I was."

"Yes, in what I didn't want to deliver. But I loved your emotional demands, because I needed them and wanted to respond."

They were quiet for a long time. "I feel I've fragmented myself into a goddamned neuter. I'm numb."

"Give it time," she said gently.

"A few months ago, before I left, a friend of mine's wife died. He took me to lunch to confide in me. Said that all he wanted to do was get lost in a sea of naked bodies. I don't even have that feeling. I don't really feel like living."

"Do you want to die?"

He smiled at her. "No."

They walked back to her house, and as she put the key in the lock, she looked at him, her worried, wide-eyed look. "Do you want to come in?"

He looked at her for a moment, then shook his head. "No."

"I understand."

"I wish I did."

She swung open the door. "I'll always be here."

Suddenly he moved to her and threw his arms around her and hid his head in her shoulder as tears came to his eyes. She held him. He was embarrassed for his tears, which seemed to ask for sympathy. But he welcomed them as a partial release from his cold numbness.

Ever so gently: "Come in."

He did not want to stay. He did not want to go. She wanted him to stay.

She went into the bathroom and came out in her nightshirt. She stopped when she saw him lying clothed on top of the bed. Then she smiled and lay down beside him, and they held each other.

It was somehow fitting that he should finally lie in her

bed like this. Over the months he had rushed to her, ready and eager for her, or he had wanted to throw her out, unable to bear the idea of her going to Scott. And in New Hampshire he had been sadly loving and confused.

Her closeness, however, finally had its effect. It was as though his body insisted on going on living, almost as an embarrassment to his sad and bewildered thoughts.

He tried to turn away, but she wouldn't let him. And so, almost reluctantly, in spite of himself, they made love. It completed her gesture.

They said practically nothing. It was as though some instinct had told her to present herself almost as just a warm body. Implicit in her tenderness, her embraces and her silence seemed to be an understanding of the part she had played in all this, as well as a sense of its complexity.

He slept a little after, but he awoke long before the alarm went off and lay there thinking. It had been different, very different. An act of mercy. A gift she thought he had wanted. She had not let him caress her or arouse her. She had wanted it to be a selfish act for him. She had made him use her.

He looked at the windows and the light from the street-lamps coming through the curtains, at his clothes thrown on the chair, and he wondered if he would ever be in this bed again.

And he began to think of Cat again. Could he ever start all over again with the inevitable cycles of joy and painful adjustment and disillusionment, haunted as he would be by their failure? They had made the failure together as surely as they had made their children, and it would bind them as surely as their children would bind them. He knew that years from now he would wake up at four in the morning someplace, alone, or if he was lucky, with someone beside him, and he would still wonder, "Why?"

He got up quietly and put on his clothes and sat on the side of the bed and kissed Kim. "Good night. Thank you."

She stirred and smiled and, without opening her eyes, murmured. "We don't thank."

"I know, but thank you."

He kissed her again, then got up and put on his raincoat and went down the stairs and home.

Robert Anderson was born in New York City and attended Phillips Exeter Academy and Harvard University, where he also received his master's degree. He has been a distinguished playwright in the American theater from his first Broadway play, *Tea and Sympathy*, in 1953, *All Summer Long* in 1954 and *Silent Night, Lonely Night* in 1959. He wrote *You Know I Can't Hear You When the Water's Running* in 1967, followed a year later by *I Never Sang for My Father*. The latter won the Writers' Guild award for Best Screenplay (Drama) and received an Academy Award nomination for best screenplay in 1970. In 1971 *Solitaire/Double Solitaire* was produced and *Double Solitaire* was later made into a television movie for the Public Broadcasting System.

In 1973 Mr. Anderson's first novel, *After*, was published. *Getting Up and Going Home* is his second novel.

Mr. Anderson was a member of the faculty of the Salzburg Seminar in American Studies and is a past president of the Dramatists' Guild. He lives in Connecticut.